SECRETLY MINE

A BIRCH CROSSING NOVEL

STEPHANIE ROWE

COPYRIGHT

CHAPTER 1

THERE WERE a lot of things Leila Kerrigan should be thinking about other than the fact that, for the first time since they exchanged vows, she was in the same town as the bad-boy rebel she'd married fifteen years ago.

For example, she should be feeling nostalgic about the beautiful lake she could see through the trees as she drove the winding road into the town center of Birch Crossing, Maine. She peeked at the sparkling, blue water, and saw a float anchored a few yards away from shore with teenagers swimming off it. She had a sudden memory of when she and Maura had spied on Dash Stratton and his friends when they were skinny dipping...

No, not that. She didn't need to be thinking about the first (and only) time she'd seen her then-future husband naked, or how he'd had muscles that a seventeen-year-old girl had dreamed of for a very long time afterward. And a tattoo on the back of his right shoulder. He'd been so dangerous and so much trouble and—

Oh, Lordy. She hit Send on her phone to call her lifeline, her best friend since college, aspiring Broadway actor, and extremely gifted singer.

Gordon Enzo answered on the first ring. "Talk to me, girl. What's happening? Have you seen the house yet? What kind of shape is in it?"

"I'm thinking of Dash naked again."

Gordon made a clucking noise of sympathy. "Of course you are. You're in an emotionally vulnerable place after your breakup with Robbie, and returning to the site of your less-than-ideal childhood. It's completely natural to be looking to feel safe and protected, and Dash is the man for that."

She snorted. "There's nothing safe about Dash. Did I tell you I heard he went to prison after I left?"

Gordon snorted. "He was your best friend's older brother, and he married you to protect you from your bastard stepfather who was stealing your inheritance. That's safety, girl. Your brain isn't going to forget that."

"Dammit. Why do you have to bring that up?"

"Because you need to deal with it. You haven't seen the man since you married him, and now you're back in town. You're going to run into him, and you know it."

Leila looked to her right as she passed Wright's General Store, the local market where all gossip began. Dash had worked at Wright's when he was in high school. "Wright's looks the same."

"Don't start talking about small-town business, girl. This is what you need to do. You need a change of man-scenery so your bruised little heart can realize that Robbie was so far below what you deserve. Dash is bad-boy sexy, right?"

"Yes." She saw a motorcycle parked in front of Wright's. "He had a motorcycle." Her heart started to race.

"Exactly. You need to ride that boy around some tight corners at high speed to remember what it feels like to live again."

She definitely shouldn't have told Clare Friesé, the estate attorney and a vague acquaintance from high school, that she'd meet the real estate agent, Harlan Shea, at Wright's to get the house key from him. Of course Dash might be at Wright's. Everyone in town went to Wright's. They used to have the best breakfasts, and people hung out there with food and coffee to gossip. Or buy groceries. Or beer. Or whatever. It didn't matter. Pretty much everyone in town seemed to go through Wright's at least once a day. "I'm not riding Dash."

Gordon snorted. "Sweetheart, the hot hunk of deliciousness is your husband, and you've never even lip-locked with the man, even when you were announced husband and wife."

"Because there's no sexual attraction between us." She pulled into a spot down the street from Wright's and put her car into park.

"Of course not. It's not as if you were thinking of him naked just a few minutes ago."

"I had a teenage crush on Dash. I'm thirty-two, and I haven't seen him since I was eighteen."

"And yet, you're still married to him. You were in a relationship with Robbie for eight years, and you never even thought about getting a divorce from Dash. And he's never once contacted you to get one either. It's not as if you're difficult to find. Ever given that any thought, my darling?"

"Divorce takes effort, and I didn't have a reason to get one. Apparently, he didn't either."

Gordon chuckled. "Again, you might want to untangle that little statement when you have some downtime."

She decided to ignore that advice. "I'm at Wright's. I need to go meet Harlan to get the key."

"Well, send my love to Auntie Bea who was nice enough to leave you her house in the will."

Bea. The woman who had opened her house to Leila when she was a teenager, scared, alone, and afraid, with nowhere else to go. "She wasn't my actual aunt."

"In your heart?"

Leila smiled. "She was the closest thing I had to a mother after mine died."

"Exactly. Go honor Bea, give a hug to the spirit of teenage Leila, because she needed it, and grab some condoms in case you run into that husband of yours."

"First two, yes. Third one? No chance." Leila laughed, her mood lightened by Gordon's humor. "I gotta go. I'll talk to you later." She hung up the phone, then leaned back in her seat, taking a moment before heading into Wright's…past that motorcycle that was sitting out front.

Maybe it wasn't Dash's motorcycle.

Maybe he didn't even have a motorcycle anymore.

Maybe he'd been in a relationship for the last fifteen years and was completely unavailable.

Maybe he stayed married so he didn't have to get serious with all the women he took home night after night.

Or maybe—

The motorcycle engine roared to life, and she twisted around in her seat to look. The rider had a helmet on already, obscuring his face, but the tee shirt did nothing to hide the broad shoulders, muscular biceps, and corded forearms.

She sank down in her seat as the motorcycle rolled forward, easing out into the road. She held her breath as he approached, not daring to look over.

The motorcycle passed, and she sat back up to look at the license plate as he drove away.

DASH12

She caught her breath. *It was him.* And he was still riding his motorcycle.

He looked so freaking hot riding that bike, and she didn't appreciate that one bit.

She did *not* have the emotional energy for this!

Then suddenly, the bike stopped. Dash twisted around on his seat and appeared to look right at her, but she couldn't see his face past the tinted face shield. His helmet was full coverage, obscuring his jaw and face from his neck up.

There was no way for her to identify him, but he was on

4

the DASH12 bike, so she was pretty safe in assuming that was her long-lost husband sitting there, yards away, staring in her direction, his face hidden from her view.

She let out her breath, suddenly hot, imagining his blue eyes staring at her.

So intense, he was. Always had been. Dangerous. Unstoppable. Heroic. And, yes, unfairly attractive.

For a long moment, she stared at him, both willing him to rip off that helmet so she could see him, and also, mentally ordering him to keep going.

I am not the woman you think you're seeing.

He kept staring in her direction, so she looked down, pretending to text, because who wouldn't?

Then she heard the engine rev, and she looked up. He was driving again, heading away from her down Main Street. Had he seen her? Did he recognize her? She'd guessed from his double take that he'd recognized her, but why had he kept going? Why hadn't he turned around to come say "Hi?"

Not that she wanted him to. Of course.

But...holy cow. Dash was still in town, and he knew she was back.

CHAPTER 2

As Leila hurried down the sidewalk toward Wright's, she kept waiting for the sound of a returning motorcycle. She hadn't known Dash well, but she'd stalked him for years when she was a teenager, and she knew that Dash wasn't the type to back down from anything.

Including her.

And yet, he'd left.

But maybe he hadn't recognized her? It had been years, and he'd barely noticed her as more than his sister's friend until he'd agreed to marry her in a quick, albeit very legal, ceremony, thanks to Bea's help.

Would Leila even recognize him? He wasn't on social media, so she hadn't seen even a picture of him in a long time.

She took a breath. Yes, of course he wouldn't recognize her. He'd probably just been looking back at something else. She could slide into her inherited house, get it cleaned up to sell, and be on her way in a week without ever seeing him.

Right. It was fine.

She pulled open the door to Wright's, and then paused as the energy of the small-town general store grabbed her. It was late afternoon, so the lunch crowd was long gone, but there were still a few folks sitting at the tables in front. The old wooden barn beams were still there, and so were the raw wood walls. The kitchen was still at the back, where Ophelia used to always be, whipping up her magic creations, but no one was cooking.

She expected to see Norm, Ophelia's husband, at the register, as he'd been sitting there for decades, but in his place was a man she didn't know, one about her age. Even with Norm and Ophelia not there, Leila still felt something inside her settle. This was home, and it always would be. A place that had always made her feel like there was a part of this world that she didn't have to hide from.

Leila took a deep breath to inhale this part of her past that felt good, then she walked over to the register. "Hi," she said. "I'm meeting Harlan Shea here, but I don't know what he looks like. Is he around?"

The man at the register flashed her a smile that lit up his eyes. He was very attractive, she noticed. Not the raw, rebel flair of Dash, but this guy's aura was probably the vibe she should be noticing instead. He was wearing a wedding ring, however, which was great, because she was done with dating anyway. "You must be Leila Kerrigan," he said.

"I am."

He held out his hand. "My name's Griffin Friesé. Clare's husband. Nice to officially meet you, Leila."

"Oh…" She looked at Griffin with new interest. Clare Gray had been a couple years older than she was, and she'd been the lawyer for Bea's estate. "It's great to meet you." She shook his hand, surprised by how strong his grip was. She was used to Robbie, who was a marketing whiz, but he wasn't exactly chiseled.

"Harlan will be around in a few," Griffin said. "Can I get you something while you wait?"

"I'm all set. Thanks. I think I'll do some grocery shopping. Clare said the house was still furnished?"

Something flickered in his eyes, but he nodded. "Yep."

She frowned. What had he not said? A part of her wanted to ask, but a stronger part of her wanted to keep her visit to Birch Crossing tightly controlled. There was so much in her past that she didn't want to have to look at it.

She had to stay focused. She was there to get the keys, get the house ready to sell, and then put it on the market. That was it. So she didn't ask Griffin to explain what he hadn't said.

"All right." She grabbed a cart from the doorway and headed toward the back of the market where the food staples were. She'd made it only to the cereal when the front door jangled.

Dash?

Her heart leapt and she spun around, then burst out laughing at the sight of the silver-haired woman walking in, wearing a pink hat with stuffed bunnies on top. "Eppie?" The eighty-something firecracker who had been one of Bea's best friends was striding into Wright's, the full force of her vibrant life force as strong as ever.

"You bet it is! I wouldn't miss the reentry of Leila Kerrigan into our town!" Eppie trotted across the worn, wooden floor, then flung her arms around Leila and dragged her into a big hug.

Leila laughed through the sudden tears, so happy to see the woman who been such a source of kindness when she was a teenager. "It's so good to see you again. You look exactly the same."

"The same?" Eppie pulled back, looking offended. "I'm ten times the women I was fifteen years ago. I'm offended you think I look the same." She bent over and touched her toes. "Could I do this fifteen years ago? No chance. Now look at me!"

Leila grinned. "You're a badass, definitely."

"Damn straight I am." Eppie popped up. "Now, listen here, Leila. I'm always here for you, but as the executor of Bea's will, I'm taking my job seriously. I'm going to be watching you."

Leila blinked. "Watching me? For what?"

"She doesn't know yet, Eppie. I haven't told her."

Leila looked toward the door of the backroom. A woman about her age in jeans, a Wright's tee shirt, and a pair of sunglasses on top of her head was coming out. She had flour on her jeans, but she looked happy. She was barely recognizable as the girl Leila remembered from high school. "Clare?"

"Yep." Clare strode right across the store and pulled Leila into a warm hug. "So sorry about Bea, Leila. She was an amazing woman."

Those same tears threatened again. "She was," Leila agreed, clearing her throat to keep her emotions in check.

"I don't even practice law anymore, but for her, what was I going to do? Say no to helping her with her estate?" Clare laughed warmly. "No chance. I'd never let Bea down."

"Who would?" Eppie agreed. "Tell Leila now. I want to see her reaction."

Alarm began to creep down Leila's spine. "Tell me what?"

Clare cleared her throat. "There are a few previsions to your inheritance of the house that I wasn't at liberty to specify until you arrived."

Oh, man. Bea had always been spirited and irreverent, much like Eppie. Leila started to laugh. "I can only imagine what trouble she left for me. Okay, lay it on me."

Eppie continued to grin, while Clare explained. "You're welcome to sell the house, but you have to live in it for thirty consecutive days before you can sell it."

Relief rushed through Leila. That was the perfect excuse to take a break from her life while she got her next steps sorted out. As long as she could still sell the house and get the

money from the sale, she had enough saved up to accommo-
date a month delay. "That's fine."

"And if you spend even one night out of the house, the
thirty days starts again."

"Wow, okay." She frowned. "Why did she do that?"

"Because she wanted you to fall in love with the house,
decide to keep it, and move back to Birch Crossing," Eppie
said. "Obviously."

Leila blinked at the sudden guilt. "I'm not moving back. I
have a life in New York." Was that really why Bea had left her
the house? She didn't want to disappoint Bea, even though
Bea wasn't here anymore. She owed Bea. Without her, Leila
would have… She didn't even want to think about it. It was
too grim.

Eppie put her hands on her hips. "You got a man in New
York, Leila?"

"Well, no, I just got out of a relationship—"

"Then it's fine to move back here." Eppie raised her brows.
"I will be checking on you every night and every morning to
make sure you slept there. My duty as executor, and as her
dear friend."

Leila nodded, accepting those terms. "I love you, Eppie.
I'd be happy to have breakfast with you every morning."
Eppie and Bea used to team up to make Leila laugh, even on
the days when Leila thought nothing would ever make her
smile again. "I could use some laughs right now. I'll cook
breakfast for you. My blueberry muffins."

"Damn, girl. I love those muffins."

Leila smiled, feeling better. Maybe it wouldn't be so bad to
be back in Birch Crossing. "I know you do. That's why I
offered them."

"Hey, little girl." Eppie waved her finger at her. "Don't
think you can bake me out of my commitment."

"I'd never think of it. It would be nice to have your company." And Leila meant it. She'd been living such a crazy, fast-

paced life for the last ten years, and with the breakup with Robbie, she'd lost everything. It would be great to have a friendly face smiling at her in the morning, one that would keep her from dwelling on things that wouldn't serve her.

Clare grinned. "I have to document it as well, so you'll see us both around."

"It'll be great to take a break from my life," Leila said. "I'm not planning to cheat Bea."

"Well, maybe you aren't at the moment, but plans change," Eppie said, with a grin that made Leila pause.

She frowned. "What's that smile for?"

"Me?" Eppie immediately stopped smiling. "I'm not smiling. Why would I smile? It's not like I'm happy to have my favorite granddaughter back in town."

Leila's heart tightened. "I'm not your granddaughter."

"In my heart you are, and that's all that matters."

Sudden tears threatened, and Leila had to look away to compose herself. She'd forgotten what it felt like to be claimed by someone who loved her unconditionally, and she'd forgotten how good it felt.

When she looked back, both Clare and Eppie were looking at her with an understanding that made the tears want to come back.

"Tough times?" Eppie asked softly.

"No. It's fine. I'm fine." She'd thought she was fine, but somehow, being back in Birch Crossing and seeing Eppie and Clare had ripped away her illusions that she was all right. Her chest felt like it was aching, and she suddenly just wanted to get out of the store and into Bea's house, where she could collapse into the emotions fighting to consume her. "Just tired from the long drive. I'll be fine after a little nap."

Eppie gave her a knowing look, but didn't challenge her.

"Okay, well, call if you need anything." Clare handed her a key. "Here's your key. I got it from Harlan. Have fun."

Eppie wiggled her brows, suddenly looking mischievous again. "Yes, have fun!"

Leila narrowed her eyes. "What kind of fun?"

Eppie grinned. "Tonight's the town fundraiser at the fire station. You're not going to miss it, are you?"

Leila groaned. "I'm tired—"

"I'll put you on the list to bring drinks." Eppie turned around, grabbed a six-pack of Birch's Best beer from the stack behind her and set it in Leila's cart. "Shopping's all done. Easy-peasy. Softball starts at five. Field games at six. Dinner at seven. Dancing at eight. Raffle drawing during dinner. What are you going to donate?"

Leila blinked. "I don't know. I don't have anything—"

"How about a gift card to Wright's?" Eppie suggested. "Griffin, ring me up for a $50 gift card. Leila's going to donate it to the raffle."

"Wait, no—"

But Eppie was already heading over to the register.

Leila bit her lip to silence her protest. She didn't want to feel too poor to afford a fifty-dollar donation. Yes, her money wasn't going to last forever, but she knew how important the fundraiser for the volunteer fire department was. She couldn't lose who she was completely.

Instead, she managed a smile. "I'm just going to get some groceries and then head to Bea's. I'll get over to the fundraiser as soon as I can." Leila tucked the key in her pocket, grabbed one more six-pack of beer for the fundraiser, and started toward the milk.

"One more thing," Clare called out.

Leila looked over her shoulder. "What is it?"

"You're not the only heir to Bea's house. There are two of you with the thirty-day live-in requirement before you can sell."

"What?" Leila turned to face Clare, her stomach dropping. "You're kidding." Crap, crap, *crap*. The house wasn't hers?

Clare grimaced. "No, not kidding. I couldn't tell you until you got here. I think Bea was afraid you weren't going to come if you knew. You have to do the co-habiting requirement at the same time, too."

Leila stared at Clare, as Eppie turned back toward them, a grin on her face. "Who is the co-heir?"

She didn't need an answer. The grin on Eppie's face said it all.

"Dash Stratton," Clare said.

Leila suddenly felt hot. Cold. Panicked. Scared. And... stupidly...the teenage Leila who still lived inside her was a little bit excited, which was completely unacceptable. "Dash," she repeated. *Holy crap.* "I have to live with *Dash* in order to get the house?"

"Yep." Clare said. "And the thirty-day live-in counts only for nights you both are there. If either of you misses a night, it starts over." She handed Leila an envelope. "Give this to Dash when you get to the house, if you will."

"Give it to Dash?" Leila stared at Clare in horror. "He's there already?"

Clare cleared her throat. "I don't know if he's there right now, but yes, he's already living there."

Oh, God. "What if I don't move in there and live with him?"

"Then the house sits there in your name until you do. You'll be paying taxes, insurance, and all sorts of fun stuff on it," Eppie said. "Racking up the bills."

"Neither of you can sell it until the thirty-day requirement is met. So if you refuse, you're also tying up Dash," Clare said.

"And heaven knows that handsome boy needs the money these days," Eppie added.

Leila raised her brows at Eppie. "You're trying to guilt me into it?"

"Yep. Guilt is magical. Is it working?"

13

"No. I can't live with Dash. I haven't seen him since I married him."

Eppie raised her brows. "Then this should be really, really good. I can't wait."

———

"YOU CAN'T TURN IT DOWN," Gordon said moments later, after Leila finished filling him in on the details of the house inheritance.

"I have to. I can't live with him—"

"You're broke, babycakes. And by that, I mean you have no money. In about sixty days, you'll have to file for bank-ruptcy if you can't pay your bills. I know it's Robbie's fault, but it doesn't change the facts."

Leila closed her eyes and leaned her head back against the seat "If I file for bankruptcy, I'll never be able to start my business."

"Nope. You'll be alone and broke forever."

She snorted. "How is that helpful? That's a little depressing and dramatic."

"Just want to make sure you're not lying to yourself about what's at stake. Especially, hello? What's so hard about living with a handsome guy for a month? I think you can manage it."

"I just—" She paused. She sighed and rubbed her forehead wearily. "It's not that easy."

"No, it's not. But you have nowhere else to go, Leila. This is your last chance. You have to do it, live-in husband or not. I have faith in you. You can do this. Just keep it impersonal and you'll be fine. But make sure you also sleep with him. Empty sex cures all."

Sex with Dash wouldn't be empty. It would be tangled up with so much past, emotions, and mess. "There's no way I can sleep with him."

"Of course you can. It's really very basic anatomy. All you do is—"

She started laughing. "Good-bye, Gordon."

"There's that laugh. I knew it was in there somewhere. Consider it an adventure."

"I don't like adventures."

"Well, then it's going to be a long thirty days, and you'll regret every minute of wasting it when it's over."

She chuckled again. "Will I?"

"You will. I know you. You're a big barrel of lifetime regret. Like, how many times have you wondered what it could have been like if you'd stayed in Birch Crossing after marrying Dash? Didn't he offer to have you move in with him for as long as you wanted? And you've always wondered why he did that, and what would have happened if you'd said yes."

She blinked. "You promised to forget I told you that."

"I lied, of course. Who's going to forget juicy details like that? No one. I need to run now. You good? Going to the house?"

Leila took a breath. "If I don't go, are you going to come beat me up?"

"Absolutely. It's totally my style. Live in terror if you choose to give up this gift from this amazing woman who clearly had some devious and interesting plan in mind when she made up that will. Go find out what it is, and save your own future while you're at it. Bye!" Gordon hung up before she could answer.

Leila tossed the phone on the passenger seat.

Go to the house.

Live with Dash for thirty days.

Then sell the house and start her life.

She could do it, right?

She had to do it. Without the money from the sale of the house, she was in so much trouble.

15

Right. "I can do this." She started the engine, put the car in drive, and headed toward Bea's house, the house that had been her sanctuary as a kid.

The house where Dash Stratton would be waiting for her.

CHAPTER 3

LEILA'S HEART was racing as she pulled into the driveway of Bea's house.

She couldn't lie to herself and believe that her nerves were because of having to go back and face so much about her past that Bea's house would drum back up for her.

It was because there was a motorcycle parked right in front of the gorgeous screen porch that extended the length of the house, facing the lake that was across the road.

Dash wasn't in sight, but that motorcycle was sitting right there, staring at her, daring her to turn around and run for the hills.

The guy she'd loved since she was thirteen was somewhere on this property right now, and she was going to have to face him for the first time since she'd married him.

What if he asked for a divorce?

What if all her old feelings for him came back?

What if...

"No," she said aloud. "This is ridiculous. It was forever ago. We were friends, and we can be friends now to get through this. I'm being silly." If there had been any spark at all, Dash would have reached out to her, or she would have tried to find him. The fact that they were married was all the excuse either of them would have needed, but neither of them had done anything.

He was a stranger. A nobody, who happened to be married to her. Literally, not a big deal at all.

All she had to do was get through this, sell the house, and get the money.

Leila pulled her shoulders back and got out of the car. She slammed the door shut, walked up to the front door, and rang the bell.

And waited.

He didn't answer.

She rang again.

Still no answer.

Was he hiding from her?

No. Of course not. This was Dash Stratton. He'd never hidden from anyone in his life.

He must be outside.

She had the key and could go inside. Find a bedroom. Set herself up.

But she didn't want to walk into Bea's home. She needed to face him, and she needed to do it now.

So she stepped off the porch. "Dash!" she called out. "Where are you?"

Again, silence.

Where was that man?

———

DASH STRATTON HAD JUST PICKED up his welder when he heard his name hollered from the front of the house.

Recognition flooded him, and he swore, spinning around. That voice sounded familiar, but there was no way Leila Kerrigan would be at his house, bellowing his name.

But he'd thought he'd seen her in that car outside Wright's.

That was twice in the span of an hour.

What the hell was going on?

She, whoever it was, shouted his name again, and something prickled along his skin. He would have sworn it was Leila.

He set down the welder and strode out of his studio. He jerked his sunglasses down over his face, and headed across the lawn around the side of his house, moving with an instinctive urgency.

He practically sprinted around the side of the house, and then stopped dead, stunned.

Leila Kerrigan was in front of the house, her hands on her hips, staring right at him.

Emotions flooded him, so many emotions he couldn't sort them out. He couldn't take his gaze off her. She was a woman now, not a scrawny, scared eighteen-year-old. She was wearing shorts and sneakers, and a blue tank top, looking like she was ready for a day on the lake, like the old days.

She had curves now she hadn't had before, the curves of a woman. Her sunglasses were on top of her head, revealing those glorious blue eyes and dark lashes that he'd begun to think he'd imagined.

She sucked in her breath. "Dash."

"Fuck." He grimaced. That was all he could think of to say after all this time. "I mean, what the fuck are you doing here?"

Her eyes widened. and he swore under his breath. "Sorry. I'm just stunned to see you in my front yard. You look great." Suddenly, he realized why she was there.

She wanted a divorce. The time had come.

Fuck. This time, he meant it.

A cute little frown furrowed between her eyebrows. "You don't know why I'm here?"

Double fuck. Had her lawyer served him? Had he missed an email? "No."

"You don't know about Bea's will?"

He narrowed his eyes. Bea's will? Not a divorce? He was annoyed by the relief that shuddered through him. "What about it? I know I got the house, because she told me many times that's what she was doing." He frowned. "What did she put in there for you?" Was there something at the house that was for Leila? He hadn't seen anything with her name on it, but Bea might have hidden it well. "Do you need me to find something for you?"

Leila stared at him, then understanding dawned on her face, and she burst out laughing. "I swear to God, I'm going to kill Eppie. And Clare!"

Ah...Eppie. He knew what kind of chaos she could cause. "What did they do?" Eppie was as much trouble as Bea had been.

"Clare gave me a letter for you." She fished around in her back pocket, then held up a folded envelope. "I suspect she explains it here."

He didn't move. If it was a letter from Bea, he didn't want to read it, hear her words, feel her presence. It was too soon for him. "You explain it."

Leila waved the letter at him. "No, thanks. Here."

Swearing under his breath, Dash walked over to her to take it, but as he neared, he felt like his world was spinning. Leila Kerrigan was back, and she was unfinished business. *His* unfinished business.

He took the envelope, and his fingers brushed against hers, sending a shock reverberating through his system. Yeah, the attraction was still there, but this time, she wasn't an eighteen-year-old he had to protect from a piece-of-shit stepfather.

She was a woman, and their age difference no longer mattered like it had when she was barely eighteen and he'd been twenty-five.

When his hand touched hers, she sucked in her breath and jerked her hand back. "Letter," she mumbled.

"Letter," he agreed, as he took a step back, folded it, and put it in his pocket. "I'll read it later."

Leila's brows went up. "You need to read it now."

"I'm good. You need anything from me?"

She stared at him. "You're as stubborn and difficult as you were back then."

"Probably."

She folded her arms over her chest. "Read the letter, Dash."

"Nope." There was no chance he was reading Bea's words right now. He missed her like hell, and he wasn't in a place to read a letter she wrote to him in front of Leila. Or anyone. Or even himself. "Anything else you need?"

She stared at him. "Really?"

"Yeah. Whatever you need." This conversation felt awkward and distant, nothing like how he'd envisioned it might be all the times he'd thought about her over the years. "Want a drink? I have water and beer." And other stuff he didn't feel like mentioning.

"Water?"

"Yeah."

She put her hands on her hips. "Dash."

"Leila."

She sighed in aggravation. "Bea didn't leave you the house. She left *us* the house."

Dash stared at her. "Us?"

"Yes." She pointed back and forth between them. "You and me. Co-heirs. We have to live in the house together for thirty consecutive nights before either of us can do anything with it. I'm moving in now."

"No." His amusement fled. Oh, wait, he hadn't been amused by anything about her sudden appearance. "It's my house. I've been living here for the last six months. She told me it was mine, repeatedly." He'd been counting on this house, and not just for himself.

21

"Well, it's also half mine. I need the money from selling it, and we can't sell it until we live here together for thirty days."

Sell it? No one was selling this house. He couldn't afford to buy out Leila. He swore under his breath, then pulled out his phone and called Clare.

She answered on the first ring. "You read the letter?"

"I'm co-heirs with Leila, and we have to live in the house together for thirty consecutive nights before we can do anything with it?" It had to be wrong. It didn't make sense.

Clare sighed. "Yes, look, I'm sorry I didn't tell you, but Bea's will specifically said Leila had to be the one to tell you."

All thoughts of his attraction to Leila vanished in a surge of irritation. He ground his jaw. "So it's true?"

"Yes, it is."

He glanced at Leila, who was watching him, chewing on her lower lip. Why did she look so damned adorable? Why did he care? He didn't have time for this. "I need this house. You know I do."

"Thirty days, Dash. You can have it in thirty days, as long as Leila agrees to give up her share."

Fuck. He couldn't afford to buy her out. "What else is in the will that you didn't tell me? There's more, isn't there? More games that Bea put in there?"

Clare cleared her throat. "It's a rather complicated will, but that's the gist of it."

He swore under his breath. "Clare—"

"Look. You could probably contest some of the provisions, but it's *Bea,*" Clare said softly. "You loved her. She loved you. Don't you want to let her do this her way? Would you deprive her of that joy?"

"No." Dash rubbed his forehead and cursed again. Bea had changed his life in many ways, standing by him when his parents disowned him. He'd spent the rest of his life giving back to her, and he couldn't stop now just because she was gone. "I'd never let her down," he admitted grudgingly.

"Bea spent a lot of time planning this," Clare said. "It's her gift to you. Not just the house, but all of it."

Dash looked at Leila. Was Leila a gift that Bea had decided to hand him? Another chance at the woman he'd let go? He ground his jaw. A year ago, co-habitating with Leila to compete for the house would have been very different than now.

Now, it didn't work for him. "Clare, she wrote the will before—"

"No, she didn't. She updated it afterwards."

That stunned Dash into silence. "She wrote it *after*?" After his whole life had changed. Rocked to its foundation. Shattered into a thousand pieces that he was still struggling to put back together. She wrote the will *after* that had happened? *What the hell, Bea?*

"Yes," Clare said. "It's your choice, Dash. You can contest it, and drag Bea's last moments of joy into question, or go with it."

He sighed. "You're very manipulative."

Clare laughed. "I know. You're welcome. Eppie and I have to confirm every night's sleepover, so you'll see a lot of us."

Roomie. Living with Leila Kerrigan for thirty days. Thirty days in which to convince her to give him her half of the house. Not sell it to him. *Give* it to him.

Fuck. He didn't like needing charity from her. Bea's promise to give him the house had been his key to getting free. To have that compromised... *What the hell were you thinking, Bea?*

He didn't have a backup plan. He'd put everything into this house on the assumption he would get it.

And in those thirty days, he also had to avoid having Leila ask for a divorce. And...he had to resist the temptation that she'd been to him for a long time.

Three bedrooms.

One and a half bathrooms.

One shower.

This was going to get rough fast.

And a part of him was actually looking forward to every minute of it.

CHAPTER 4

DASH WAS EVEN MORE attractive than he'd been when she was in high school.

Leila narrowed her eyes as she watched Dash talk on the phone to Clare. He still had a dimple in his right cheek, and his eyes were a radiant blue. He looked like he hadn't shaved for a couple days, just enough roughness to make him look even more dangerous.

Dammit.

She didn't like dangerous anymore.

She'd never liked dangerous.

She'd been *tempted* by dangerous, but she hadn't actually *wanted* dangerous.

And yet, here, in front of her, stood a man who was a danger to her in so many ways, and she couldn't stop noticing how freaking attractive he was.

He finally hung up, shoved his phone in his back pocket, and glowered at her.

Glowered. At her. As if it were her fault.

Screw that. She was over being treated like there was something wrong with her. "Don't look at me like that."

"Like what?"

"Like it was my idea. I'm going inside to pick my bedroom." She turned and strode toward the house, but to no surprise, Dash jogged after her and caught up before she even made it to the porch steps.

He stepped in front of her, literally blocking the door. "This isn't going to work."

She put her hands on her hips. "What isn't? Being room-mates? It's a big house." She was upset, and she knew it wasn't simply being back in her childhood town. It was because Dash was being such a jerk about it.

How many times had she imagined running into him again? It would be romantic. Electric. Both of them declaring that they'd stayed married because they loved each other, and the time was finally right. She'd imagined him taking one look at her and unleashing a string of curses as only Dash could create, followed by him declaring how beautiful she was, how he'd been waiting for her all this time, and he was ready to be her knight in shining armor.

Instead, all he'd done was grump, curse, and glower. Not even a single appreciative look.

Stupid husbands.

"This co-heir thing," he said. "Look, I need this house. I was counting on it. I've been living here for the last six months."

Oh, no. She wasn't going to let him sweet-talk her into giving it up. "I need it, too," she said. "I need to sell it and make the money from it."

His eyes narrowed. "Sell it? You can't sell it. It was Bea's home."

She tried to ignore the guilt that clogged her stomach. "I have to sell it. We'll live together for thirty days, and then sell it. The house looks good. It'll sell quickly."

He scowled. "It looks great because I've been taking care of it for years. She let me work in the workshop so I took care of stuff. Anything she needed." He paused, and she heard his voice catch. "She was a champ."

He missed her, Leila realized. Grumpy Dash was out of sorts because he *missed* Bea.

Her heart softened a little bit, just a little, because she knew how he felt. "Bea was amazing," Leila said softly. "She was there for me."

"Yeah."

They locked gazes, and suddenly the chasm between them was bridged by their common grief, their shared love for a woman who had taken both of them, and Dash's sister, under her wing when they'd needed it. "Was she happy?" Leila asked. "Did she have a good rest of her life?"

Dash nodded. "Her friends were always around. She had a boyfriend for a while, too. A good guy. Norm's brother. She was always a sparkling light, all the way until she crashed that kneeboard."

Leila smiled. "How many one-hundred-year-old women die kneeboarding on a lake?"

He laughed softly. "It was the only way Bea would ever go. There's no way she'd die in a bed. I think she knew her time was up, and she decided how it was going to happen."

"That's just like her." They met gazes, and Leila's heart softened at the emotion in Dash's eyes. "I'm glad she had you, Dash."

He nodded. "I was lucky to have her."

Silence fell for a moment, but the awkwardness was gone. Remembering Bea had humanized Dash from the image she'd been holding in her mind all these years. "How was the funeral?"

Dash grinned. "Eppie had a bouncy house, a lobster bake, a DJ, and a whole bunch of kids games at the town beach. She even had fireworks in the evening. Best party Birch Crossing has seen in years."

Leila's throat tightened. "Exactly how Bea would have

wanted it." She hadn't even known about Bea's death until several weeks later. Would she have gone to the funeral? She hoped she would have, but it had been difficult enough to come back today, even when she was desperate.

"That's why Eppie did it," he agreed softly. "No one messes with Bea, even after she's gone."

She met his gaze, finally understanding the situation. "Which is why we're going to live together for thirty days, aren't we?"

He swore under his breath, but she saw the resignation in his eyes. "Yeah," he said. "Can't mess with Bea."

She smiled, remembering all the times when she was a kid when Bea had laid down the law. "No, we can't."

It was settled then.

She was going to live with Dash Stratton for the next thirty days. "How many bathrooms are there?"

"A half bath downstairs." He walked past her, opened the front door, and held it open. "One full bath upstairs."

One shower.

Thirty days.

And the rebellious bad boy she'd loved since she was a teenager.

What could possibly go wrong?

———

DASH DROPPED the last of Leila's bags at the door of the bedroom he'd given her. There were only three bedrooms, and two of the others were occupied.

Not one bedroom.

Two of them were occupied.

One by him. And one…soon.

He'd kept both doors firmly closed so she wouldn't see what was inside. He didn't know why he was hiding from her, but he was. His life…fuck. He didn't even know what his life was right now, but he had to figure out how to deal with it in two days.

Leila was all that he'd been imagining since she'd left. And more.

And now she was back. And it was too late. The timing was wrong. So fucking wrong.

Leila tossed her bag on the bed and turned to face him.

The tension that had been gripping him since he'd first heard her voice coiled even more tightly. "You look good," he said. She did look good. Beautiful, but also interesting. She had lines at the corners of her mouth and eyes. She had weight in her eyes, and also a sparkle. She looked complicated, and he liked that.

Her brows went up, and something simmered in her eyes. "Thanks. You're still riding the bike?"

His motorcycle. "Not much. I had a chance to get out on it today, but I mostly drive a truck. I work construction, so yeah."

She folded her arms over her chest, which accentuated her breasts.

He tried not to notice.

"I always thought you were going to be a tattoo artist," she said.

He laughed, surprised by her comment. "Really?"

"Yeah. You always used to draw those cool designs for Bea's husband to build with his iron works, but I figured you were too dangerous to be a painter. So, I decided on tattoo artist."

"Dangerous?" Fuck. He hadn't been dangerous. He'd been on the run his whole damned life. He understood that now. He'd come to understand a lot of things over the last year. "Just trying to survive."

Understanding flickered in her eyes. "Me, too."

He cocked his head. "Things were rough for you?" He didn't like that at all. He'd married her to keep her safe. He'd let her go so she could have a better life than what she'd find in Birch Crossing.

She smiled, a smile that didn't quite reach her eyes. "It's fine. Glad for a break from my life, if I'm honest."

What the hell? The same protectiveness that had prompted him to say yes when Bea and his sister Maura had asked him to marry Leila surged to life again. "What's going on?"

She frowned at him, and he remembered that he hadn't seen Leila in fifteen years.

He had no business prying into her life. Shit. "Never mind." But he couldn't sit around and let her carry that weight. He had a couple days off from the life that had taken him hostage, so he could use that time how he chose. "You going to the fundraiser tonight?"

Leila laughed softly. "Eppie made me buy beer to bring and donate a gift card to the raffle." There was warmth in her voice, but also an edge that he couldn't quite read.

"Want a ride?" He made the offer before he'd consciously thought it.

Wariness flickered across Leila's face. "I'm good. I want to be able to leave whenever I want. I'm pretty beat."

"Perfect. I'm not planning to stay long. I want to get some time in the studio tonight."

"The studio?"

He nodded. "I took over Roger's workshop after he died. He used to build fire escapes and stuff, and I went from there."

She cocked her head. "What do you build?"

He shrugged. "It's iron art, I guess. I'm heading out now to do some errands, but I'll be back at five to pick you up. Bike or truck?"

Interest piqued in her weary eyes. "When I was younger, I used to dream about riding on your motorcycle. I thought it would be so badass."

He laughed, even as her comment rolled around inside him. "Yeah, I know."

"You do?"

"Yeah. Whenever you were with Maura and I'd pull up on my bike, I'd see the way you looked at it." He laughed again when her cheeks turned pink. "I'm not gonna lie, Leila. Sometimes I would pull up just so I could see the look on your face. It was good for my ego."

She laughed then, and her embarrassment faded. "You're an ass."

"I was an ass," he corrected. "And now I'm…"

She raised her brows. "Not an ass?"

"It's complicated." He shifted, suddenly wanting to get out of there. Something about Leila was captivating him, and he couldn't afford to be distracted. "See you at five. We'll take the bike."

Then, before she could protest, he turned and jogged down the stairs.

But even when he shoved open the front door and headed toward his bike, he couldn't get Leila out of his mind. All was not fine with the woman he'd married.

His wife. Felt weird to say those words, but they were true, for now, at least. Her presence could tangle that up in a hurry. But for now, legally, they were bound.

He swung his leg over his bike, started the engine, and then put on his helmet. What was he doing, offering to take Leila to the fundraiser? He didn't have time for that. Not right now.

A year ago, yeah.

Today? No. He didn't have time for anything except trying to clean up a lifetime of mistakes.

But he'd seen the way Leila's face had lit up when he'd mentioned the bike, which meant he was taking her.

He got his helmet fastened, and took a look back at the house. Living with Leila for thirty days? He barely knew the woman he'd married so long ago. How the hell were they going to work this out? Settle the house? Live together?

Maura would get a kick out of it—

He swore at his thoughts, and sudden darkness settled down on him.

Maura.

Anger tore through him, and he hit the gas. The rear tire skidded in the dirt before the bike leapt forward. The wind whipped past him as he raced out of the driveway and onto the road.

Needing to escape.

And knowing he couldn't.

But he didn't know how to stay.

CHAPTER 5

LEILA BRACED her hands on the window, watching Dash speed away.

She let out her breath. "That man is much too dangerous for me."

Dangerous because he awakened all the same feelings in her that he had when she was a teenager. Silly, stupid emotions like lust, desire, infatuation.

Except, now, it was more. When she was a teenager, he'd been so much older than she was, that he'd been only a fantasy.

But now? The age gap was nothing between them.

It was two adults, living together.

The man she'd married.

And was still married to.

Why were they still married?

It was a question that Gordon had been right to ask, because she didn't know.

It was a question she'd been afraid to look at, for fear that if she looked at it too closely, she would break the spell and she'd find herself no longer tied to Dash.

Why did she care? Why did it matter? She didn't even know him.

And why hadn't he cut the ties either?

Leila let out her breath and tore her gaze off the road where Dash had disappeared. From the second-floor window, she could see the lake through the trees. Just one road and a row of houses were between Bea's house and the lake.

She saw the footpath they'd used to go between two houses and down to the lake. Did the current owners still allow kids to use the path and swim from their dock and float, like she and Maura had?

Involuntarily, her gaze wandered to the right, to the house she'd grown up in.

There it was. A tiny, rustic cabin still taking up space on the lake. She could barely see it through the trees, but she could see enough to remember how it felt to live there. Scared. Sad. Confused. Lonely.

Leila tore her gaze off her old home and looked down at the yard of Bea's house. The old picnic table was still in the shade, and that same tire swing still hung from the majestic oak tree. The rope was bright white, new. And the picnic table had a new coat of sky-blue paint with flowers painted across it.

The rose bushes along the side of the yard were bountiful and colorful, and Bea's butterfly garden was wild and thriving.

Dash had indeed kept things beautiful.

Guilt edged into her gut, and she turned away. She didn't have an obligation to keep the house because Dash and Bea had loved it. She could sell her half to Dash and move on. Then he got what he wanted and Bea's house would still be with him.

It was fine.

She leaned on the windowsill and looked at the room.

34

How many times had she slept here when she was scared to go home?

Her gaze went to the closet. Would it still be there? Surely Dash or Bea would have cleaned it out by now.

But maybe not.

She pushed a chair over to the closet, then climbed up on it. She used her phone to shine a light into the back corner of the top shelf.

The box was still there. Tucked back in the corner.

No way.

She leaned in and grabbed the box, dragging it across the shelf. It was lighter than she remembered, but there was definitely still something inside. She pulled the box out, climbed down and set it on the bed. The shoe box was still covered in the flowers she'd drawn. They were so faded now, but she could still see some of the outlines.

She opened it and her heart turned over. Inside was a little wooden loon, small enough to fit in the palm of her hand. Its black and white checkered feathers, white breast, and red eyes were a little faded with time, but it brought back memories of the haunting call of the loon that she'd listened to every night while she lay in bed.

Dash had carved this little loon, painted it, and given it to Maura, who had gifted it to Leila.

Leila picked it up and turned it over in her hand. It was worn smooth now, from all the hours she'd clutched it in her hand, using it to give herself courage that she couldn't find on her own. She used to imagine that Dash's boldness lived in that little loon, and if she held it, then she would have that same courage.

She smiled, and then set it aside to pick up the little journal with the blue flowers on it. She opened it to the first page. *I hate Willie.*

Her stepfather.

The old emotions came surging to the front, and she

closed the journal. She didn't need to relive her childhood. She was long past that. She was a grown woman, smart, talented, healthy, newly liberated to live her own life on her own terms.

She didn't need Dash's loon or to stagnate in the past.

Maybe that was why Bea had made her come back. So Leila could finally let go of the shadows that still clung to her. So, she could finally get up every morning with a light heart, laughter in her soul, and eyes that saw only love and possibility in the world.

And maybe, Bea wanted her to finally let go of the safety net of Dash. Because as long as she was still married to Dash, she always had an excuse to keep men at a distance, like Robbie.

She hugged the journal to her chest and looked up at the ceiling. "What's your plan for this whole thirty-day thing, Bea?"

The ceiling said nothing, but Leila felt the warmth that she'd always been surrounded with when she'd been in this house, in this bedroom. She'd trusted Bea back then, and it was time to trust her now. "All right," she said. "I'm in. To the fundraiser with Dash, and then…to whatever comes next."

She put the journal and the loon back in the box, didn't even bother to look at the rest of the contents, then put the lid on it. For a long moment, she stared at the box. She should put it in the trash. She wanted to put it in the trash. But she couldn't yet. It was her past, which helped define who she was today.

But she didn't want it in her room. In her closet.

Leila tucked it under her arm, then headed down the stairs. She stepped out onto the front porch, and looked around, but everywhere on the property still felt too close. She didn't want to look around and see the box, or know that it was there.

Maybe Clare would hold it for her.

She felt stupid putting it in the back of her car, but she didn't know what else to do. "And to think I thought I was over it all," she said aloud as she shut her car door.

Bea knew better, which was why Leila was back.

"Thirty days," she said. "I have thirty days to get my life back."

Not get her life *back*. Because it had always been attached to the shadows of Birch Crossing and her phantom husband.

To get her life *started*.

Beginning with the fundraiser with Dash.

CHAPTER 6

DASH STAYED AWAY from the house until it was time to pick up Leila.

But when he pulled in on his bike and she walked out the front door, he immediately regretted that he'd been gone all day.

She was absolutely compelling.

Leila gave him a little wave as she jogged down the porch steps. She was wearing denim shorts that revealed a hell of a lot of thigh, and a fitted tank top, and she was carrying a white sweater. Her legs were muscled, and she was wearing hot pink sneakers with lime green trim.

She looked like summer freedom, and he wanted to be around that vibe. He wanted to be around her. Which was why he'd stayed away.

He was still so thrown by the fact she was there. In his house. In his life.

He turned off the bike as she reached the driveway. "Hi."

She smiled at him, and he felt her nervousness. "Hi." She cleared her throat. "Do I just get on?"

He nodded. "I have a helmet for you." He reached behind him to get the helmet he'd picked up for her, and his arm brushed against hers. Electricity seemed to shoot through him, and she sucked in her breath at the contact. "Sorry."

"What? It's fine." She laughed softly as she took the helmet from him. "I'm sure we'll have plenty of accidental touches living in the same house for a month."

His gut tightened at the thought of repeatedly running into Leila. *Shit.* He couldn't believe his reaction to her. It was intense, relentless, and riveting. And not okay, for a multitude of reasons.

He had to keep focused and on-point. He'd decided to help her get unstuck from whatever she was dealing with for the next few days, not to seduce her into his bed, even though that felt like the exact place he wanted her.

She thought he was dangerous?

Not a damned chance. Not anymore. At least not to her. He'd never, ever be a danger to her, no matter what he had to do to make certain of that.

He watched her as she put the helmet on and strapped it beneath her chin. His fingers itched to help her, but he kept them on the handlebars. She looked so damn cute in that helmet.

What the hell was he thinking? Noticing? Feeling?

Leila wasn't there to be his distraction from his life. She needed to feel safe in the house, and that meant she didn't need to feel worried about what he was thinking.

"Good?" She dropped her hands.

He put his hand on the helmet and moved it to make sure it was secure. "Yeah, good."

"Great" She pulled the sweater on. "I feel like we're supposed to be wearing Kevlar."

"Yep. That's the usual recommended gear for riding a bike."

She hesitated at his honesty. "Are you a good rider?"

"Not dead yet."

She put her hands on her hips. "Really? What kind of

breezy remark is that? You know I'm asking if I need to make up an excuse not to ride with you. I'm not ready to die."

Her words hit a chord in him that it wouldn't have hit a year ago. "No one ever is. But you're going to go at some point. But for every day until that time, you're not going to die. So, you get to decide how to live while you've got the chance." He nodded at her car. "You want to live in a car or on a motorcycle this afternoon?"

She stared at him. "That's quite a speech."

He shrugged, suddenly restless. He felt like his mind was in total chaos, and having Leila here was adding to it. "Let's go." He didn't want to talk anymore. He just wanted to move forward. With Leila. Without Leila. It was her choice.

She lifted her chin. "All right." She flipped down the face shield, then swung her leg over the bike and settled in behind him.

Hell yeah.

"I've never ridden a motorcycle before," she said. "What do I do?"

"Tuck up tight against me," he said. "Wrap your arms around my waist, and lean with me around the curves in the road. I'll go slow." He pointed to the bars by her ankles. "Feet go there."

She put her feet in place, then scooched up securely behind him. Her arms slipped around him, and he looked down as she locked her hands around his waist. He could feel the heat of her body against his back, her legs flanking his hips and thighs, her trust as she put her life into his care.

He rarely gave anyone a ride on his bike, but it felt damned good to have Leila tucked up against him.

"Ready," she said.

"All right." He started the bike again. He tapped the back of her wrist twice to let her know he was moving, then let out the clutch. She tightened her arms around his stomach the moment the wheels began to turn, and he grinned.

For the first time since he'd married her fifteen years ago, they were together.

Touching.

Trusting.

Mind. Blown.

CHAPTER 7

THE MINUTE DASH'S motorcycle began to move, Leila decided she'd been an idiot to get on the bike.

She'd thought she'd feel exhilarated and free to have the wind blowing through her hair, but she just felt sudden, raw terror at her complete vulnerability.

The pavement was right below her feet. Right there. If she put her foot down, the asphalt would rip her sneakers off. She had relinquished all control to Dash, which went against everything she'd come here to work on.

She gripped him tightly, her heart pounding as he headed down the road. She had no idea how fast they were going, but it felt like the world was spinning by at a reckless speed.

She pressed her face shield to his back and closed her eyes, fighting off the sudden panic. What had she been thinking, getting on the motorcycle? She'd had a crush on Dash because he was the adventurer that she wasn't.

And she still wasn't.

She'd been an idiot to think that just because it was Dash, that she would spontaneously transform into a woman who liked danger, took risks, and delighted in a total lack of control over her life.

She wanted to be back in her condo. In her relationship with a man who didn't light her up, but who didn't scare her either. She wanted to be getting up every morning, going to her safe job, and coming home to her predictable life.

But she'd lost it all.

She didn't have a safety net anymore.

She only had a motorcycle, and a very muscular husband to hang on to.

The motorcycle slowed, and she opened her eyes as he pulled off the road into a scenic pull-out beside the road. Relief rushed through her as the motorcycle came to a stop, and sudden tears threatened. She'd made it.

Then she looked around and saw they were alone on the edge of the road, surrounded by trees.

They weren't there yet.

They would have to keep going.

Noooo.

Dash pulled off his helmet and turned around to face her. "Leila."

He sounded tense. Oh, God. "What's wrong?" She looked around, but she didn't see anything overtly terrifying. They were in the middle of the woods. A small house was in a clearing across the street, and a little stream ran alongside. But that was it.

"Nothing. Take off your helmet for a sec."

"Why?" She quickly unbuckled it and yanked it off. "What's happening?"

He smiled at her, that same, endearingly cocky smile he'd had so long ago. "You remember when you agreed to marry me?"

Her heart started to race. "What about it?"

"You decided to trust me enough to legally bind yourself to me, right? Your life was falling apart, and you trusted me to help you save it. Right?"

She nodded again. "Yes, why?"

"How did it feel to trust me?"

She swallowed. "Why are you asking me that?" There were so many reasons she didn't want to dive into her past. She remembered how scared she'd been, and she also remembered what it had felt like when Dash, Maura, and Bea had sat down with her at Bea's kitchen table and proposed she marry Dash. When she'd looked at Dash and realized he was willing to marry her, she'd felt like her knight in shining armor had swept in to save her.

She'd felt like a princess when she and Dash had taken their vows. She'd thought all her problems were solved.

And then, he'd sent her on her way, all alone, to find her path by herself.

"I can feel how terrified you are by the way you're hanging on to me," he said. His voice was non-judgmental, which kept her from getting defensive.

Instead, she laughed softly. "I thought I was brave. I'm not. Is it too far to walk the rest of the way? It turns out, I don't like motorcycles."

"You're not riding a motorcycle."

She raised her brows. "No?" She patted the seat. "Is this a horse? My mistake."

"Nope. Not a horse."

"Then...?" She was actually a little curious as to what he was trying to say. Now that the bike was stopped, her tension had faded, and she could actually process what he was saying.

"*I'm* riding a motorcycle. The same motorcycle I've been riding for years, and never crashed."

She couldn't help but grin. "Then what am I doing?"

"You're trusting me, just like you did before."

Her smile faded, and she stared at him. Into those blue eyes that she hadn't seen for so long. "I don't even know you. That feels like a stupid thing to trust my life with someone I don't even know."

"True." He inclined his head in acknowledgement. "But I protected you back then, and I wouldn't start putting you in danger now. So, when I start the bike up again, instead of thinking about the fact you're on a motorcycle and you don't know how to ride one, focus on the fact that for the next few minutes, you've entrusted me with your well-being, just like you did before. That's it."

"Just trust you?"

"Yep."

"That simple?"

"Yep."

She started laughing. "That's such an arrogant caveman mentality. You order me to trust you, and then claim that will make all my worries disappear?"

He grinned. "It didn't work?"

"No," she said, but she was still smiling. "That was ridiculous."

"I'm very trustworthy," he said, still grinning that insanely charming smile.

"Trustworthy enough to marry when I was eighteen," she agreed, "but that doesn't translate into trusting you not to skid off the road and send us plummeting down into the lake."

"Hmm..." He studied her. "How about the fact I did motocross racing in my early twenties and won a bunch of races?"

Oh, man. He was a motocross racer? Of course he was. Why was that so sexy? "Really?"

"Yeah." He grinned. "I was a lunatic back then, and I still survived. So, a little roll and stroll with you isn't even going to challenge me."

She couldn't help but giggle at his ridiculous verbiage. "Roll and stroll? Did you just make that up?"

"I did. You like it?"

"I do," she admitted. "It sounds very innocuous and safe."

"So safe it's almost boring." He took her helmet and fiddled with it. "We were supposed to be synched on Bluetooth so we could talk while we were riding, but yours wasn't on. It is now. I'll roll this beast along, and if you need a reminder about how damned good I am at driving it, just ask."

She smiled. "I do feel moderately less certain of death after our chat. A motocross racer is kind of badass."

"Fantastic. I'm a badass, then. Let's go with it." He handed her the helmet, and put his back on at the same time she did. "Can you hear me?"

His voice came through the helmet, right in her ear. "Yes!"

He grinned at her. "All right, then. Enjoy this leisurely tour of your old stomping grounds, Ms. Kerrigan."

She pulled down her face shield. "Thanks so much, Tour Guide Dash."

"You got it." He started the bike back up. The engine roared to life, but before she could think about being nervous, his deep voice echoed in her ear. "Don't be alarmed, fair traveler. T'was only the horses preparing to move out."

She laughed as she wrapped her arms around his waist and tucked in against him again. "T'was?"

"It's my favorite word. That and 'plethora.'" He pulled out into the road. "And whenever I have a plethora of t'wases in a conversation, I'm pretty much in heaven."

She shook her head, chuckling at his silliness. "I didn't know you were such a word nerd."

"Imagine. After fifteen years of marriage, we're still learning new things about each other."

"It's a stunner," she teased. "I thought you were an open book. What else have you been hiding from me?"

"I sleep naked, for one."

Sudden heat coursed through her. "I can't believe I never noticed that."

"Right? You never pay attention to me. I spend hours in

the gym every day, but my biceps just go unnoticed day after day."

Of course, as soon as Dash said that, all she could think about were the corded back muscles she was pressed up against. "Maybe if you would flex for me more often, I'd notice them."

"You want me to flex? I can do that." He took his left hand off the handlebars and flexed. "You like?"

Good gravy. He wasn't kidding. His arms were the stuff of fantasies. She itched to palm his arm, but instead, she said, "Did I mention the rule that both your hands need to be on the handlebars at all times?"

"I can't believe you were more worried about crashing than admiring my biceps." He did put his hand back on the bike, though. "What kind of marriage do we have?"

"Pure sex," she blurted out, before she had a chance to think about it. Damn him for showing off his ridiculous bicep and making her mind go into the gutter.

Dash made a sound like he was choking. "Is that what we have?"

Oh, God. What door had she opened? "Well, on the nights that aren't Scrabble competitions."

"Right. Scrabble and sex. That combo is the foundation for every lasting relationship."

She started laughing. Where had this conversation gone? "And ice cream."

"Of course ice cream. Life is nothing without ice cream. We're here. Welcome to the Birch Crossing Firefighter Fundraiser."

They were there already? She was startled as she looked ahead and saw all the trucks and cars in the parking lot. She'd been so caught up in their banter that she hadn't even noticed the ride. "Did you do that on purpose? Distract me so I wasn't scared?"

"If I said yes, would you be impressed?"

She giggled. "Since when are you so funny? I thought you were a moody, reserved bad boy."

"I am." He pulled into a spot beside a big, black pickup truck that had a bunch of construction equipment in the bed. "That was weird how I was funny there for a few minutes. I'm sure it'll go away. Don't get worried."

"You can be funny," she said as he turned off the bike. "It feels good to laugh."

He flipped the whole front of his helmet up and turned back to look at her. "Yeah, it does," he agreed, his blue eyes twinkling at her. "Forgot what that felt like."

She smiled. "Me, too. You can keep being a goofball. I give you permission."

He grinned. "Hot damn. You made my day. Can I buy you dinner at this all-you-can-eat buffet for six dollars a person?"

She pulled off her helmet and shook her head to free her hair. "The way you spend your hard-earned cash on me makes me feel like a princess."

He stared at her hair for a second before dragging his gaze back to her face. "You know that makes me crazy when you flip your hair like that."

Her stomach fluttered. Was he serious or teasing? She swallowed, and flipped her hair again, whacking him across the face with the ends. "Like that?"

He started laughing. "Yeah. Exactly like that. Being face whipped by the ends of your hair is my favorite kind of foreplay."

He had the most gorgeous laugh. Deep, heartfelt, and authentic. She loved it. "My favorite foreplay is you buying me a cheap dinner, so let's get this night started." She handed him her helmet, and this time, when his fingers brushed against hers, there was no mistaking the heat that shot through her.

She wanted him. There was no way to deny it. He was hot

as heck, funny, irreverent, and a protector, and he'd been under her skin for about a billion years.

Dash's smile faded. "Leila, the way you're looking at me is saying all sorts of things I'm not sure you mean."

She met his gaze. "What way?"

"Like I'm the buffet you want for dinner."

Oh, Lordy. "That's how I'm looking at you?"

"Sure is."

She slipped off the bike and stepped away from him. She wanted to come back with some funny quip, but her brain seemed to be frozen by the sudden heat between them. "That's funny," she said, with brilliant, unmatched wittiness.

"Is it?" He swung his leg over the bike and set their helmets on the seat.

"It's not?"

He walked to her, moving right into her space. "Leila."

She swallowed. He was only inches from her, and she had to look up to make eye contact. "Dash."

He was quiet for a moment, standing there, staring down at her.

Each moment that passed made her heart start to beat faster. She wanted him to kiss her. Right then. Right there. "We never kissed after we got married," she said.

His eyes darkened. "Nope. We didn't."

Again, the heat coiled between them. There were a million things she could say right now to cut the tension, send them back into silliness and jokes. She could step away and head right over to the corn on the cob and trays of burgers cooked by muscular firefighters. But she couldn't make herself do it.

Instead, she stood there, in that moment, and faced it.

Dash didn't move away either. He didn't crack a joke. Instead, he said, "This could get dangerous."

She nodded. "I know."

"You don't like danger."

"I know."

He was silent for a long moment. Leila was vaguely aware of the hustle and hubbub around them, but in their little bubble, there was only smoldering sexual tension. "It's been fifteen years. It's too late to start anything," he said.

"I don't want to start anything."

"What do you want, then?" he asked, his gaze so penetrating that she felt like her insides were going up in flames.

"My wedding kiss."

"That's it?"

"Yes," she whispered. "That's it. I deserve it."

"Yeah, you do." He slid his hand along her jaw. "One long-awaited wedding kiss coming up."

Her heart raced faster than it ever had at the feel of his touch on her skin. *He was going to kiss her.* After all these years, he was going to kiss her.

He met her gaze, slid her a smile that made her stomach flutter, then leaned in and kissed her.

His mouth was hot and delicious, everything she'd ever dreamed of, and so much more.

She'd been expecting a quick kiss, but he lingered, tasting her mouth as if she were the most decadent chocolate he'd ever experienced.

When he set his other hand on her face, she instinctively put her hands on his hips, leaning into the kiss.

The moment she touched him, he wrapped his arm around her waist and pulled her in for more.

CHAPTER 8

DASH KNEW he was in trouble.

Kissing Leila was like diving into a mirror-smooth lake at sunrise, with the loons calling, and the fresh, clean water wrapping around him and sweeping all the noise and chaos out of his body, mind, and soul. Everything inside him became about the feel of her body against his. His entire awareness became the taste of her mouth, the feel of her breath against his lips, the heat of her body against his.

There had been so much churning inside him for so long, whipping faster and darker with each passing day. And suddenly, for the first time in ages, maybe ever, he felt like he could breathe, think, be present.

He angled his head and deepened the kiss, desire coiling through him when she leaned into him, kissing him back just as fiercely as he was kissing her. Leila wasn't keeping him at a distance. She was drawing him in, and meeting him with unfettered passion.

More than peace now. Desire, life, vitality were coming alive within him. A lust for her, but also to be alive, to feel, to experience this moment, this woman, the fire that was suddenly burning between them with such gorgeous heat and temptation.

She let out a little noise of desire and pressed herself more tightly against him. He swore under his breath and accepted her move, locking his arms around her back. He slid his tongue past her lips, and when she responded in kind, his whole body ignited with a raw need that seemed to consume him—

"Okay, kids!" Eppie's voice sounded right in his ear, jerking him back to the present. "This is a family event. No butt-grabbing allowed until after the kids leave!"

Leila jumped back with a little gasp. "Oh, God. I totally forgot where we were."

"That's okay," Eppie said cheerfully. "A little hankie-pankie is always a good thing. I just wanted to make sure you two weren't headed toward the full Monty."

Dash couldn't take his gaze off Leila. Her face was flushed, and she was breathing a little heavily. She looked like she'd just been thoroughly kissed and had loved every minute of it.

Yes. Satisfaction, the kind that his sister would have called smug, male satisfaction, pulsed through him.

"Dash!" Eppie hit him on the shoulder. "Stop undressing Leila in your head! It's much too obvious."

Leila's eyes widened, and he dragged his attention off her to focus on Eppie. "Better in my head than in real life, though, right?"

The older lady cackled. "Only when in public, my dear boy. Only when in public." She was wearing a bright yellow hat with crocheted daises all around the rim. Each one was at least four inches in diameter, and she'd stuck a few real daises on as well. The brim was wider than her shoulders, and it sat low on her head, making her ears stick out, but that was barely noticeable because of the two-inch yellow daisy earrings dangling almost all the way to her shoulders.

Dash grinned at her. "Excellent point, Eppie."

"I'm full of excellent points," Eppie said, before turning to Leila. "My darling, you must come with me." She stuck her hand through the crook of Leila's elbow. "Do you like babies? We're having a baby fest with the ladies." She shot a look at Dash as she spoke, and just like that, all his tension came back.

"Babies?" Leila frowned. "I'm not really a baby person."

Fuck.

"We'll fix that," Eppie said. "Dash, we saved you and Leila seats at table twenty-two. We'll meet you there when it's time to eat."

Leila looked back at him as Eppie towed her away, mouthing "help me."

He grinned and waved at her. They both knew that no one turned down Eppie, and no one actually wanted to. Eppie was infectious with her zest for life, and he was lucky that she'd been such good friends with Bea that he'd gotten to know her.

But...*fuck.* Leila wasn't a baby person.

"Hey Dash."

He looked over as Blue Carboni walked over. Blue was a former kidnap recovery field agent, and he'd come to Birch Crossing a while ago, after his partner, Harlan Shea, had settled in town with his new wife. Blue was a great guy, and he and his wife Chloe had been a lot of help over the last few months, when Dash's life had gone sideways. "Hi. How are Chloe and the girls doing?"

Blue grinned. "We have a date to adopt Jess and Makayla now. We'll be a family of six in August."

"Damn, man. That's fantastic." Blue and Chloe had opened their huge, old home to girls in the foster care system. They'd decided to only take girls, to create the safest space they could for them. They'd adopted two of their foster kids so far, and then Jess and Makayla would make four. "You feeling overwhelmed by all the girls?"

Blue's face lit up. "You kidding? I was born to be a girl daddy. You should see me braid. I'm faster than Chloe now. I'm the braiding champ in the household. I can do French braid, reverse French braid, and pig tails." He grinned. "I've been watching videos so I can learn how to do designs with the braids. These girls have high fashion standards, and there's no salon near Birch Crossing that specializes in Black hair. I'm all they've got, and I won't let them down."

Dash grinned. "Nice work."

"You ain't seen nothing yet," Blue said. "I'm amazing."

At that moment, they both heard the shout of "Daddy!"

Blue spun around and crouched, sweeping Tonisha up into his arms as she screeched with delight. True to his claim, the little girl had an intricate pattern of braids, complete with dozens of pink beads on the end of each braid. Damn. That was impressive. "You really did that?"

"Sure did. I have all that finger dexterity from handling weapons for so long. It's a great crossover skill, apparently."

Tonisha held out her braid to Dash. "I'm a princess," she said. "See the pink beads?"

Dash grinned. "I do. And the shirt."

She pulled her shirt away from her body to show him a glittery pink shirt. "And my shoes." She kicked her pink sneakers at him, shoes that had a princess on the side. "A princess can do anything, and so can I!"

Dash nodded. "You sure can."

Blue grinned. "What else are you?"

She held her arms up and flexed her biceps. "I'm strong!"

Blue nodded. "And smart."

"I'm smart!"

"And beautiful."

"I'm beautiful!"

"And brave."

"I'm brave!" Her arms were still above her head, and she was shouting the words like she meant them.

Blue was a hell of a dad. Dash hoped he could be half of what Blue was, but the man gave him hope.

"And Daddy's my favorite," Blue added, winking at Dash.

Tonisha shrieked with laughter. "Mommy's my favorite," she shouted. "Mommy!" She squirmed to get down. "I see Eppie! I want to see Eppie! Eppie!"

Blue set her down, and both men watched as Tonisha raced across the roped-off parking lot toward Eppie and Leila, who had just reached the gathering where Chloe, Clare, their two best friends, and their kids were gathered on a spread of blankets. The men weren't around. It was just the women.

The sight of all the women together caught Dash unexpectedly, and he was hit with sudden grief. He turned away and took a breath. "Fuck."

Blue was watching him with understanding. "It takes time to heal, but it'll come."

Dash looked up at the sky, trying to focus on the bright blue. "Sometimes I don't want to heal. I feel like if I heal, I'll forget."

"You'll never forget," Blue said softly. "I'll remember every person I lost on every mission for the rest of my life. I'll remember their faces, their voices, and their last words. And those were strangers, not someone I loved. You won't forget, but when you can remember without all the pain, it's better."

Dash looked over at Blue. "Is it?"

"It's better in the right ways. You can breathe again. You can live again. You can feel joy again." He held up his hand before Dash could speak. "And it's right to feel joy, Dash. It is. You can't bring them back, no matter how much you suffer or punish yourself. But you can keep their spirit alive by allowing yourself to thrive again."

"Maybe." Dash let his gaze wander back over to the group of women, but this time, he searched out Leila and focused on her. She was sitting on the ground next to Clare, and she was shaking hands with Chloe, who had moved to town after Leila had left, so Leila had never known her.

"Your wife, huh?" Blue said, following Dash's gaze.

"My wife," Dash repeated. "That sounds weird to say. She was a girl I married a long time ago to help her out. She was Maura's best friend. A kid, compared to me back then."

"And yet, you're still married."

"Yeah." Dash smiled when he saw Leila laugh at something Chloe said. He loved her laugh. "She made me laugh on the ride over. For a little bit, I forgot about everything, and I was just happy."

"That's good," Blue said. "Keep her around, then, for a bit. Let her make you happy."

Dash looked over at him. "I have to live with her for thirty days to get the house."

Blue started laughing. "Bea did that?"

"She sure did."

"I love that woman. I didn't know her well, but damn, that's good work right there."

"Yeah." Dash paused. "Leila doesn't know."

"About?"

"Any of it."

Blue let out a whistle. "Damn, Dash. You need to tell her."

"I know." He ran his hand through his hair. "It's just nice to be around someone who isn't looking at me through that lens. She's willing to be silly and laugh, and it feels good. It's a break." Plus, Dash sensed that Leila was dealing with her own issues. He didn't want to burden her with his. He felt like they both needed some levity in their lives.

"She's your wife, Dash. She was Maura's best friend when they were teenagers. She needs to know."

"I guess I'm hoping that maybe someone else will tell her." He looked at Blue. "I don't want to talk about it."

Blue's face softened with understanding. "It'll get better. Maybe telling Leila will help with that."

"Maybe." Suddenly, all the passion and intensity that their kiss had ignited felt like a tease. A lie. That wasn't his life. He wasn't that guy.

"A little advice?"

"Always welcome, coming from you," Dash said honestly.

"Don't be the guy who's afraid to have the hard conversations, especially with Leila. You can't be that guy anymore."

Dash ground his jaw. "It's not who I am."

"It has to be." Blue smiled. "Trust me, I was a thousand times more closed off than you are, and I made it out the other side. You just have to decide that it's worth it. You have to decide you want to be that guy for them."

Did he? He didn't want to be that guy. He didn't know how to be that guy.

"Hey!" Griffin Friesé, who was both the owner of Wright's General store and Clare's husband, strode up. "Softball's starting in a few. You guys in? It's over thirty-five versus under thirty-five this year." He grinned. "The Unders are calling it the Has-beens versus the Future. I need some good firepower or we'll go down in flames."

Blue grinned. "I'm in. Let's go, Dash. It'll be good for you. Take your mind off things."

"Women love athletes," Griffin added.

Dash raised his brows. "I'm already married to her. I don't need to impress her."

"Marriage is the first step. Keeping them is a life-long focus." Griffin blew a kiss to Clare. "Let's go, boys."

Blue and Griffin headed toward the softball field, but Dash didn't move. Maura and Leila had both played softball in high school. Maura had lost interest in sports after she'd graduated, but maybe Leila?

She was smiling and laughing, but her shoulders were tense. Was it being around the kids? The women? He recalled that Leila hadn't been all that social when they were kids, which was why she hadn't had anyone to turn to besides Maura, Bea, and himself when things got bad for her.

Decided, he strode over to the little gathering. "Hello," he said.

There was a rush of greetings from kids and women, then he focused on Leila. "The town softball game is starting. Over thirty-five versus under thirty-five. You in?"

Her face lit up. "Yes! I would love to! Can I pitch?"

He grinned as she shot to her feet, pleased he'd thought to ask her. "I'm not in charge, but I'm assuming so. Griffin is the captain of the over thirty-five."

Leila grinned at him. "I'm under thirty-five," she said. "We're enemies now, my friend."

He groaned. "I forgot you're a baby."

"I'm not a baby," she quipped as she waved good-bye to the women and walked beside him toward the softball field. "I'm a gloriously awesome woman who just happens to have a lot less miles on my body than you."

He laughed, his spirit already lighter just by being around her for a minute. Did he want to screw that up by getting all serious with her about his life? Nope. He didn't. "The miles look good on you."

Her brows shot up. "They look good on you, too, old man."

He laughed again. "You won't be calling me old after we dust you young 'uns."

"You won't beat us. I'll be pitching."

"It's slow-pitch. You're not allowed to strike anyone out."

Her face fell. "Not even you?"

He laughed. "You can try me."

She grinned. "Awesome."

"Won't work. I'm a stellar athlete."

"I'm a stellar pitcher."

"You were. It was a long time ago," he teased.

"Not as long ago as it was for you," she shot back.

"Want to make a wager?"

Interest sparked in her eyes. "What kind of wager?"

All sorts of interesting ideas popped into his mind, ones that definitely weren't appropriate for family-friendly venues, or even for an evening with the wife he'd just kissed for the first time today. "Backrub."

She stared at him for so long he began to feel like he shouldn't have said that. "Or folding laundry," he amended. "Or cooking dinner. Cleaning the bathroom for the month. There are a lot of options when we live together. "

"I'll take the backrub."

Heat poured through him. "All right."

"Warm up those hands. I want at least an hour after we win and I strike you out." She flipped her hair at him, then turned and jogged away toward the younger crowd gathering on the third base side.

There were plenty of women playing on both teams, and he liked that. Birch Crossing wasn't a place where the women stayed on the sidelines, and that was good. A good place for girls to grow up… *Fuck.*

"Ready?" Griffin tossed him a glove. "I brought extras."

He caught it. "Thanks." He'd been so focused on Leila when he'd come back to the house that he'd forgotten about getting his gear for the game.

But he was okay with that. He liked focusing on Leila. She felt good.

He looked over at the third base bench. Like him, she'd found a glove, and she was already tossing a ball, warming up. She looked adorable out there, tossing a softball in her shorts and tank top. She looked comfortable and happy, and he could see her laughing with the others.

He paused, watching more carefully. She did look happy. Maybe that was what she needed. Time with a crowd that was closer to her age, without all the baggage he carried with him. Not that he was old, but seven years became a big gap when it was weighted with shadows and crap.

Blue put his hand on Dash's shoulder. "She's cute."

"She is."

"You going to keep her this time?"

"No." Dash turned away. "She's not mine to keep."

"Just to marry?"

"Yep. Until she doesn't need that either." But hell. Now that he was with her again, the idea of cutting that one tie that held them together didn't feel good at all. "Let's play ball."

Dash saw the look Blue gave him as he jogged out onto the field, but he didn't care. Yeah, he was shoving his emotions into a cave, but that was where he needed to keep them, despite what Blue thought.

Right now, he was going to play softball against the woman who was still his wife, and that's as far as he was going to think.

Except for the backrub that was at stake.

He was probably a jerk for suggesting it, but now that it was on the table, he was damned glad it was.

Whoever won, he was going to lean into it. Live for the moment that he got, because he knew all too well that everything could change in a heartbeat.

CHAPTER 9

L<small>EILA WAS</small> happy for the first time in a long time.

She forgot how much she loved softball, and she'd never played it for the town before. She loved the crowds cheering her on, and all the people who had learned her name and were shouting it every time she came to bat.

The teasing and trash-talking had been hilarious.

And the best part had been looking across the infield and seeing Dash. He always seemed to be watching her, ready to give her a thumbs up, or a grin. She felt like she had her own personal cheerleader, and it felt great.

Dash was hers, and only hers, by law, and she loved how that felt.

There were a few women on his team who were funny and nice, but Leila never felt threatened by them, because Dash's focus was on her.

They might be married in name only, but he made her feel like it was real while they were in public, and she would forever be grateful to him for that.

It was the last inning, now. The Unders were up by one run, and the Overs were down to their last out…which was

Dash. He had a runner on third, which meant any hit would tie the game.

Despite his promise that she could fastpitch him, she hadn't. She'd tossed him some soft pitches and he'd launched home runs into the woods all three times he'd been at bat. He was a fierce athlete, and she loved it. Her husband was hot stuff, and it was freaking awesome.

Robbie had been a softy. Smart and successful at business, but athletically and physically? He'd been a nothing.

But Dash was all that, and more.

Everyone started cheering as he walked up to the plate, but he held up his hand for silence. "This woman on the mound," he called out, "was a great pitcher in high school. I challenge her to pitch to me for real. Let's make this an actual battle for the win."

Everyone started cheering, and Leila felt her energy rise.

"You sure?" she shouted to Dash. "The game is on the line." And a backrub, but she wasn't going to yell that to the crowd. "You have the chance to be the hero." They both knew he'd probably jack a home run if she just tossed him the ball, the way she'd been doing to everyone all during the game.

"I want to earn my hero status," he yelled back. "Bring it, Leila! I'm ready."

The crowd erupted into cheers, and her teammates started chanting her name.

The Overs started chanting Dash's name.

The fans were shouting for both of them.

The field became electric, and she couldn't contain her joy. Dash and everyone else were inviting her to tap into her power. She hadn't felt powerful in a long time.

"Go Leila!" Clare yelled, and Leila looked over. The little group she'd been sitting with had moved over to watch the game, and all the women gave her fist pumps and started yelling encouragement.

She felt like a star. "All right, Dash," she shouted over the crowd. "Let's do this!"

He blew her a kiss and stepped into the batter's box.

Leila took a breath. It had been a very long time since she'd thrown a pitch for real. "Can I take a throw, just so I don't blow out my shoulder?"

Dash gave her a thumbs up and stepped back.

All right.

Leila positioned herself, closed her eyes, and envisioned throwing the ball. Her balance. Her grip on the ball. Her timing. She felt her mind settle, and her muscle memory kick in.

She opened her eyes, nodded at the catcher, and then unleashed a pitch. It smacked right into the catcher's mitt, and the place erupted in cheers.

Damn. That had felt good. It had been a little low, but still. Wow.

The catcher shook out his hand, as if she'd broken it, and she burst into laughter as he tossed it back.

"Take a couple more," Dash shouted. "I'm watching your delivery."

"All right." She threw a few more pitches, and each one felt better than the last, and the ball speed and movement increased. Her muscles felt good. Her body and mind remembered. Each time she threw, the crowd went crazy, making her laugh.

Clearly, this was a crowd that appreciated the power of women's softball pitchers.

Finally, Dash held up his hand. "All right, champ. You good? Warmed up?"

She caught the ball. "Ready."

Dash blew her a kiss and then stepped into the batter's box.

Her heart smiled. After the teams had been trash-talking

all afternoon, he hadn't trash-talked her now. He'd blown her a kiss instead.

Not that it was going to get him mercy from her, but she did think it was pretty sweet of him.

Dash did a practice swing, and she positioned herself, summoning her focus.

The catcher set up to the inside of the plate, closer to Dash, and she nodded. Her catcher, Ryan, had played baseball. He knew how to catch, and he apparently knew where to pitch to Dash.

Did she have that kind of control right now?

Probably not. But it would be fun to try.

She took a breath, focused, and then pitched.

Dash swung and missed, and the crowd erupted as Ryan threw the ball back to her.

She grinned. "You were a day late," she shouted.

"You were early," he yelled back, making the place laugh.

"Try again!" she shouted.

"You try again," he yelled back.

She grinned, settled, and then threw again. This time, her pitch went sailing above both their heads. Ryan got his glove up fast enough to catch it, but it was a disaster of a pitch.

Everyone burst out laughing, and instead of feeling stupid, Leila grinned as Dash dove to the ground, mocking fear for his life. They were a comedy duo, the two of them, and it felt great.

"Try to keep it a little lower," Ryan yelled as he tossed the ball back to her.

"Lower?" she quipped. "I didn't realize."

Dash stepped into the plate, and she threw again.

Another swing and miss, and she couldn't help but laugh. She could tell he was trying, but her pitches were coming in at a different angle than baseball pitches, and she was so much closer than a baseball pitcher that he couldn't get the timing.

Plus, she was still good, and that was fun.

She leaned in, watching Dash as he got ready. She didn't need to be fancy. All she needed to do was get it over the plate. She wasn't going to let him win, and she knew he wasn't going to let her win either. They were both going to earn it, and she was going to beat him.

Because she was better.

She nodded at the catcher, took a breath, then threw the ball. It leapt off her fingers and shot toward the plate. Dash swung, but he was too late again, and she could hear the whoosh as his bat whipped through the air, completely missing the ball.

"Strike out! Unders win!"

The field erupted, and her teammates raced out onto the field, whooping and shouting, sweeping her up in a hug. Dash grinned at her and then bowed to her.

She blew him a kiss before she was swept up in the celebration.

Damn. It felt amazing to be good at something, to feel like a star, and Dash had given her that by telling her to break the rules of the game and fastpitch to him. He could have been the hero of the game, but instead, he'd given her the chance to be the hero.

And to get a backrub.

CHAPTER 10

LEILA WAS STILL BASKING in the softball victory when she made it to Table Twenty-Two a short while later. Dash was already seated, and he was bouncing two little girls on his lap. The seat next to him was the only one open, which made her choice easy.

She sat down next to him, then grinned when the table burst out in a round of applause. It was a long table, with enough space for fourteen people. All the women and kids she'd met earlier, plus Griffin, and two other men she didn't know, but from the way they were interacting with the others, she was guessing they were the husbands of Clare's friends, Astrid and Emma, both of whom had been very warm and welcoming to Leila.

It was a full table, with a lot of people and kids, but Leila didn't have time to feel awkward as the group erupted into cheers when she walked up.

"Let's see the medal!" Astrid's auburn hair was held in place by a beautiful turquoise beaded headband, and she was wearing all sorts of cool silver jewelry. She'd told Leila that she was a jewelry maker, and invited Leila to stop by to buy something, which she definitely would. She felt like it would be her statement piece to remind her that she could build a new life for herself that she loved.

Leila pulled the medal over her head and handed it over. "Dash was awesome, letting me fastpitch to him like that."

"He's a guy," Clare said. "His ego demanded that he win the hard way. Can't just take the win, can you, Dash?"

Leila looked over at Dash, and smiled when he winked at her. "I couldn't take the win without giving Leila a chance to fight back. She deserved it, and she killed it."

Happiness settled in Leila. "It was fun," she admitted.

"So fun!" Emma, who was friends with Clare grinned. "Girl power all the way."

"Princesses!" The little girl on the lap of the woman who had introduced herself as Chloe held up her foot, showcasing a pink sneaker with a P on it. "Princess power!"

Leila grinned. "I had a princess doll when I was a kid. I loved her."

"One?" Chloe rolled her eyes. "I think we're up to about fifty princess dolls now. Blue built a castle for them, a horse-drawn carriage, and a sports car because modern princesses like sports cars."

Leila smiled. She might have had only one, but that princess doll had been her best friend when she was little. Was that sad? Maybe, but she was too happy right now to think of it that way. She was just glad she'd had one that she'd had the chance to love.

Clare waved the table to quietness. "I want to introduce Leila to everyone." She gestured toward the man sitting next to Chloe. "This is Blue Carboni. He's new to town, but we love him and pretend he's lived here his whole life."

Blue was handsome in a rugged, rough way, and he had a scar across his cheek, but there was a warmth to his smile that belied his tough exterior. "Great to meet you, Leila. I've been looking forward to meeting the woman who tied Dash down so long ago. Now that I've seen you pitch, I can see why he couldn't stay away."

She grinned, then sucked in her breath when she felt Dash's arm around the back of her seat. "Great to meet you, Blue," she said.

"And this is Harlan Shea," Clare said. "He's both Astrid's brother, and Emma's husband. He and Blue were partners in their kidnap recovery field work, but the great women of Birch Crossing dragged them into a civilian life of chivalry, daddyhood, and town fundraisers."

"And we love every second of it," Harlan said, putting his arm around Emma and kissing her cheek. "Nothing like the love of a magnificent woman to make a guy get his life together."

"And this..." Clare gestured to a sassy senior cackling at the opposite end of the table from Eppie. "Is Judith. She's the other half of any trouble that Eppie causes."

Judith had sparkling white hair, bright blue eyes, and a grin that was pure trouble. "You'll be seeing me around," she said. "Where Eppie goes, I go!"

"Yes, we need to spy on Dash and Leila," Eppie said. "Did you all hear that Bea made Dash and Leila co-heirs to the house, and they have to spend thirty consecutive nights in the house together before they can inherit?"

There was a burst of laughter, hoots, and cat calls, and Leila found herself laughing.

The group was so warm and rambunctious, and she felt completely included. She knew Clare and Emma from her teenage years, but she didn't know them well. She vaguely recalled seeing Astrid around, but Astrid had skated with the more trouble-making kids, so she hadn't known her either.

But they were all making her feel welcome, and it felt so great.

Maybe the next thirty days would be all right. Maybe indeed. She looked over at Dash, and saw he looked happy too. His eyes were twinkling, and he gave her a wink when he saw her look over.

Yep, maybe it would be okay, after all.

And as for the backrub? It might be very dangerous to collect on that bet.

And she might do it anyway.

CHAPTER 11

DASH LEANED back in his seat, feeling weirdly content as the group moved on to dessert. The band had just begun playing, and some folks had already started dancing. Kids and parents mostly, but he knew from experience that the demographic would shift after the first half hour or so when the kids went home and the evening started for the adults.

He watched Leila chatting with the folks at the table. She was vibrant and sparkling, and he could sit there and watch her forever.

Was this what he could have had if he hadn't been such a dumbass for most of his life? He hadn't ever thought he wanted this, to sit around a fundraiser with a bunch of married people and their kids, but he was decidedly at peace.

The noise that had haunted him for so long was at bay, and he liked it.

He was just thinking about asking Leila to dance when he heard someone mention his sister's name.

His attention jetted back to the present, and he leaned in, trying to track the conversation to see where it was going.

Leila was nodding. "Yep, Maura was my catcher on the team. We were great together."

Oh, *fuck.*

Blue shot a look over at Dash as Clare smiled. "You two were close, weren't you?"

Leila nodded again. "She was my best friend. I haven't seen her in a long time, though." She paused. "Maybe I should look her up. Being here makes me want to connect again."

Clare shot a look at Dash. "You don't know about Maura?" she asked Leila, her voice soft.

"What about her?" Leila looked around the table, which had suddenly quieted. "What happened with Maura?"

This was what Dash had been waiting for. The chance for Leila to find out the truth without him having to do it. He could get up right now and walk away, and let them tell her, let her work through it on her own.

Clare took Leila's hand. "Sweetie, Maura—"

"Dance with me." Dash shot to his feet and grabbed Leila's hand. "I love this song. Come on." He couldn't let her find out this way, at a table full of almost strangers. He knew suddenly that it had to come from him. He owed it to Maura and to Leila. "Let's go."

He caught Blue's look of approval as he dragged Leila unceremoniously to her feet, but he hadn't done it for Blue. He'd done it for Leila.

"What? Wait." Leila stumbled to her feet, caught off balance by him tugging her hand. "Dash—"

He didn't answer. He just led her out onto the dance floor and pulled her into his arms. "Dance with me," he said softly.

Leila settled into his arms, but she looked up at him. "What was that about?"

He glanced around them. Townspeople were around, and the entirety of Table Twenty-two were watching them. "Not here. I'll tell you later."

Leila stopped dancing, her brow furrowed. "What's going on, Dash?"

He shook his head. "This isn't the place. Let's dance, and

then we'll hit the road. I'll tell you at home." At home. As if they shared the house. Which they did, he supposed, but it felt different.

"I don't like being lied to," she said softly. "Don't lie to me, Dash."

He swore. "It's something that needs to be discussed in private. Not here. I won't do it here."

Her eyes were wary. "You're making me nervous."

"I'm not a serial killer. Nothing like that." Dammit. He'd really liked that moment of holding her in his arms, when they had started to dance. He'd blown it. "You want to go back home and talk?"

"I don't want to go anywhere. I want to know."

Fuck. He didn't want to do this. Not now. Not this way. But he'd lost control of the situation. "All right. Come with me." He took her hand and led her off the dance floor, exiting at the opposite end from Table Twenty-Two. He said nothing as he walked around to the back of the fire station, to where his bike was parked. "Let's go for a ride."

She put her hands on her hips. "No. Tell me."

"It's better if we don't do this here."

"I don't care. You're freaking me out. I need to know what's going on."

Dash narrowed his eyes at her. "You're stubborn as hell."

She said nothing. She just stood there with her hands on her hips waiting.

He closed his eyes. Fuck. He didn't want to have this conversation, but he couldn't spare either of them from it, not forever.

"Dash?" Her voice was softer now. "What's wrong?"

He opened his eyes. "When was the last time you talked to Maura?"

She shook her head. "A long time ago. I got...caught up in my life. Lost sight of a lot that mattered."

He ground his jaw. "Do you know that she moved to New

York to pursue her art? She met an art gallery owner named Sophia Reardon, who believed in her art and took her on as one of her artists."

Leila brightened. "That's great. I'm so happy for her!"

"She and Sophia fell in love. They got married a few years ago."

Leila cocked her head. "That sounds fantastic. Why doesn't your tone sound like that's fantastic?"

Fuck this was hard. He took a breath. "They had twins last year."

Leila stared at him, waiting for the news she could sense was coming.

He didn't know how to say it. His throat was thick. "They... *Fuck*."

Tears glistened in Leila's eyes. "Tell me what happened, Dash."

"Car crash."

Leila put her hand over her mouth.

He took a breath. "Sophia and Maura died immediately. The twins were at home with a babysitter."

"Oh. God." Leila sat down on the bike. "I didn't know."

"I know. I wasn't sure how to tell you. I didn't know if you'd care. I mean, it's been a long time since you've seen her."

"Of course I care. She was my best friend." She looked at him. "But you...she was yours too."

He nodded. The situation was so complicated. He decided to get it all out. "Maura and Sophia named me guardian of their daughters. Sophia's parents sued to get custody. They figured I was a bad choice because I'm a single guy with a shitty job, a motorcycle, and a prison record."

Leila's mouth dropped open. "You're a born protector."

He shrugged. "I know that. Maura and Sophia knew that. So I used all my savings to fight back. I wasn't going to let them down. They chose me, and I had to make sure they got what they wanted." What hell that had been.

"What happened?"

"I won."

She stared at him. "You're their dad?"

"Yeah. As of a couple days ago." He still couldn't believe it. What was he getting himself into?

"Holy crap. Where are they?"

"Still with Sophia's parents in New York. They got the judge to order that the girls lived with them during the trial, and then got a few extra days with them to adjust." That had still pissed him off, but he'd won the big game, so he'd focused on that. "I'm going to go get them on Friday."

Leila let out her breath. "That's a lot."

"Yeah." He didn't know what else to say. He knew it changed everything. "So, yeah, not the bad boy rebel you married anymore."

She cocked her head. "Were you ever a bad boy rebel?"

"I don't know." He suddenly felt tired. "I don't know anything anymore. I'm still trying to figure it out." He ran his hand through his hair. "Honestly, today with you has been the first time in a long time that I've felt normal. I'd forgotten what it felt like to laugh. I just wanted to say that I appreciate that you bring some levity and fun into my life."

She smiled, and suddenly she looked tired as well. "I could say the same thing too. My life imploded recently, and I was happy to come here and get a break from it."

He grabbed onto the chance to talk about something other than his sister. "What's going on?"

She shrugged. "Nothing like suddenly becoming a dad or losing family, but it wasn't easy for me."

"I want to know."

She looked up at him. "I dated a guy for eight years. We lived together and started a business together. Then, recently, he told me that he had another girlfriend, she was pregnant, and he wanted to marry her. Then he fired me, because, as it turned out, I didn't have any actual equity in our business. He had it all. He said he needed it for his baby. I was left with all our debt but none of the assets. He was very clever how he handled it, and I hadn't done my job to know what was going on." She managed a smile. "So, new life direction for me. I just don't know what it is yet."

He laughed softly. "You're homeless then?"

She nodded. "Except for the house I live in with my husband, yes."

He whistled. "And his two kids, as of Friday."

She grimaced. "I'm not good with kids."

"Doesn't matter. I'll keep them out of your way." But even as he said it, a weight seemed to settle in his gut. He'd loved what he'd found with Leila today. But it had to be over before it even began. He didn't want to resent the two little girls who would be calling him Daddy as soon as they learned to talk, but a part of him was still trying to adjust to what his life was becoming. He loved them. He did. But…could he be the guy they needed? That Maura and Sophia believed he was?

"No, it's okay. You don't need to keep them out of my way." Leila managed a smile. "It's your house as much as it's mine. And kids are…chaotic. You can't live worrying about them getting in my way."

He frowned. "You okay with that?"

She lifted her chin. "Of course."

He could see in her eyes that she didn't believe it, but he appreciated that she was unwilling to add to his weight. "I'm sorry," he said.

"Oh, Dash. Are you kidding? No apologies ever. You're an amazing man who is going to be a great dad. I just wish…" She stopped.

His attention sharpened. "You wish what?" There were a thousand things she could be wishing for, because there were a lot that he was thinking about as well.

She met his gaze. "Nothing."

Nothing.

He wanted to ask again. But he didn't. Instead, he simply said. "What do you want to do?"

She sighed. "About?"

He gestured back and forth between himself and her. "About this?"

Her gaze sharpened. "This what?"

He couldn't believe he was bringing it up, but he needed to. He felt like this was his chance, his last chance, before his life became about something else, someone else. "There's so much electricity between us. A backrub owed. A wedding kiss I'm still thinking about."

Leila sucked in her breath. "Me, too."

"I've felt like I've been on the edge for so long. When I'm with you, I feel…like my soul has life again."

She nodded. "I feel the same way."

"I'm going to be a dad in two days. Of twins. But until then…" He hesitated. What did he want? He wasn't even sure. "I owe you a backrub."

She stared at him, her blue eyes wide and alert. "You do," she agreed.

"I honor my bets."

She took a breath. "I don't even know what we're getting into."

"Me either."

They stood there, at the edge of the parking lot, by his bike, silence looming between them. "How about that dance?" he finally said, back peddling away from the backrub. "Start there. Take it one step at a time."

She lifted her chin. "How dangerous can a dance be?"

"Depends." He held out his hand to her. "Take a risk with me, Leila?"

She raised her brows. "Didn't we already establish on the ride over that I'm risk averse?"

"Yep. And didn't you then realize that riding a bike with me was pretty damned fun?"

She inclined her head in acknowledgement, a little twinkle in her eyes. "You were very sassy."

He grinned. "Imagine me on the dance floor. I'm ten times as entertaining."

"I'm pretty certain this is going to wind up being a terrible idea, but let's do it." She put her hand in his and let him pull her to her feet. "I do love dancing."

"As do I. I'm a great dancer." He slipped his arm around her waist and pulled her against him, not even bothering to head back to the dance floor just yet. He could hear the music, and it was enough for him.

"As good as you are at hitting fastpitch softballs?" She let him draw her in until her body was against his.

"So much better." Then, because he wanted to, and why the hell not, he leaned down and kissed her.

And, just like before, she kissed him right back.

CHAPTER 12

AN HOUR LATER, Leila sat at Table Twenty-two, and watched Dash sitting with Blue. He had one of Blue's daughters asleep on his lap, and Blue had two of his foster girls on his.

Chloe and Blue had eight little girls living in their house right now.

Eight.

And everyone at the table was taking turns with the girls, creating an entire family around them, supporting them. The girls might be temporary in Chloe and Blue's home, but the love and belonging they received was forever. She knew each of those girls would have a place with every single person at that table for the rest of their lives. They could come back in ten years, and they would still be welcome.

Dash included.

She knew why Maura and Sophia had chosen Dash. Because he was amazing with kids, and he brought with him an entire community of support. Once his daughters were home, they would have a forever home just like the foster girls, no matter what ever happened to Dash.

It was the security that Leila had clung to with Bea, but it had never been like this, because Bea could not have protected her from her stepfather. But Blue, Harlan, Dash, and all these women *would* protect the children. Really, truly protect them.

Leila felt so happy with the group earlier in the evening, but now that she knew what she knew about this Dash and his circle, Maura, and his future daughters, it was different.

She and Dash had had fun dancing. Kissing. Laughing.

But now, there was a weight to the evening, at least in her heart.

There was no future with her and Dash. In two days, he would be fully focused on the girls. And she would be...what?

She didn't even know.

But she did know that maybe it was time to let go of the fantasy of Dash Stratton someday becoming her husband in every way. His daughters would have to come first. And he already had this whole community surrounding him. There was no place for her, but being here made her realize that she wanted a place. A real place. A home that would envelop her in a way that she'd never had, not even with Robbie.

Eppie pulled out the chair beside her. "What's happening, girl?"

Leila cleared her throat and turned to Eppie. "It's been a great night. Thanks for getting me to come."

Eppie cocked her head. "What's that sad ass look on your face for?"

Leila immediately put on a smile. "I have a great look on my face."

"Do you?" Eppie picked up a plastic cup of white wine and sniffed it. "I think you're looking at your husband like you lost him. Odd, since it looks to me like you just found him."

Leila raised her brows. "Matchmaking, are you, Eppie?"

"Damned straight," Eppie said. "Bea's goal was to get the

two of you together, and that's my job to help make her dream come true."

Leila stared at Eppie. "Bea really wanted us together?"

"Yep. Why else would she make the two of you live together for a month? Obviously."

Leila frowned, thinking about that. "Why?"

Eppie cocked her head. "Guess she thought it was better than you two not being together."

Leila laughed. "That's not an answer."

"It's the only one I'm giving you at this point, so roll with it. So why are you looking so damned depressed?"

"Dash told me about Maura and Sophia. And the twins," she said as she took a bite of one of Clare's cupcakes, which Clare sold at Wright's General Store and a few other shops in the area. The chocolate was decadent, and Leila paused to experience it. It was incredible.

Eppie's face softened. "Ah... Life gets complicated, doesn't it? You don't want to be a mom?"

"A mom?" Leila choked on the cupcake. "A *mom*? To whom?"

"Dash's kids, of course."

Oh, God. She sat back. "Eppie, you're heading down the wrong path! I haven't seen Dash in fifteen years, and we were never more than passing acquaintances. Being a mother to his kids isn't even remotely on the radar. The fact I was kissing him is not the same thing as anything long-term happening." Especially now. She didn't want anything serious, and there was no way to get tangled up with Dash on a non-serious level now that he was a freaking single dad.

Eppie cocked her head, making the dangling pompoms on her hat tilt across her face. "But would you like it?"

"Kissing him? Yes. It was great. But that doesn't mean—"

"Not what I asked," Eppie snorted. "Would you like being a mom to his kids?"

"A *mom*? No." Leila didn't hesitate. "I'm not a kid person. Or a baby person."

Eppie studied her. "Some people aren't," she said thoughtfully.

"Yep. That's me. I'm the one who always makes a break for the coffee room when someone brings their new baby by the office."

Eppie ignored her. "But sometimes, it just takes the right situation. The right baby."

"Heavens, no. No one wants me near a baby anyway. I don't have that instinct." Leila took another bite of cupcake, deciding to lose herself in the fabulous dessert. "Besides, I'm not sticking around. I have to rebuild my life, and I'm doing that in New York. It's where I have contacts and a foundation."

"Then why are you here?"

"Because Bea was a crafty old lady in her will."

Eppie grinned. "That she was." She raised her coffee cup. "Here's to crafty old ladies, and their easily manipulated heirs."

Leila laughed. "Absolute truth there." She raised the remains of the cupcake and tapped it against Eppie's cup. "To old ladies and heirs."

"And the delicious husbands they kiss at family events," Eppie said with a grin, her gaze going behind Leila.

Leila felt her cheeks heat up when she felt a hand on her shoulder. She didn't need to turn around. She could see from Eppie's face who it was. "Is that him?" she asked cheerfully.

"It is," Eppie beamed at him. "You two getting ready for your first night together? Pretty exciting stuff."

Leila looked over her shoulder at Dash. "Eppie wants us to get together."

Dash's eyes widened slightly, but then he grinned. "Eppie is a matchmaker. Many couples in this town are victims of her interference."

"It was Bea's last wish," Eppie said. "You wouldn't let down an old lady, would you?"

"Hell, no. In fact, let's just get this over with right now." Dash went down on one knee. "Leila, will you marry me?"

Eppie rolled her eyes, and Leila burst out laughing. "I can't marry you, Dash. I'm already married."

He swore. "To whom? I'll call him out for a duel at dawn."

"He'd kick your ass. He's a scary biker dude. Don't mess with him."

"Scary?" Dash leaned on his knee, pretending to ruminate over that bit of info. "Damn. You married a scary biker? No man's going to mess with you."

"Right? It's perfect." She leaned in. "My husband is actually imaginary," she whispered loudly. "He doesn't really exist. I just use him to keep men away from me."

Amusement flashed in Dash's eyes. "That's fucking brilliant. I'm in awe of your manipulative deception. Have sex with me tonight."

"Absolutely," she said, trying to blatantly ignore the sudden hit of desire at his proposal. "I would love to." Then she grabbed him by the face and dragged him in for a sloppy, hot kiss, that had them both laughing while they were trying to kiss.

"Oh, for heaven's sake," Eppie snorted. "You two are impossible. Have you no respect for the deceased's last wishes?"

"We have respect." Dash slung his arm around Leila. "We're going to have sex and get married."

"Not necessarily in that order," she agreed, "but that covers the bases."

"What else did Bea want us to do?" Dash asked. "We'll add that to our list tonight."

Eppie rolled her eyes. "And to think I agreed to follow the two of you around for a month. My head will explode before the thirty days is up." She got up. "I resign."

She glared at them both, then strode away, grabbing Blue on her way to the dance floor as her dance partner.

Leila's smile faded as she watched Eppie. "Is she really mad? We aren't mocking Bea."

"Hell, no," Dash said, rising to his feet. "Eppie has a great sense of humor. She just likes to pretend she's grumpy. Right now, she's out there thinking 'I made Dash and Leila think about having sex tonight. I'm a star. I should make the big bucks for this.'"

As he spoke, Eppie looked over at them. She wiggled her brows at Leila, and then nodded at Dash and gave a thumbs up.

Leila burst out laughing. "Okay, you're right. She's not mad."

"It's all part of her evil plot to manipulate us." Dash held out his hand. "One last dance and then head home?"

"Sure." She put her hand in his, and let him pull her to her feet. She followed him out on the dance floor. It was a fast song, but he didn't release her. He pulled her into a hold and then began to sway around the dance floor.

"You don't know how to swing dance, do you?"

Leila grinned. "You mean, from the Friday night town dances that happened all summer? Maura and I used to go and dance with each other to practice."

"All right. Let's see what we remember." He stepped back, and set her in hold. They watched each other, listening for the beat, and then jumped in at the same moment with their rock step, and then they were off.

The music was upbeat, and they weren't the only ones who had reverted to the swing dance of old. Leila was laughing so hard as Dash escorted her around the floor, spinning her and bringing her in and out. He was a great leader, and what she didn't remember, she could easily follow. He was admirably light on his feet for a man with his amount of muscle, and she was laughing breathlessly as they gallivanted around the dance floor.

She'd been thinking Dash was going to pull her in for a slow, seductive dance when they'd first walked on the dance floor, but this high energy gallivant was a thousand times better. She couldn't stop laughing, and he was grinning too.

Her heart was racing, she was breathing hard, and she felt so gloriously alive.

How could something so simple as a swing dance at a Birch Crossing fire fighter fundraiser make her feel so alive?

The song ended, and the place erupted in cheers. "Another one," someone shouted. "More swing dances!"

Leila joined the cheers, shouting and calling for another one.

The band leader checked with her team, and then shouted. "One more for the ladies!" And then the band started playing another song that was perfect for swing dancing.

Leila grinned at Dash. "We can't leave now!"

"We sure can't." He took her head and spun her around as the music started, "Let's go, darling!"

Leila shouted with delight as they started dancing again, her voice joining the crowd's cheers. For so many years, Dash had been an unapproachable enigma in her life. First, when she was a teenager, and then after she'd married him. He'd been a dangerous bad boy who was so much more vibrant and alive than she was. She'd never believed she could be enough to interest him, to make this larger-than-life protector come down to earth long enough to notice her.

And yet here she was, in his arms, laughing, dancing, and having the best time of her life.

She never wanted the night to end.

CHAPTER 13

IT WAS after midnight by the time Dash drove into their driveway.

He'd decided to take a scenic route home from the fundraiser, because he'd wanted to show Leila some of the lake, and because he hadn't been ready for the night with her to end.

Being with Leila had been completely unexpected, but even more unexpected was how damned fun it was to be with her.

Fun wasn't his thing, at least not wholesome, swing dancing fun. But hell, he'd had a night. He'd barely known the girl he'd married, and he hadn't added to his knowledge over the years.

But tonight? He felt like maybe he'd missed out on a whole lot.

He parked the bike, and Leila let go of his waist. "What an amazing night," she said. "Thanks for the tour. It was wild to see so many things I'd forgotten about."

"We can go again tomorrow. Lots more to see when it's light out."

She paused. "You know, that would be fun. Let's do that."

Anticipation raced through him. "Maybe some skinny dipping on Eppie's dock."

She laughed again, a gorgeous sound he was already becoming accustomed to. "Honestly, I think she'd just come out and cheer us on. She wouldn't be shocked. In fact, she might even join us."

"Oh, hell, no. I can't be swimming naked with Eppie." He pulled off his helmet. "Some things are just wrong."

Leila swung her leg over the back of the bike and hopped off. She handed him her helmet. "That was super fun tonight, Dash. I haven't enjoyed myself like that in so long. It was a gift."

He secured the bike and got off. "I feel the same way. It's been rough for a while."

Her smile faded. "Me, too."

He slung his free arm over her shoulder and kissed the top of her head as they headed up the front steps. It was such a natural move, and it felt normal and right. He had no idea how it could feel so natural with a woman he barely knew, but since she was leaning into him, he was going to go with it.

He opened the front door. "After you, milady."

She slipped past him, and he followed her, nudging the door shut with his foot before setting the helmets in the closet.

She watched him. "You don't lock the door?"

"Never. It's Birch Crossing. I gave up trying to get Bea to lock the front door, and I guess I just kept going with it."

"I can't imagine not locking the door. We'd never do that in New York. I locked the door even when I ran down to the lobby to get my mail."

"Welcome to Birch Crossing then." He came to a stop in front of her. "I owe you a backrub."

He heard her tiny intake of breath very clearly. "You do," she agreed cautiously.

"You tired?" He wasn't. He felt like he could run up the side of Mt. Washington right now without breaking stride.

She searched his face. "No."

Right. "Me either." Anticipation coiled through him. "Great. Meet you on the living room couch in five."

"Make it fifteen. I want to take a quick shower. Bug spray and sweat isn't sexy." Then her cheeks turned pink. "Not that I'm trying to be sexy. I just…" She threw up her hands. "Whatever. I'm going to go shower. I'll be down in a few."

Sexy. She was thinking about *sexy*. Dash let out his breath as he watched Leila race up the stairs.

He was thinking about sexy, too. Mostly because she was sexy as hell. Wholesome. Sweet. Fun. No edges at all. And sexy.

He'd married her because she was a gentle soul that he'd felt the need to protect. All these years later, she still had that same core. Yes, she was a woman now, and she had a grit and sass he hadn't seen before in his limited time with her, but that beautiful core that awakened the need to protect her? That was still there. Evident. Calling to him.

He let out his breath and headed to the kitchen to make coffee.

What the hell was he doing, offering her a backrub tonight?

Leila was his damned wife, and a stranger in many ways.

If he scared her off, he might lose her forever. This hidden, secret marriage had bound them together by invisible threads for so long, and he'd liked it. It had made him feel grounded, like there was a person in this world who his soul was linked with.

And if he fucked it up by taking it too far, he could lose her. And now, there was more at stake, because he was pretty sure they were friends now.

A secret wife was one thing.

A not-so-secret wife who was now a friend that ignited his

soul and gave him the laughter he'd forgotten about? A whole lot more to lose.

He leaned on the counter, and thought about it. Was a backrub a really stupid idea?

Yeah.

It was.

He should rescind the offer.

Then he saw a bottle of organic, earth-friendly dish soap on the edge of the sink, one that he hadn't seen there before tonight. Leila must have put it there.

She was already leaving her mark. And she was stuck with him for thirty days. No matter what happened tonight. No matter if one of them wanted to run…they couldn't.

Not for thirty days.

Which meant…he had time to see what it could become, to make mistakes, and fix them.

Because after tonight, he wanted to get to know the woman he'd married.

Decision made: the backrub was still on the table.

―――――

Leila stood in her room, her wet hair coiled in a towel on top of her head, and looked at the bra in her hand.

A good backrub never included a bra.

A good backrub went with bare skin.

It was late at night. Why would she put on a bra after her shower to get a backrub?

But if she went down there without a bra, what message would she be sending? Would she be sending a message? And if she was sending a message, would he notice? And if she didn't mean to send a message, would he think she was?

"Leila," she said aloud, "you're completely overthinking."

Nothing would happen with Dash. They were roommates for the next month who apparently were attracted to each other. A little kissing? No problem. She liked it. She thought he was still insanely hot.

But he was going to be a dad in a couple days, and that was not her cup of tea, at all.

So, this was just a thing. A little brief moment of opportunity for both of them to take a break from their lives.

"Overthinking again," she said aloud.

It wasn't an affair.

It was literally a bet to pay off because she'd struck him out. That was it.

She looked at herself in the mirror. "Do you want to wear a bra?" she asked herself.

No. And the answer had nothing to do with Dash. It was after midnight, she had just showered, and her mind was on pjs and fuzzy socks. Dash was safe. Whatever happened between them tonight would have nothing to do with whether or not she was wearing a bra.

She just wanted to be comfortable, and she felt safe enough with Dash to do that.

"Right. There we go." She tossed her bra back in the drawer, and instead, pulled on her purple sleep shirt with the yellow happy faces. It was old, but it was the softest piece of clothing ever created, and she wanted the security of it.

Plus, the fact that it was faded, had a tear in the hem, and was a couple sizes too big would make it clear that the fact she was braless had nothing to do with seduction, and everything to do with comfort. That was the message she wanted to send, and it was clear enough that he'd understand it.

Perfect.

She pulled on a pair of cotton sleep pants that had pink hearts and flamingos on them, then grinned when she caught sight of herself in the mirror. There was literally no way that he would think she was trying to be sexy.

CHAPTER 14

SHE WAS SEXY AS HELL.

That was Dash's first thought when he saw Leila walk down the stairs, wearing the cutest damn pjs he'd ever seen in his life. The happy faces all over her shirt. The freaking flamingos on her pants. Her hair was still wet, leaving droplets of water on her shoulders. Her feet were bare, showing her pink toenails. Her breasts were that shape that told him she'd liberated them from her bra and was letting them be free.

She'd probably dressed to make it clear she wasn't interested in seduction, with her clothes baggy and loose, faded and old, but Dash fucking loved it.

It was exactly the side of her that he was attracted to: her soft inner core. Her total lack of airs. Her realness. The side of her that felt like comfort and home.

He took a breath. With Leila, he didn't have to be what he wasn't. She was that sensation of acceptance, which was funny, since she'd apparently married him because he was a bad boy rebel, which he wasn't anymore. Not even close.

She flipped him a smile as her feet touched the last step. "Do I smell coffee?"

His gut actually turned over at her relaxed smile. She wasn't just sexy as hell, she was also cute as hell. "Decaf. It's a local brand. They sell it at Wright's. Vanilla roast. I made extra." He didn't even know if she drank coffee. That was funny. Ironic. He'd been married to her for well over a decade, and he had no idea about the most basic aspects of her likes and dislikes. "Want some?"

"I'd love some."

"Great." He'd enjoyed making her coffee. It felt intimate, in a normal, casual way. "I'll grab you some. Couch is yours."

"Thanks." She flashed him that same relaxed smile again, and then headed toward the living room.

Dash paused for a moment to watch her walk. The way her hips swayed was pure temptation, even though her pants were so baggy he could barely see the outline of her ass. But his imagination was working overtime, and it was doing a great job.

She glanced back at him, and then cocked a brow. "That look on your face is dangerous," she said "Eppie would love it."

Shit. "I live to make Eppie happy." He turned away and strode into the kitchen. He grabbed a loon mug out of the cabinet. Not one of Bea's, but one of the ones he'd brought in when she'd passed and he'd taken over the house. He loved Bea, but he'd needed to make the space his, not live in the shadows of the woman who had meant so much to him.

Other than her personal items like clothes, Dash hadn't gotten rid of any of Bea's belongings. He'd just made a little room for his sparse possessions. A balance he was still sorting out. "Want cream or sugar?" he called out, again noting the irony that he didn't know how Leila liked her coffee.

"No thanks."

"All right." He poured the steaming coffee, set the two coffee mugs on the tray with fresh local strawberries, and

Birch's of Maine chocolates, added a couple napkins, and then headed out to the living room.

He grinned when he saw Leila sitting on the couch, her feet propped on the coffee table, looking through a hardback tabletop book that Bea had given him for Christmas a year ago. "What are these photos of?" she asked. "Did Bea's husband make these?"

He set the tray down. "They're my iron projects. Bea went around town and took pictures of all my installations and items people had bought. She then put together in a book for a Christmas present last year." He grinned. "I have three boxes of books in the front hall closet if you want some. I think I have two hundred copies."

Leila smiled. "Bea was the best." She paused to look through some more pages. "Did you learn the craft from Roger?"

"Yes." He'd spent many hours with Bea's husband, from the time he was in high school until Roger had died eight years ago. "When I was a teenager, I was his second set of hands on the heavy projects, like fire escapes. He was a true artist, and over time, I picked up skill from him. When his hands started failing, I did most of his work for him, while he directed me. I finished up all his commitments after he died so Bea would have the money, and now I play around."

Leila cocked her head. "What do you make now?"

He shrugged. "I do a few commissioned projects, like railings, and signs for people's camps, fire escapes. Sometimes I just make things I think are cool. All on the side. My job is construction, working for Jackson Reed."

She turned the book so he could see what page she was looking at. "This fire escape? How it spirals around, and how you have the loons on every level? And how the rails look like tree branches? It's art. Roger was brilliant, but you've taken it to a whole new level."

He shrugged. "It's a fire escape designed to look attractive, not like an eyesore."

"How much did you charge for this one?"

He leaned over to look at it. "I think that was two grand."

She raised her brows. "Two thousand dollars? How long did it take you to make it? Did you even break even?"

"I charged for the cost of the materials. Labor was on me."

"*On you*." She stared at him. "Did you just say that the labor was 'on you?' You mean, free?"

"Yeah."

"How many hours did you spend on it?"

"I don't know. A hundred. Maybe two. Not that much." He handed her a cup of coffee. "Here."

"A hundred?" She set the book down and took the coffee. "You should have charged ten thousand dollars for that. Or more. Twenty, even."

He stared at her. "Twenty grand? You think that fire escape is worth twenty thousand dollars?" The idea was staggering.

"At least! It's art, Dash. And it's brilliant. It's your gift."

"Thanks." He was strangely pleased by her reaction to his iron work. Bea had always told him he was talented, but it was different coming from Leila. "But it's not my style to charge that kind of money."

"But it's worth it."

The idea that his fire escape was worth twenty grand was interesting, but irrelevant. "Doesn't matter." He sat down next to her. "The woman I made it for didn't have that kind of money. She had grandkids and wanted them to be safe, but I wanted her to have something pretty to look at, that would make her feel good. So, free labor." He braced his arms on his thighs and leaned over to look at the image. Bea had made sure that Rita, the woman who owned the house, was in the picture. He grinned, remembering how happy she'd been. "I'm never going to charge for my labor for my iron works. It's fun for me that I get to do it."

Leila set the book down and took the coffee. "You're very talented, Dash."

He grinned. "Thanks. It's fun. I do it to chill. Won't get to do it much after Friday, so I'm trying to finish up a few pieces." Regret flickered through him. "I'll miss it," he admitted. "It's where I find my peace."

Leila nodded. "Your free time will be taken up by kids."

"Yeah. I have childcare lined up with Clare and the gang, so I can still go to work no problem, but when I'm not at my construction job, I need to be present here. I can't justify leaving them with a sitter so I can do something fun. To earn money to take care of them? Yeah. To play? Nah." He leaned back. "I'll play again when they're teenagers and running loose on the town like I used to do."

Leila's eyes twinkled. "They're girls, Dash. You want them running loose on the town when they're teenagers? You know what teenage boys are like."

Alarm flashed on Dash's face. "Fuck. You're right. I'm not going to get back to the iron work for at least thirty years."

She laughed then. "I hope it's not thirty years. That would be a shame."

Dash shrugged. "People are more important than iron. It happens." He fought for the words, but they still made his gut tighten. His people were gone. Bea. Maura. Sophia. His parents, not that they were dead, but he hadn't spoken to them in over fifteen years, and he never would.

Leila cocked her head. "You all right?"

He cleared his throat, fighting his way back to the present. "Yeah, I'm good. How about that backrub? It's getting late and I don't want us to fall asleep."

She was still watching him with insightful concern. "You don't have to give me a backrub. It was just a silly bet."

"That all the world heard!" he said, chuckling. "Eppie will ride my ass until all eternity if I don't pay up." He set his mug on the red fox coaster on the coffee table. "Let's do this. You can experience the magic of my artist hands."

Her brows shot up. "You're going to mold my back like hot iron?"

"Exactly. It's a rare skill, but someone's got to do it."

"All right." She put the coffee down. "It doesn't have to be long. Seriously."

"Don't tell me how to pay off my bets. Face down. Ass up. Now, woman."

She burst out laughing as she rolled over and stretched out on her belly. "It's a good thing I have your sense of humor or else I'd have to throw my coffee in your face, call you a jerk, and storm out of the house."

"Hell, don't throw coffee. My face is too pretty to be destroyed by tenth degree burns." He studied her stretched out. "If you were my girlfriend, I'd be straddling your butt to deliver the best massage."

She buried her face in the pillow. "I'm your wife, you forgetful idiot. Straddle away."

Oh, *hell*. Dash stood up, shook out his shoulders, then grasped the back of the couch to support himself as he slowly lowered himself onto Leila's pink flamingo ass, making sure not to put his full body weight on her. Her body was warm and soft beneath him, and desire coiled through him like a whip, quick and hot.

Leila sucked in her breath, and for a moment, they both went still. The position was intimate and personal, and he loved it...and at the same time, he wasn't sure it was a good idea. He was so damned attracted to her. *Compelled* by her. "You okay?"

She let out her breath in a long, intentional release. "Yep. Good. Go for it."

He flexed his hands. "It's been a long time since I've given a massage. It might take me a minute to get my groove going."

"I'll give you two minutes. After that, I expect to get my money's worth."

"The zero dollars you spent on this?"

"Unhittable pitches have tremendous monetary value. I'm thinking about a million five."

He grinned. "That's a hell of a backrub."

"I'm worth it."

"Yeah, you are. And I can deliver." He leaned forward and set his hands on her lower back. He pressed his thumbs along the side of Leila's spine while his fingers wrapped around her sides.

It was shockingly good to touch her.

There was a tight cord of muscle under his thumbs, and he began to work it, focusing on each fiber of muscle and coaxing them to unlock.

"Holy cow." Leila groaned. "You have magic hands."

"That's what my tools tell me." He grinned and began to relax, focusing into his craft. He loved her body. He loved the human body, women's bodies, but right now, all he could think about was *hers*. He loved her contours. Her body, with its muscles, its curves, its beauty, was like a canvas, a solid piece of iron, waiting to be unleashed into the magic it was meant to be.

He worked his way up her lower back, feeling her ribs. Her shoulder blades. The tautness of her muscles holding on so tight. "You meditate?"

"Meditate?" She laughed softly. "No."

"I can tell. You carry a lot of tension in your body." He found a knot on her right shoulder and he began to work it, closing his eyes to focus on the feel of each fiber beneath his fingers. He connected with it, allowing his mind to move with it, easing the tension from it.

"What are you doing?" she whispered.

He paused. "No good?"

"It's freaking amazing. Please keep going and never, ever stop."

He chuckled and resumed his work. "Feels good?"

"Good's not the word," she said. "It's more like…I can feel this weight leaving my muscles, and this humming relaxation coming to life."

He smiled with satisfaction and closed his eyes as he moved his hands down her lower back again, lower, and lower, to the curve where her back merged into her buttocks. Her muscles were wound tightly here as well, and he focused his work, coaxing every fiber to let go.

He kept working, his thumbs working lower and lower, following the tension, until suddenly, he realized that he was lower than he'd meant to go. He froze. "Sorry."

"Are you?"

He smiled at her sassy tone, and then resumed his massage. "No. I was focused on your body, not where your pants were."

Her pants, which were now almost halfway down her ass, almost, but not quite revealing parts that he had no business seeing.

"I was too." She sighed. "I can't believe I've been married to this magic for so many years and I had no idea."

He laughed as he raised her waistband to a more proper place, and then began to work on the back of her right thigh, high up, where her hamstring connected to her glute. "More tension in here."

She let out her breath, and he knew that he was digging deep. "How do you know how to do this? I thought you were going to give me some half-assed backrub that was actually about trying to get me naked. But you're actually working on me."

He grinned. "I am," he agreed. "But I'm not going to lie and pretend that I'm not noticing your body as well."

She laughed. "Well, thank heavens for that, because I can't

stop thinking about how freaking strong and talented your hands are."

"Sexual tension is rampant right now."

She groaned. "I'm so glad it's not just me. I'm having all sorts of naked visions in my head. Naked and sweaty."

"Hell. Me, too." He wanted to bunch her wet hair to the side and kiss the damp skin on the nape of her neck. "After more than a decade of marriage, it's a good sign that we're still attracted to each other." He moved to her left leg and began to work her upper thigh.

"Right? It's as if this whole thing between us is brand new, full of the unknown."

"Exactly. It's like I've never had my hands digging into your gorgeous ass before."

"I would never get tired of your hands on my body."

Desire began to coil inside him more tightly. "I'd never get tired of having my hands on your body."

She didn't answer, and the only sound became the rustle of her pajama pants as he worked on her, along with the sound of their breathing. Intimate and intense. Coiled with awareness.

"Dash?"

"Yeah."

"Is it weird that I want to roll over, hold out my arms, and pull you down on top of me?"

His cock got hard. "Why would it be weird? I'm a physical specimen. It would be weird if you weren't wildly attracted to me."

She groaned. "Your ego should really annoy me."

"It doesn't?"

"No. It's hot."

"Because I'm mocking myself. Self-mockery is hot."

"Is that it?"

"I'm sure it has nothing to do with the way your ass fits so perfectly in my hands, and how good it feels to have my thighs locked around yours."

She groaned again, then hit his thigh. "Up, rebel boy. I need to move."

He raised himself off her, and she twisted around so she was facing him. Her cheeks were flushed, and the desire on her face went right to his gut.

He settled back down on her, his thighs over her hips.

She searched his face. "I didn't come here for this. For you."

He nodded. "I know. I didn't get up this morning expecting this. You."

"What do we do? It can't go anywhere. You're getting kids in a couple days, and I'm going back to New York to restart my life."

"Well, we got married and that didn't go anywhere, so maybe taking action that won't lead to anything is how we do things."

She folded her arms over her chest. "I just got out of a relationship. It was bad."

Something dark coiled inside Dash. "You mentioned that."

Leila nodded. "He kicked me out of our home and our business so he could marry that woman. Apparently, they'd been dating for two years, and I didn't know it." Her voice was soft, but there was a shit ton of hurt and emotion under the surface.

What Dash was feeling wasn't soft. "What's his name?"

Her eyes widened, then she started laughing. "Are you going to beat him up?"

"I'm thinking about it. Name?"

"You'd crush him with your pinkie. He'll sue you. Way too much effort."

"To defend you? Never too much effort." He was trying to keep his voice calm, but anger was coiling deep inside him. "I don't like it when people in my circle of protection aren't treated well." It was why he'd spent so much time in New York with Maura and Sophia. Why he'd married Leila. Why he'd helped Bea. Why he'd taken on two baby girls when he had no idea how to be a dad, and he'd had no intentions of ever being a father.

Leila cocked her head to look at him, and her arms relaxed slightly. "The great protector," she said softly.

"Fuck, yeah. What's his name?"

Leila held her arms out to him. "Kiss it out of me, you over-protective rebel."

He was still tense. He'd given Leila his legal protection so she would have a great life. It did not sit well with him that she'd been in a position with some asshole who hadn't honored her. If the guy was cheating on her for at least two years, then there was no way he'd ever made her feel valued and worthy.

And then, some piece of shit worth nothing, had dumped her, like he was better than she was.

Leila sat up. "Kiss me, Dash. Kissing you makes me forget about everything else, and that's what I want right now. To be consumed by you, for just this moment."

Heat coiled tight in his gut, but he didn't move. How could he move on her? She'd been jerked around already. He was her safe space, which meant he didn't start making out with her when there was no future, when there was no commitment, when there was no—

She grabbed the front of his shirt, dragged him down, and kissed him.

He meant to hold back, to protect her from him, but the minute her mouth closed on his, and he felt her fists bunch in his shirt, he was hers.

CHAPTER 15

ELECTRICITY SPARKED through Leila when Dash dragged her against him and kissed her back. Hot. Fierce. And earth-shattering.

Kissing him hadn't been planned. He'd just looked so angry and so intense about her breakup with Robbie that something inside her had taken over, and she'd needed to kiss him.

His anger had been on her behalf. To protect her. To defend her. And it had been too much for her to resist.

Dash moved over her, kissing her with desperate, relentless kisses, using his body to coax her back down to the couch. *Yes.* She kept her hands in his shirt, pulling him down with her, so that when her shoulders touched the pillows, he was right there with her, his weight pinning her to the couch.

She'd been fantasizing about this with Dash since she was sixteen. Or younger. And ever since.

To feel his body on hers. His mouth consuming her. His tongue. His hands on her hips, roaming her ribs, sliding down her thighs.

He was all male and temptation, and he was as great a kisser as she'd imagined he was.

He slid next to her on the couch, so they were on their sides, facing each other. He hooked his leg over her hip and dragged her against him. His kisses were pure fire, his mouth hot and delicious.

Her heart fluttered with nerves as she kissed him back. This was *Dash Stratton*. The man she'd had a crush on forever. And he was an amazing kisser. What was she doing, kissing him back? She was in way over her head! She pushed at him. "Dash. Stop."

He stopped immediately, pulling back. He jerked his hand off her hip, launched himself off the couch, and bolted to his feet, moving so fast that she almost didn't even see him move. "Fuck. I'm sorry." He held up his hands in apology. "That was an asshole move."

She propped herself up on her elbows, confused that he'd bolted. "Why are you standing on the other side of the room?"

"Because I took your kiss to places you didn't intend." He ran his hand through his hair. "I just…kissing you was unexpected. I didn't realize I'd react the way I did."

She stared at him as he shifted his weight and ran his hand through his hair again. "Are you *flustered* by kissing me?"

"Fuck that." He dropped his hands to his sides. "I don't get flustered. I just wanted you to feel safe and I blew that. Shit. You can have the house. I'll bow out—"

"Wait a sec." She quickly stood up and caught his wrist. "Why are you freaking out?"

He glanced at her fingers around his wrist. "Because it's my job to protect you, not tackle you on the couch until you're forced to tell me to back off."

Holy crap. The guy was even more a protector than she'd realized. "Dash," she said quietly, encircling his other wrist with her fingers. "I feel safe with you."

He scowled at her.

"I literally demanded that you kiss me, then grabbed your shirt and dragged you down on top of me."

He continued to scowl at her. "You had to tell me to stop. I felt you getting tense. I should have stopped immediately. I shouldn't have pushed to the point where you had to tell me to stop."

Leila pressed her lips together. "Well, I'm not scared of you, but now I'm annoyed."

He narrowed his eyes, listening.

She sighed. "Look, the reason I got tense and told you to stop was because I was freaking out about kissing you."

"Why?"

She let go of his hands. "You're such a beast to make me admit this, but it's because I've had a crush on you for so many years that I felt like my head was going to explode kissing you. It was a little overwhelming to have the man of my fantasies kissing me the way you were."

He continued to watch her. "Good overwhelming, or bad?"

She threw up her hands. "Great. Awesome. I started to freak out because I have you on this pedestal, and then you became a real man who was kissing me like it was the only thing you ever wanted to do for the rest of your life, which means that I'm on that pedestal trying to keep up being as great at kissing as you are!"

Dash stared at her for a long moment, then, to her surprise, burst out laughing. "I have to say, I've never heard that speech before."

"Because no woman will admit it. I'm sure every woman you have ever kissed was secretly freaking out. You're Dash Stratton!"

"I think you're the only woman who ever cared that I was Dash Stratton," he said, still grinning. "But I do have some concerns about getting you naked now. If we got naked, would you be with a fantasy, or with me?"

Some of her tension eased at his laughter. "Always the

fantasy. You're not real. And we can't get naked. We're married."

"Right. Of course. Married people should never get naked with each other. But in theory, it's a valid question." He cocked his head, watching her. "I find myself in a dilemma. Now that I know that kissing you has a green light, I want to kiss you pretty much all over your entire body, but it would crush my tender heart to think you weren't actually with *me*."

Her heart started racing again. "I'd like you to kiss me, but I do think it would be better for my emotional well-being if you were simply a man and not a god when I was kissing you."

"Hmm…" He walked over to her and peered down at her, not touching her, not kissing her. "What would make me human?"

Why did he smell so good? He smelled amazing. "I don't know. My teenage girl fandom is an intricately woven part of my soul."

He studied her. "I was in prison for two years."

She took a breath. "I knew you were in jail."

"Prison. Not jail. Jail is for less than six months. Longer than that, and you get the real deal."

"Why?"

"I was a stupid idiot who was mad at the world. I got in trouble as often as I could to piss off my parents. Of course, they'd already disowned me by then, so not sure it really had that payoff."

Her heart got a little ache in it. "You don't see your parents?"

He shook his head. "Neither Maura nor I had them in our lives. They weren't good people."

Leila vaguely remembered Dash's parents. They were a very wealthy family from New York who came to the lake for summers. She and Maura had become summer friends, best friends, first meeting at the town beach for swim lessons when they were little, playing summer league softball together. "Is that why you stayed in Birch Crossing?"

He nodded. "I didn't go back to New York with them after I turned eighteen. They didn't want me and I didn't want them." He leaned in. "I was a fuck up, Leila. I hated the world, and marrying you was the only decent thing I did for a long, long time."

Her heart turned over at the intensity in his voice. He believed that. He didn't see himself the way she'd seen him. "Thank you for marrying me. You saved me."

"Did I?" He took a strand of her hair between his fingers. "What about the asshole who broke your heart?"

"I would never have had the chance to meet him if you hadn't helped me escape my stepdad," she said honestly. "I'm grateful for the life I have led, even if it hurts."

He swore. "You look at me like I'm a saint, Leila. I'm not. I'm…" He paused. "If it weren't for Bea, I think I'd be dead by now. I was headed in that direction. The choices I made for so many years were just…self-destruction, and I feel like I'm barely out of it. But I have to get it all together in two days, and I don't know how."

His words hung between them, and she felt the weight of them.

And suddenly, Dash was human to her. A man who was flawed and vulnerable, even while he was this massive protector.

She held up her arms. "Kiss me, Dash."

He didn't move. "Who are you kissing?"

"An ex-con who has made a bunch of stupid decisions in his life, but who, underneath it all, has a beautiful heart that you couldn't hide from Bea, Maura, Sophia, and me."

He swore under his breath. "You're insane, Leila. But as it turns out, I need that right now." He encircled her waist with his arm, pulled her against him, and kissed her.

The kiss was different this time. Or, maybe, she was different. Her heart wasn't fluttering out of fear. Instead, she felt connected, like this man she'd idolized for so long was actually…

She couldn't think of the word. Accessible? Human? Safe, but in a different way than she'd thought before? She sighed and slid her arms around his neck, surrendering to him once again.

He kissed her with the same passion as before, but this time, there was a tenderness to it that made her heart turn over.

All the other kisses since she'd come to town had been rooted in the fantasy past, but this one was built on what was happening between them right now, in this present, and that made it different.

What *was* happening between them? This was not what she wanted or needed or had emotional space for. She shouldn't have told him about her fantasy issue. It was better to be kissing Dash, her Super Crush, than Dash, a man who was real, because the real one tugged at her heart in a way that her idol never had.

But she couldn't stop kissing him. It felt too extraordinary to be in his arms, to feel the heat of his body against hers, to bask in the decadence of his kiss.

He grabbed her around the waist, and then hoisted her up. She wrapped her legs around his hips, surrendering to him completely. He didn't break the kiss as he set her on the couch, once again, his weight pressing her to the cushions.

It felt so amazing to be with him. She gripped his shoulders, feeling the muscle beneath her hands. Dash was so fit, and she loved it. His shoulders were probably twice the size of hers, and he moved like a predator, athletic, capable, delicious.

Except when she'd struck him out, of course….

He angled his head, deepening the kiss, and she sighed with contentment, wanting nothing more than this moment.

His hands moved to her hips, and then to her belly, and then slid beneath her shirt.

She sucked in her breath at the feel of his palm on her bare skin. Warm. Strong. Tempting.

Dash broke the kiss, and kissed down the side of her neck, sending chills down her spine. She knew she wasn't in an emotional place to get involved right now, but she didn't want to stop. She'd waited too long for him. Was she kissing her fantasy man right now? The real, present man? Or some tangled-up version of both that she couldn't sort out?

He nibbled along her collarbone, and she sucked in her breath. "That feels amazing," she whispered.

"You taste fantastic." He kissed across her chest, the stretched-out-neckline of her tee shirt doing nothing to impede his progress.

Her heart began to race as his hand spanned her ribs. His thumb brushed against the underside of her breast, and desire shot through her. "Why does it feel so good when you touch me?" she whispered.

"I don't know, but I feel the same way." He moved his hand to cup her breast, and then took her mouth in his again while he thumbed her nipple.

Was she glad she hadn't worn the bra right now? Or wishing she had? Both? Neither? Leila could barely think right now. She was so consumed by the physical sensation of everywhere they were touching, and of the emotions and desire spinning through her so frenetically.

Dash pressed a kiss to her breast through her shirt, and she let out a little moan. "God, Dash. That feels amazing."

He pulled back, searching her face. "I want to make love to you, Leila. I've got nothing to offer except this moment. That's it."

She met his gaze. "I don't have anything to offer either, but I want this moment." She swallowed. "I want you to make love to me, Dash."

A smile lit up his face, and his expression suddenly became so tender she wanted to cry. "Since this is basically our wedding night, I vote we move it off the couch. How about my room?"

Her heart was racing now. "Is it romantic?"

"I'll be there, so it'll be romantic."

Oh, God. "You say the most self-deprecating things. How do I stand it?"

"It's rough being with me, but you've been managing it for fifteen years, so I know you can handle it." He kissed her again, then got up. He held out his hand. "Carry or walk?"

She hopped to her feet. "I'll walk. I can't lose my power to you—" She laughed as he swept her up in his arms.

"I wasn't really asking," he said. "I'm supposed to carry you across the threshold, at least according to every cheesy movie that I've never actually watched."

Leila looped her hands around his neck as he literally jogged up the stairs, carrying her as if he hadn't even noticed he was lugging a human being with him. "I guess I'm lighter than carrying around massive pieces of iron, huh?"

"Different."

"Different? I'm *different* than iron?"

"Yeah." He grinned at her as he walked into his room. "Is that not romantic enough for you? I feel like that was pretty good."

She laughed again as he gently tossed her on the bed. "It was pretty weak, but since you waited a decade and a half for our wedding night festivities, I guess my expectations should stay pretty low."

"Exactly." He crawled onto the bed, moving like a predator, with a wicked gleam in his eyes that made her heart start to race. "Expect nothing and life will overdeliver." He braced himself above her and lowered just his head to envelop her in a decadent, tantalizing kiss that was all skill and finesse.

"Yes," she whispered. "More of that."

He laughed, a deep, delicious laugh that made goose-bumps pop up on her arms. "Your wish is my command, my bride." He kissed her again, tangling her emotions and needs into chaos, and they paused. "Is it warm in here?"

She grinned. "Very. Aren't you hot?"

"I am hot. That's what all the ladies tell me." He sat up and ripped his shirt off.

"Holy crap." Leila let out her breath. Dash was *sculpted*. He had a tattoo over his heart that said *Freedom*. Another tattoo on the front of his left shoulder that was a lake vista, with a loon floating on the water. They were beautiful art, on a body that defied humanity, at least the humans she'd been around. She recognized his artistic style, and knew he'd designed them himself.

He cocked his brow at her, then held up his arms and flexed them, showing off biceps that were literally ridiculous.

She burst out laughing at his silliness. "That's just wrong."

"What? My pose? Do I have the angle wrong?" He turned his hands to the side and raised his brows. "Or the tattoos? I got them done by an amazing tattoo artist who used to live in Bass Derby. She had a store at Eagle's Nest Marina. She was brilliant."

"The tattoos are beautiful. It's wrong that I've been married to those biceps for so long and never been able to enjoy them properly." She held up her arms. "Come to me, you big lug. Show me all you've got."

He let out a low growl that made her giggle in anticipation, and then he tackled her. She shrieked with laughter as he pinned her to the bed, roaming her body with his hands and his mouth, making the silliest comments even as he stoked a fire inside her.

She's never laughed so much in bed, but Dash was just a goofball, even as he melted all her defenses and inhibitions with his kisses.

"We need this off," he muttered as he grasped the hem of her shirt. "Arms up, my darling."

"I'm definitely not your darling. We're strangers." She sat up and raised her hands over her head. Her heart was racing as he pulled her shirt over her head, not quite able to shake the nerves. This was *Dash,* plus, he was even more delicious than she remembered.

"My strange bride," he corrected. "Probably strange in more ways than one." Then he sat back to look at her, and all her fears vanished. His expression was pure male appreciation, and reverence.

Feeling deliciously bold, she raised her arms over her head and struck a pose that made her feel sexy and powerful.

And when his eyes widened, and he sucked in his breath, she knew it had worked. She was hot! Whoohoo! Robbie had never made her feel hot, but Dash sure did, and she loved it so much.

This time, when Dash came back to kiss her, the laughter was replaced by raw intensity and need. He kissed her like a man who'd been starving for her, and she kissed him back with equal desperation.

The way he kissed her and touched her made her feel beautiful. Vibrant. Revered. His touch was slow and deliberate, as if he were savoring every curve of her body, so she did the same for him. She embraced how beautiful his body was, and she ran her hands over his muscles, not even trying to pretend she wasn't infatuated with his body.

It was a mutual admiration session communicated with touches, kisses, and whispers of need and appreciation, and she felt glorious and safe.

Soon, the rest of their clothing was gone, on the floor or somewhere. She hadn't even noticed when they'd become naked, she'd been so consumed by the wonderful sensations pulsing though her.

Dash broke the kiss he'd been teasing her with. "This is insane, Leila. How are you doing this to me?"

She put her hands on his hips and pulled him over her. "Doing what?"

He didn't answer. He just caught her mouth in another kiss that poured heat into every cell in her body and every recess of her soul.

She sighed into the kiss, then smiled when he grabbed a condom from the nightstand. "Yes," she whispered.

Dash paused, searching her face. "No going back if we do this, Leila. Not sure what it'll change or how it will change, but it will."

She nodded. "I know."

He still waited, poised over her, his gaze searching hers. She saw the vulnerability in his eyes and suddenly remembered all he was going through, all that he'd lost, and in that moment, he lost all the sparkling shine of a fantasy crush.

He truly became Dash Stratton, a man who was fighting his personal battles. Real. Flawed. And the man who'd saved her and then let her walk away.

That man, she could relate to. This was the man she wanted to be intimate with. "Make love to me, Dash. We'll figure it out."

He laughed softly. "That's probably a bad plan, but I've never been great at making plans." And with that, he sheathed himself inside her, slow, easy, deliciously.

Leila met his gaze as they came together. There were no jokes. No witticism. No teasing. Just an unspoken connection that went deeper than she'd ever realized. She smiled and pulled him down to her so she could kiss him.

He kissed her back as he began to move inside her, a rhythm that sent sparks of the most amazing sensations dancing through her. The rhythm intensified, more and more, deeper, hotter, until she was completely lost in him, in the moment, in the gloriousness of how he made her feel. His hand went between her legs, adding to the cacophony of sensation, until it exploded through her.

He came as soon as she did, holding her tight as his body bucked against hers. Together they climaxed, tumbling off the precipice into a glorious landing in each other's arms.

Sated, Dash collapsed beside her and pulled her into his arms, pressing his face into her hair.

He was wrapped around her, holding her tight, as if he'd never let her go, as if he'd never leave her unprotected. Emotions welled up inside Leila, emotions that spilled over until she suddenly couldn't breathe. Tears filled her eyes, and she had to choke back a sob.

Dash raised his head to look at her, his forehead etched with a frown. "What's wrong, sweetheart?"

Leila shook her head, not trusting herself to talk. She didn't want to start sobbing all over him after their amazing experience. All they'd had was fun since she'd arrived. There was no place in this moment to get emotional and weighty.

Dash drew her hand to him and pressed a kiss to her knuckles. "I've been married to you for more than a decade, sweetheart. I know when you're upset. You can't lie to me."

She started laughing through her tears. "I'm literally crying. It doesn't take a genius to realize I'm upset."

"Thank God for that, because I'm no genius. And in case you haven't noticed, I haven't really been the most attentive husband."

"I know. I've had to sleep with other men to fill my life."

"Yeah, maybe we need to talk about that."

"No. I'm good." She wiggled out from under him. "I'm going to go take a shower, then go to bed. I'm beat." Then she bolted for the bathroom, leaving him in bed, staring after her with a look of surprise on his face.

She hoped Dash was the kind of guy who wouldn't feel the need to follow a crying woman into a bathroom.

But she had a feeling he wasn't.

CHAPTER 16

DASH FROWNED as his bedroom door slammed behind Leila.

What the hell had just happened?

He tossed back the covers, vaulted off the bed, and jogged after her.

He caught up to her just as she was closing the bathroom door. "Leila."

She looked at him, and he saw pain in her blue eyes. "Go away, Dash."

"No." He leaned on the door, not to force it open, but just enough to keep her from shutting it. "What's going on?"

"Nothing." She gave up on the door, and instead turned on the shower.

She was absolutely breathtaking naked, but he knew it wasn't the time to focus on it. "Liar," he said. "Look, Leila. I know pain when I see it, and I'm not going to let you deal with it alone. What's going on? Was it me? Something I did? Or said?"

She stuck her hand in the shower to see if it was warm yet, but it took forever, so he knew he had a few minutes. "Look," she said, "I'm sorry I got emotional. I know that's not what today is about for us, or anything. So, I'm taking it off the table."

Dash leaned against the sink and folded his arms. "Give me the short answer. One thing that upset you. Then I'll leave."

She glared at him. "You're so difficult."

"I know."

"Did you annoy Bea like this?"

"Yeah. Often." He got more comfortable against the sink. "What's up?"

She looked over at him. "I just...I have a lot going on right now. That moment in your arms, I felt...safe. Like everything was going to be okay. I haven't felt like that in a while, and it was just so amazing, as if all this weight had suddenly lifted off my shoulders for a brief moment."

His gut tightened. "I understand," he said quietly. "I've been in a freefall since Maura and Sophia died, and then Bea. I'm completely fucked up right now, but today, with you, I've felt normal for the first time in a long time. Happy, even. Felt good."

She sat down on the edge of the tub. "It's not real, this moment, this thing between us."

"It is real." He leaned forward. "Of course it's real. We felt good today. Carefree. That's real."

"But it won't lead to anything. You're going to be a freaking *dad,* and I'm..." She looked at him. "I'm not okay, Dash. I know I seemed like it today, but I'm not."

He closed the toilet lid and sat down on it, so he was level with her. "I know. I saw it in your eyes this afternoon."

"Robbie wrecked me," she said softly. "I feel like I'm so broken right now. I completely trusted him, and I had no idea what he was doing behind my back. I feel stupid. I feel lost. And I'm completely broke. He had everything set up in his favor, and I was too trusting to realize it or even think about making sure I was protecting myself."

Anger surged through Dash, anger on her behalf, but he kept it in check. Instead, he leaned in. "Leila. I'm wrecked too. We can be wrecked together."

She looked at him. "There is no 'together' for us, Dash."

"There is, because we have to live together for a month."

She sighed. "How are we going to live together? The attraction between us is real. You're sitting there naked and all hot, and all I want to do is tackle you and spend the night in the middle of mind-blowing orgasms, laughter, and intimacy-induced emotional overload."

He grinned. "That's not a bad way to go."

She managed a small smile. "Okay, I admit that the way I phrased it didn't really support my point."

"Not if you're trying to talk me out of joining you in the shower, no," he agreed. The shower had finally gotten hot, and steam was beginning to fill the small room. "Should we talk in the shower?"

"No!" She threw up her hands. "Dash. I can't be involved in anything right now. Look at what just happened! I melted down just from being in your arms. I've been with someone for eight years, who then betrayed me. I need to be with me. Figure out a plan. I don't know. Find a way to stop being so freaking scared about what comes next."

He got that. Hell, he got that. "Maybe we can do that together. Since we're stuck with each other."

Leila shook her head. "Maybe I should move out. Maybe we should try another time."

Alarm shot through him at the idea of her moving out. "Clare didn't tell you?"

"Oh, God. What now?"

"It was in her note to me. We have six months from Bea's death to live here together and complete our quota. If we don't, then the house gets sold and the money goes to charity."

Her eyes widened. "How long has it been since she passed away?"

"Almost five months. We have to do it now."

She leaned her head back and closed her eyes. "I don't think I can do this, Dash."

"I need this house for the twins, Leila. I spent all my savings on lawyers fighting for them. Maura and Sophia left some money in a trust for them, but it's for their care and education, not for a house. It's my job to provide a house for them."

Her eyes snapped open. "You want to keep the house?" At his nod, she frowned. "I'll need the money from the house to pay off my debt, and to get my head above water again."

The grim reality suddenly struck him. "I don't have the money to buy you out."

She stared at him. "I don't want the house but I need the money from it, Dash. What if we sold it and split it? You could buy a smaller house."

Sell this house? It was the only roots he had left. The only thing he had. Fuck. He and Bea had talked about how he would raise the twins in this house. He'd never thought of how having a co-heir would change things. "No. This is the house. Bea and I talked about it. I can't give them less. They lost their parents and have only me. I can't move them into some crappy house."

"No." Leila held up her hands. "That's not fair using that guilt on me. I would give them the house if I could. But I literally am in massive debt from the whole debacle with Robbie. I have to have the money from the sale of the house. I'm not a bad person, Dash. I'm not. But I can't—"

"I know." He cut her off, trying to stay calm. "It's okay. We'll work it out. You don't want the house, so that's good, right? I'll find a way to buy it."

She gave him a look. "You don't have the money."

"I don't. But I'll see what I can do."

"It's hundreds of thousands of dollars."

"I know." He braced his forearms on his thighs and grimaced. *Hell.* Things kept getting more complicated. "You know what?" he said quietly.

"What?"

He looked up at her. "It never bothered me to stay married to a woman I'd met only a few times, because I had no plans to become a family man. You said you're not a baby person? Well, I'm not either. I didn't want to get married, have kids, or settle down. I have never cared about money or owning my own home. Fancy shit doesn't mean anything to me. And now…" He spread his hands. "I have to become the man I never wanted to be, and care about things I never wanted to care about. I'm running absolutely blind here, and it keeps getting bigger."

Leila studied him. "If being their dad isn't right for you—"

"I'll make it right." He cut her off. "Sophia's parents are not the right people for those kids." He met her gaze. "Leila, we both know what it's like to be raised by the wrong people. I'll do whatever it takes to make sure those girls never grow up feeling scared, unloved, or not enough. I might not have any idea what the hell I'm doing, but I'm a good guy, and I love them. That's better than you or I had."

He felt the words in the core of his very soul. Something inside him had gone into a fierce protector mode when he'd found out that those kids were his. "Nothing will stop me. I will love the hell out of them and make it right."

Leila smiled, her face softening. "I believe you, Dash. You're a protector."

"I am." He bounced his foot restlessly. What the hell had Bea been thinking to make Leila the co-heir? It messed up everything for him.

Maybe she hadn't realized he'd use up all his savings to fight for custody.

Maybe she hadn't realized the tough financial straits he'd be in.

It didn't matter. He couldn't ask her, because she'd gone and gotten herself killed on a kneeboard. "When Maura and Sophia died," he said, "Bea was still alive. She said she'd help me with the girls. I thought I could do it with her help, right? She'd be their grandma, and I'd fill in. But then she died."

"Oh, Dash." Leila's face filled with understanding and empathy that made him squirm.

He didn't want to be weak. He didn't want anyone, especially Leila, to see him as weak.

He hated when he thought about the loss of Bea, Maura, and Sophia. He needed to stay focused. "It's fine. I'll figure it out." He stood up. "Shower's yours. I need to start thinking." He couldn't pick up extra shifts at work, because he'd have kids at home. So, what the hell?

Leila watched him. "Well, you're stuck with me for thirty days. I need my money, so I'll help."

"No." Crap. He hadn't meant to put his crap on her shoulders. That wasn't his style at all. "Leila, you have your own things to work through. Take care of yourself. I can handle it." He started out the door, then stopped.

What was he doing? Walking out on her when she was sitting there naked on the edge of the tub?

He wasn't an ass, and even if he was, Leila deserved more.

He swung around and came back to kneel in front of her. "Look, tonight was incredible. I needed it more than you'll ever know."

She smiled and touched his face, her fingers lingering along his jaw. "Me, too." But her eyes were heavy, and he hated that.

"We'll get this figured out," he said. "No guilt over the fact you need the money."

She laughed softly. "My need for the money will rip a

home away from two kids who lost their parents. It's a little difficult not to feel like a selfish frog."

"Frogs are a necessary part of the food chain around here," he said. "Without frogs, mosquitoes would overrun us."

She laughed softly. "Well, thank goodness even selfish frogs have a purpose in this ecosystem."

"Everything has a purpose." He couldn't get over the guilt in her eyes. Shit. His life added weight to hers, and that wasn't okay. He paused, then said the words he never thought he'd say, but he had to. "Look," he said, dragging the words out of him. "Since we're married, the fact I now have kids could put you on the hook for them in some ways. If you want a divorce, then, just ask."

Her eyes widened. "A divorce?"

"Yeah." He laughed softly. "I'm not gonna lie. I liked being married to you. Felt good. But it's different now. It's not just a piece of paper from a long time ago."

She stared at him. "I like being married to you, too."

Relief rushed through him at her words. It felt good to know he wasn't alone. "What does that say about us?" he mused. "That we liked being married to someone we barely knew, who we hadn't seen for fifteen years? A marriage that was literally no more than a piece of paper?"

"That we knew one day we'd have amazing sex?"

He grinned. "That was worth it, for sure."

She looked up at him. "I have a friend, Gordon, who always asks me that. Why did I stay married to you? Why did you stay married to me? He likes to point out that I was in an eight-year relationship, but I never thought about getting a divorce from you."

Huh. Dash hadn't thought of it in that way, but he found that interesting. He liked it, in fact. This Robbie jerk had never tempted Leila away from him.

"I used our marriage to keep women at a distance," he said. "I'll admit it. Whenever a relationship felt like I'd had enough, I'd tell them I was married. No one wanted to stick around. What about your ex? Did he know you were married?"

"Yes."

"Did he ever ask you to get a divorce?"

"Never." Her eyes widened. "I'm such an idiot," she said softly. "He clearly never wanted anything more with me, or he would have wanted me to get a divorce."

"Well, you didn't want more either, or you would've come looking for me. Don't forget that," he said. "It sounds like you were both on the same page." He paused. "Except he was an asshole who cheated on you and took advantage of you financially. I'm not exonerating him from that. Just that neither of you wanted more."

She stared at him. "So, I'm lying to myself that I'm upset that the relationship is over?"

"No. Maybe the relationship you had with him, before it went sour, was what you wanted. No long-term commitment. Maybe it was exactly what you wanted."

She sighed. "Is it wrong to admit that I don't even know which way to turn right now?"

"No." He rested his forearms on her thighs, and set his hands on her hips. "I'm lost as hell right now, too. Scared shitless about a lot of things, but most of all, how to give two little girls a life they deserve. My parents were not good people. I don't know anything about being a good dad."

Leila set her hand on the side of his face. "I'd love to offer some advice on that, but my childhood was from hell."

Her hand felt so good on his skin. Grounding. Connected. Calming. "Which I know."

She sighed. "Yes, you do. I guess maybe that's why a paper marriage works for me. Marriage trapped my mother to a terrible man, and trapped me to him as well. Only my knight in shining armor got me out of that one."

He grinned. "That might be an overstatement. I'm no knight."

"You were to me, then." She smiled. "All I wanted was a piece of paper that kept me safe from my stepdad."

"And I got a piece of paper that kept me from having to get serious with anyone."

She cocked her head. "Why didn't you ever want more?"

"I don't know. I just never did. I don't want to settle down or need to think about anyone else's welfare over my own."

"And now you have to."

"And now I will," he agreed. He fell silent. "You were always at the back of my mind. I wondered how you were."

She smiled. "I always fantasized about you, even when I was with Robbie. You were this Greek god in my memories and my imagination." Her eyes widened. "Oh, God. I hope that's not why I chose Robbie, because I was always obsessed with you, and no man could compare to the image I had of you."

"No man can compare to the reality of me," he agreed. "I'm financially obliterated, emotionally unavailable, and I'm an ex-con with two kids." He paused. "Is that not the image you were fantasizing over?"

She laughed. "No, it wasn't. In my fantasies, you were incredibly hot—"

"That's true." He flexed his arm, making her laugh again.

"It *is* true. You over-delivered on that one."

"What else about your fantasies?" He was fascinated that she'd had fantasies about him all this time. Yeah, his ego liked it, but it also just…created a bond.

She raised her brows. "My fantasies? I had this one where I'd come out of work after a long day, and I'd be so tired. You'd be standing in the parking lot, leaning against my car, with a whole bunch of roses and chocolate."

"I brought you chocolate and strawberries tonight. That's pretty close."

She smiled. "It's almost exact."

"Tell me the rest."

Her smile widened. "When I saw you with the goodies, my heart would go all soft and mushy. You'd give me this big smile that was pure love, and then you'd walk over to me, pull me in for a glorious kiss, hand me the roses and chocolates, and tell me that you'd come for me. That you were there for me now, and everything would change. That our marriage would be real, and it would be amazing."

Damn. He was stunned by her admission. And he wasn't going to lie, he loved the hell out of it. This incredible woman had fantasized about him? What man wouldn't like that? "When you were with Robbie, you actually dreamed about me coming after you and poaching you away from him? I just want clarification on that one."

"Yes." Her cheeks were a faint pink of embarrassment. "Quite often, in fact."

"Awesome." Dash wasn't a moral enough guy not to like the fact that this douchebag who'd jerked her over had come in second to her fantasies about him. "Did you tell him?"

She raised her brows. "No, I didn't. Should I have?"

"Maybe. It might have gotten him to raise his game if he'd known he had such competition."

"You were a fantasy. I'm not sure he would have found that threatening."

"I went to prison. I can be very threatening." He wasn't lying about that. He didn't play that card often, but he had it available to him at all times.

Something flickered in her eyes. "Why are bad boys so freaking attractive?"

He leaned in, starting to become more aware again of the fact they were both still naked. "Why are women who sass us so freaking hot?"

"I have breasts. That makes me attractive to men like you.

But just for the record, in my fantasies, you were rich, too. So real life was a failure on that obviously."

"Fuck. I almost had you. If only I were wealthy."

"Right? So close, and yet so far." Leila smiled. "I see you as a real man now, and it's better that way. The fantasy was a little much. Too intimidating."

He started laughing. "You're saying that I'm enough of a loser that it works for you?"

She grinned. "Exactly what I was trying to say. I'm so glad we have such great communication skills."

"That we do." He was quiet for a moment, tracing circles on her hips with his thumbs. "What now, Leila?"

"In what way?"

"Us."

Panic flashed across her face. "You mean the divorce?"

"Shit, no." He was already regretting bringing up the divorce. "I was actually thinking about the fact we're both still naked and the shower is going to run out of hot water soon. And my bed is nearby. And so is yours. And the fact that we still have the house to ourselves for another forty-eight hours."

She dropped her hand from his face and folded her arms across her chest, visibly retreating. "I have no idea what to do about that. And about us. Is it better for us to pretend tonight didn't happen?"

"Can't do that. It happened. Next option." He was completely focused, his body taut, waiting for her answer. For permission to pounce, because that was all he wanted to do right now. Leave the conversation and weight behind, and just steal one more moment of fun before he had to wake up tomorrow and start to figure stuff out.

Her blue eyes were wary, searching his face. "We could make tonight a one-night stand, and just go the friend route for the next thirty days, because both our lives are a wreck right now?"

"That doesn't feel right," he said, resistance building hard and fast inside him.

"I know." She sighed. "But we're in no place for this thing between us."

"I agree. We're not in a place to make anything work between us." But he didn't move away. He couldn't move away. He couldn't give up on this. He always gave up fast when it came to women, but with Leila? No. Not yet. "Is there a third option?"

She rolled her eyes in visible exasperation. "Chaos, confusion, and possibly heartbreak."

He swore. "My heart's trashed right now."

"Mine, too." She searched his face. "But it feels good to be with you," she whispered. "You make me laugh, and I need that."

"Hell, yeah," he agreed.

They sat there in the bathroom, studying each other.

"I guess another option would be to enjoy the sex and the fun while we can," she said hesitantly. "Embrace this as our rebound relationship and then move on when the thirty days is up. Or the forty-eight hours because I'm not sure about naked time with you when kids are around."

"Thirty days and then call it quits?" He didn't really like the second half of that proposal.

"Or forty-eight hours of romance, then twenty-eight days of friendship, then call it quits? No breaking of hearts allowed. Just healing."

He slid his hands into her hair. "Let's start with tonight and then see what happens."

She gripped his wrists. "But either way, we agree to end it when the thirty days is up? We agree that it's nothing more than that. And we have to keep things fun. We both need fun and levity. No emotional drama. Just the healing power of laughter and fun. Promise?"

"That sounds great." But even as he said it, his mind

lingered on the "no emotional drama" rule. He wanted to help her deal with her situation, and if they dealt with Robbie, it wouldn't be easy. But he'd deal with that when it happened. He also didn't like the "end it" part of the deal, but he didn't have to talk her out of that yet. "Agreed. Now kiss your loser husband and let's get naked."

She started laughing. "We are naked."

"Then let's get wet and naked." He stood up and grabbed her hand to pull her to her feet. "My shower or yours?"

"We only have one."

"And it belongs to both of us."

"For now."

Reality flickered between them, dampening the moment for a brief second. "Now is all we have." Then he picked her up, stepped into the shower, and proceeded to show her how great the "now" could be.

He hoped it far exceeded all those fantasies she'd ever had about him.

Because it sure did for him.

CHAPTER 17

F RIDAY MORNING CAME WAY TOO QUICKLY.

Leila kept an eye on Dash as he carried stuff to his truck. She was cleaning up from their breakfast, and he was installing car seats in his truck.

They'd spent two days with each other.

Neither of them had worked on anything they'd needed to work on: his money, her financial future, any of it.

They'd just had fun. They'd taken Bea's boat out on the lake. They'd made love. A lot. They'd gone skinny dipping. They'd hung out at Wright's General Store after hours with Clare and Griffin. They hadn't talked about babies, loss, or divorce. They'd just had fun. Laughter.

They'd both needed it. But at the same time, every minute had been the awareness that it was just a hiatus. They were hiding from life, and that hiding spot was about to disappear.

Dash came to stand behind her. "I'm ready to go." His voice had a slight reserve to it, so different from the laughter and warmth that it had held the last two days.

It was all right. She didn't take it personally. She'd known it was coming.

But she couldn't simply let it go. She couldn't let their time together simply end unacknowledged, as if it had been nothing.

She'd meant for it to be nothing. And she was pretty sure Dash had as well.

But now that the ending had come, she couldn't lie to herself anymore.

It had been everything. That didn't change the fact that it was still ending, but it did mean she had to make a choice.

She had to simply let it go, without fanfare, guilt, or regret.

Or, she could embrace the turbulent emotions cascading through her for the last hour, as she watched the man who'd held her all night prepare to drive out of her life for good as the man he currently was. When he came back, he'd never be this man again, and she knew it.

Maybe she was breaking the rules, but it didn't matter. Leila had fought for so little when it came to the people in her life, and she didn't want to do it anymore. She wanted to be more, to open herself more, to acknowledge the gifts when she got them.

And that gift had been Dash for the last two days.

"Leila?" He touched her shoulder. "Did you hear me? I'm ready to go."

She took a breath and turned to face him. "I need to say something."

Wariness flickered in his eyes. "All right."

She put her hands on her hips. "I know that neither of us accomplished anything the last two days. All we did was have fun. I know it was unproductive. But I needed it so much. You made me feel whole again. Safe. Happy. And I want to say thank you now, before you leave, because I don't know what will happen when you come back."

He stared at her for a long moment, long enough that she started to feel stupid.

No. She was done letting herself feel stupid. For anything. So she lifted her chin. "I wanted you to know that."

He didn't answer her. But he put his hands on either side of her face, bent down to her, and kissed her. It was the most tender, most heartwarming, most intimate kiss she'd ever experienced.

And he didn't stop.

He just kept kissing her until tears started to pool in her eyes.

When he finally stopped kissing, she had to fight for composure. "That felt like a kiss that a soldier would give his true love before heading off to war. A kiss of good-bye."

Dash brushed his thumb over her lower lip. "That's exactly what it was. The last two days have been a precious gift I will remember for my entire life, Leila. On a lot of levels. Another time, another place, I'd be all over the chance to keep going with you. But when I come back, it won't be the same. I'll be different. Our relationship will be different. The clock will be ticking on getting the house sorted. So, yeah, thank you, and good-bye."

She lifted her chin. "It's not that much of a good-bye. I'm still living here."

Emotion flicked in his eyes. "I know," he said softly, his words laden with the truth that it was a good-bye, and they both knew it. He kissed her again, then, without another word, he turned and walked out.

Leila stayed where she was as the door slammed shut and his boots thudded across the porch.

Loss gripped her when she heard his truck start. But she didn't rush to the window to watch him leave.

She simply stood there, in that empty house, listening until she couldn't hear the crunch of his tires on the dirt driveway, or the sound of his engine. Sadness flowed through her, over her, into her, making it difficult to breathe, but she didn't fight it. She let it fill her, somehow needing that sadness to process that everything she and Dash had had was real.

She'd been happy, truly happy for the last two days. He'd made her laugh, cooked her dinner and breakfast, loved her like crazy, and made her feel like she mattered. Like she had value.

She hadn't trusted anyone enough to let them take care of her like that before. Maybe the fact that she knew it was temporary had made her able to surrender so completely. Maybe it was that they were tied by marriage, so she knew that at least today, he couldn't walk away from her. Maybe it was simply that he fit her in a way no one else had, and she'd let him in.

Either way, Leila was grateful for it. Grateful for the glimpse into how happy she could feel, and how nice a day could be...even if it meant the loss of it was a surprisingly painful ache in her heart.

As the sound of Dash's truck faded, and the magic they'd shared drifted into a past that couldn't be reclaimed, the silence of the house expanded, wrapping around her like a shadow that had been waiting for the sunset.

She became aware of the emptiness of the house that had been so full of life and laughter when Dash had been with her, so full of love and warmth when Bea had filled it with her vibrant laughter.

Now, Leila was alone, really alone, in the house that was all about her past.

Dash's presence was no longer there to demand Leila's focus and attention, and the ghosts she'd tried to hide from for the last fifteen years suddenly came to life, drifting out from the crevices and shadows they'd been hiding in.

Her gaze went to the living room, and the faded blue couch that still sat by the fireplace. The couch where Dash had given her that backrub. The couch that her teenage self had cried on when she'd run from her stepdad, scared to go home.

She looked over at the sink, at the dishes she'd eaten breakfast off of this morning. They were the same dishes that Bea had served spaghetti and meatballs on when Leila hadn't had a meal all day.

The backyard was the same one where she and Maura had played croquet, screaming with laughter whenever they got the chance to pound each other's balls into the bushes.

All these memories were things Leila had vaguely noticed when she'd first arrived, but they'd been eclipsed by the intensity of Dash.

But without him as a distraction, suddenly the house felt very full of old memories that didn't feel very good, and Leila didn't want to be in the middle of them by herself.

She turned away from the living room, pulled out her phone, and called Gordon.

He answered on the first ring. "Girl! I've been waiting for updates! What is happening?"

She smiled at the sound of his voice. Just hearing his irreverent joy made her stomach loosen, and the tension crowding her eased. She realized suddenly that Gordon was like Dash, in that they both made her laugh, lightened her heart, and made her remember that life was supposed to be fun. "Lots of sex, Gordon. There's been lots of great sex."

He let out a whoop that made her laugh. "Hot diggity, Leila! You dirty dog, you! Tell me everything!"

Leila did, as she walked around the house, looking in the rooms, using his upbeat company to keep her emotions in check as she looked through all the memories that the house gave her. By the time she reached the backyard, the stories were complete, and so was her tour of the house.

She sat down on the porch swing and leaned back, gazing out over the yard.

"That's it, then?" Gordon asked. "Just a good-bye kiss and then off to become a daddy?"

"Yep."

"So, your thirty days starts over when he gets back then, right?"

Crap. She hadn't thought of that. "Maybe they'll give us a break since Dash has to go get the girls."

"Doesn't sound like it. What are their names?"

She paused. "I don't know. He just calls them the twins."

"Holy cannoli, Leila. You're about to become a stepmom and you don't even know their names? What is that?"

Stepmom. The word made her belly clench. "I'm not their stepmom."

"You're married to their dad. That makes you a stepmom. Face it, girl. You got the babies you never thought you wanted."

"No. Dash and I don't even have a relationship. We barely know each other. It's not like that."

Gordon made a tsking sound. "Lift your hand off the panic button, Leila. If you didn't call to tell me you're excited to be a stepmom, then what?"

She let out her breath, voicing the worry that she'd pushed aside for the last two days. "I need the money from the sale of the house, Gordon. But Dash can't buy me out. I can't kick them out just because I need the money. I just can't."

Gordon sighed. "You're a great person, sweetie. But you're also in tough straits. You gave up everything for Robbie and it burned you. You can't do that again. You won't recover financially or emotionally. Bea left you a gift and you owe it to yourself to take it."

She gazed at the shed where Bea's husband had his iron workshop. The sign over the door still said Roger's Iron. "I don't know how I can do that, Gordon."

He sighed. "I know. I'm not a monster. I understand the twins issue. But I feel like I failed you by not realizing what a douchebag Robbie was and pulling you off that train. Okay, let's think. If you can make the money, you won't need the house, right?"

"Well, yes, obviously."

"So, we have thirty days to earn you all the money you need to get back on your feet."

"To earn several hundred thousand dollars?"

"Doubt is unattractive. Shed that now, girl, and get thinking. This is your time to shine."

She bit her lip. "Any ideas?"

"None whatsoever, but that's always a great place to start. I'll brainstorm. You brainstorm, and we'll reconvene later today. I want a list of fifty ideas."

Leila started laughing. "So, I'm going to start a side hustle, then? Is that my plan?"

"Maybe. Or maybe this will be your new career. Let's go, babycakes. Let's go big and make this happen. You got this."

She wanted to feel like she had this. And Gordon was right. She needed to believe it. But that felt so far away from where she was. It was too big of a leap. Before her two days with Dash, she hadn't even felt like she could manage a shower, let alone reinvent herself financially overnight.

"Leila? What's happening over there? I'm just getting silence."

She smiled. "All right. I can write down some ideas."

It wasn't a belief in herself. It wasn't actual money. But it was a step, and a step was something.

"Perfect. And get out of the house. Go somewhere that energizes you. Go ask that Eppie spitfire if she has any ideas. She sounds like a trip."

Leila chuckled. "She is. Okay, maybe I'll go to Wright's and see if anyone is around."

"Perfect. Go do your thing, Talk to you later. Smooches!"

"Bye." She was still laughing as she hung up the phone. Gordon was on the edge of crazy, but he always made her feel better. He was an aspiring Broadway star, who hadn't quite had his breakthrough yet, but he'd had a few lead touring roles that had been amazing.

She'd met him when she first moved to New York. He'd been in the theatre program at her college, and they'd bonded over the terrible food, and been friends ever since.

He was eccentric, always broke, but he had a zest and passion for life that she'd always envied when she'd gotten up every day to head to work with Robbie.

Maybe this was her chance to find the spark like Gordon had.

Dash had made her feel vibrant. Maybe there was more of that inside her.

Maybe the total catastrophic implosion of her life was exactly what she'd wanted, and she just didn't know it yet.

CHAPTER 18

ON HIS WAY out of town, Dash pulled his truck over in front of Wright's General Store, parking behind Jackson Reed's pickup truck.

He knew he had to get on the road, but seeing Jackson's truck had prompted him to pull over. He jogged into Wright's and saw his boss at the register, chatting with Griffin, Blue, and Harlan. "Jackson!"

The four men looked over at him, and greeted him with the same smiles they always had, even though he wasn't that far out from his total fuck-up days.

He strode up to them. "I'm on my way out of town to pick up the twins," he said.

Jackson grinned. "You look terrified."

That hadn't been what Dash had been planning to talk about, but Jackson's words brought him to an abrupt halt. "Of being a dad? Hell, yeah."

Griffin leaned forward. "I'll tell you right now, Dash, you're going to screw up. A lot."

Fuck. "Thanks for that. You sound like Maura's in-laws. You want to sue me for custody? You and Clare would be great with them."

Griffin frowned. "That's not what I meant. You'll be great. My point was that there's no right answer when it comes to kids. Every minute is a guessing game, and you make the best choice you can, and that'll be enough."

"I don't have enough tools to make guesses. My parents sucked."

Understanding flickered across Harlan's face. "I get that," he said. "When I wound up an accidental dad when I married Emma, I was pretty sure those kids would be a thousand times better off with anyone but me."

Dash frowned, listening. He knew he was better than Maura's in-laws, but that wasn't saying much.

"Our kids went through hell before we adopted them," Harlan continued. "*Hell.* They deserved the best, and the dad they got was me. I had nightmares about fucking it up."

Dash nodded. "I've had those."

"But in the end, I realized that it was meant to be. I love the hell out of them, and I give them my best, and it's enough. My gritty past makes me able to understand where they came from, and I can help them heal."

Dash shifted. "Aimee and Ashley had a good home—"

"And now they have you and Leila. You guys will do it."

Dash's gut tightened. "Leila and I aren't together."

The men exchanged glances, but it was Griffin who spoke. "Sorry for the assumption. Based on how you guys were together this week, I figured it was on."

"It was temporary. We were just having fun."

Harlan grinned. "There's no 'just having fun' when it's with the woman you're married to. Trust me, I know."

"It's not like that." But Dash was on edge now. Had he led Leila on? "We talked about it. Neither of us are in a place for a relationship." He tried to laugh. "Hell, we're enemies now," he added.

None of the men looked impressed. "Enemies in what way?" Griffin asked.

"The house," Dash said. "She needs the money from the sale of it, and I don't have the cash to buy her out. That house is for those kids. I owe it to them." He turned to Jackson. "That's why I came in here. I know I asked for a couple weeks off to get adjusted with the twins, but I need to start building the cash reserves. Can you put me back on the schedule this week?"

Jackson raised his brows. "Nope. Can't do that."

Dash swore under his breath. "I know you can use the extra hands—"

"I know, but you have to be a dad. You can't pawn that off on someone else."

Dash narrowed his eyes. "I'm not pawning it off. I need to earn money. I'm trying to be responsible for the first time in my life."

But Griffin was shaking his head. "Never sacrifice time with your kids to work. Took me a long time to learn that."

"Agreed," Harlan said. "Those kids need you. They don't even know you."

"I've been down to see them every single weekend for the last six months," Dash retorted. "Every damned weekend I drive down there Friday night and come back Sunday. I sleep in my car so I don't waste money on a New York hotel. They know me." Fuck. He didn't know what else to give. "I appreciate that you guys think that they have to take priority, but I have to work. I literally have to."

Empathy flickered in Griffin's eyes. "A few extra hours this week working for Jackson isn't going to create that money you need. I've earned a ton of money in my life. You have to think bigger. Bigger than you think is possible."

Dash felt the stress prickling down his spine. "Any suggestions?" He couldn't keep the bitterness out of his voice.

This was why he'd spent so many years rejecting mainstream society. The crap about needing money, being obligated to play the game, getting stuck in the grind…it all made his skin crawl.

He'd do it for the girls, but *fuck*. He had no idea how to navigate it, and he didn't want to.

Griffin shook his head. "No idea. It's your path. Your inspiration. What would work for me wouldn't work for you. What are you great at? What's your magic that no one else can do? Figure that out, then figure out how you might earn money from it."

Harlan started laughing. "It's not that simple for the rest of us regular people, Griff. Money loves you."

Griffin grinned. "It does. And I love it. Gotta own your love for money before it'll love you back."

Harlan snorted. "Birch Crossing has made you soft, Griff."

"Happy," Griffin shot back. "Birch Crossing has made me happy as hell. Got my kids, my woman, my store, and you lazy sods to distract me."

Dash wasn't in the mood to hear how happy they all were. "Look, Jackson, I need to go. Can I pick up those extra hours?"

Jackson sighed. "Yeah, I'll give you a few, but honestly, focus on the kids. You'll never get those two weeks back."

"I know." Fuck, he knew. "I don't want to go to work," he admitted. "I've never liked working for anyone. But I have to. So thanks." He spun and strode away, too on edge to talk any further.

He shoved open the door and stepped outside. He knew what his speech had sounded like. *I never liked work.* He'd never liked the idea of work, of being forced to do things for money.

But he wasn't lazy. He worked his ass off for Bea, for free. He did his iron installations at cost. He loved working. He just didn't want to be forced to sell his soul for money, and he'd worked hard to make sure he had that option.

But not anymore. When Maura and Sophia had died, he'd

called up Jackson for a job that day, because he'd known what he needed to do. But it ate his soul. "Fuck!"

"Dash?"

He looked up, grimacing when he saw Leila walking toward him. His heart started racing at the sight of her. She looked so damned adorable in her sneakers, shorts, and tee shirt. Her hair was tumbled down around her shoulders in loose, carefree waves, and he knew exactly how soft they were. "Hi."

She frowned as she reached him. "What's wrong?"

"Nothing." He touched her hair. "You look gorgeous."

She smiled and he saw her take a deep breath. "Thanks. But tell me why you're shouting epithets while you're walking down the street."

He shook his head. "I'm not putting my problems on your shoulders."

She sighed. "Men are so freaking uncommunicative. No wonder no one wants to marry them." She pushed past him. "Bye."

He started laughing. He couldn't help it. "Many people, men and women, want to marry men."

"Not me!" She didn't turn around.

"You're literally married right now."

"I'm going to go find some women to bond with." She started up the stairs to Wright's.

"No women in there," he said. "Just Griffin, Harlan, and Jackson. They're men, *and* they're married. The worst of both."

She stopped on the top step with a sigh. "Where do the women in this town go?"

"Probably to Chloe's house."

"Chloe?" She turned to face him.

"Married to Blue. He did kidnap recovery with Harlan. They were partners."

"I know who she is. Why are they at her house?"

"She has a knitting store. The women go there to hang out and knit."

She stared at him. "Knit. They *knit*."

He grinned. "Yep. And they gossip and eat, from what I hear. I haven't been there much, but the men talk."

She walked back down the stairs to him. "And Eppie? Is she there, too?"

"She basically runs it. She's already set up a space there for the twins. When she's babysitting, she's going to have them there most of the time. The women are committed to turning them into knitters by age one."

"Dammit."

He grinned as she marched back toward him. Why did every minute seem better if Leila was in it? Even when she was mad and sassy, she made him feel better. "Why? What do you need?"

"I want to brainstorm ideas about how to start earning money and fast, so I don't need to throw your kids out on the street like a ruthless wench."

His heart softened. "Thank you."

She smiled, her eyes warming. "Don't thank me yet. I don't have a single idea."

He understood that. "If it helps, I was just talking to the guys about that. Griffin, who is rich as sin and owns a number of hugely successful businesses, told me to figure out what I'm great at, better than anyone else, and then figure out how to make money from it."

She nodded. "You picked your iron work, right? That makes sense. I don't have anything like that."

He stared at her, startled by her comment. "My iron work?"

"Of course. You're a genius." She put her hands on her hips. "Oh, for heaven's sake, Dash. Don't even tell me you're going to deny it. I've seen that photo book. Roger was great, but you're an artist."

Resistance settled inside him. "I told you, I do that for fun."

"Imagine doing it for fun and money?" Her voice got more energy in it, and excitement flashed in her eyes. "That's the answer. Do you have any unsold pieces in the workshop?"

He folded his arms over his chest. "No one around here can, or should, pay me for that."

"No? You think that you should give away your gift for free?"

"Yes. It's to make people happy."

"And what about you? And your kids? You think you guys should be unhappy, broke, and living in a cardboard box so others can be happy?"

He scowled at her. "That's not what I meant."

"It's the choice you're making," she shot back. "Whether you admit it or not, you're choosing to honor the well-being of others over yourself and the twins."

He ground his jaw in frustration. "The choice I'm making is to let my work spread happiness to those who need it," he said. "If I try to turn it into a business, I'll lose my joy and I'll lose the joy of making others happy. I need it to be as it is. Maura was the artist. I'm not."

"You *are* an artist, Dash. And you can do both. Make some pieces for locals, but then take the time to make others and sell them. Making money from what you love won't ruin your love for it unless you decide it will."

"No." Anger coiled inside him. "Creating with iron is my peace. I need it to stay that way."

"But—"

"No." He was adamant, and starting to get annoyed that she was pushing at him. She was cute as hell even while she was annoying him though.

"What if it's the only answer?" she pushed.

"There's never only one answer." He was restless now.

"What about you? Don't you have a special gift? You never told me what your business with Robbie was."

She paused. "Marketing." Her face brightened. "I could help you market them outside the town—"

"So, that's it? That's your big idea? You'll take a commission on my work and make yourself money, too?" He couldn't keep the frustration out of his voice, and regretted it immediately when her eyes widened.

She took a step back. "I was trying to help."

"I told you I'd handle my problems." Dammit. She was already shutting down on him. He could see it. Fuck. He wasn't that guy anymore, the one who didn't want to deal with the world. Especially not with this woman. He wouldn't be that way. "Shit, Leila. I'm sorry. I know you're trying to help. I just…my iron work is the only thing that's been mine my whole life." He didn't know how better to explain it. "The only thing that never judged me."

"Dash," she said softly. "I know that you have rejected a lot about the world for a very long time. But you need to realize that I'm not the enemy. I'm on your side. See me for who I am." She touched his arm. "Look at me, Dash. See me." She paused. "I need you to see *me*."

He fought against his need to turn his back on her and walk away, treating her like the world he'd shunned for so long. Instead, he made himself look at her, really look at her. Into her blue eyes, that were filled with concern.

He saw her. Her caring. Her kindness. The beauty of her soul. The woman he'd felt connected to since they were young. *"Leila."* He swore under his breath, then reached out and pulled her into a hug.

She wrapped her arms around his waist and pressed her face to his chest.

He closed his eyes and breathed in the scent of her hair. He absorbed the feel of her body against his, warm, real, and strong. He took a deep breath, and then another. "I'm freaking out about going to get them," he admitted.

She laughed softly. "I would be, too."

He pulled back. He wanted to ask her to come with him. The words burned inside him. But he didn't do it. He wouldn't trap her. He wouldn't put her in the position of having to say no. "I need to hit the road. You can go find the women at Chloe's. Do your brainstorming…" He managed a smile. "But leave my art out of it."

She didn't smile back. "You don't look good."

"Thanks. Every guy loves to hear that." He dropped his hands from her shoulders. "Fortunately, I have a fantastic ego, so no damage done." He gave her a smile. "See you soon."

He started walking back down the sidewalk toward his truck, then paused when she called his name. "Dash?"

He looked back at her. "What's up?"

"Do you want me to come with you? Would that help?"

Something flickered inside him, something that nearly took his breath away. This woman, who owed him nothing, who didn't even like kids, had offered to drive to New York City to pick up two babies with him, just because he was losing his shit. He walked back over to her, pulled her into his arms and kissed her.

She softened in his embrace and kissed him back, her hands resting on his biceps.

When he finally broke the kiss, her cheeks were flushed and her eyes were sparkling. "That was quite a kiss."

"You're quite a woman."

She smiled. "So, that's a 'yes, Leila, please come with me and save me?'"

"No." He traced his thumb over her lower lip. "I'd like you to come, but I need to do this. I need to be able to handle them on my own, and I won't let you sacrifice yourself to do it. I've got this. But your offer…it's stunning. I appreciate it more than you could ever know."

Her brow furrowed. "If I go with you, maybe we don't have to start the thirty days over. Maybe it will count if we're together, even if we're not in the house."

"Four more days with you is fine with me."

Emotion flickered in her eyes. "Dash—"

"I gotta go now or I'm going to let you come with me. See you Sunday." Then he turned and strode for his truck, making a break for it while he still had the willpower.

He got in the truck, checked to make sure he still had the two car seats and the bags of baby gear, then he put the truck into drive. But as he pulled out, he couldn't help but look in his rearview mirror.

Leila was standing where he'd left her on the sidewalk in front of Wright's.

She lifted her hand to wave to him, and he tooted the horn.

As he drove away, he felt a deep sense of peace settle over him. When he got back on Sunday night, she'd be there. Maybe it was because Bea's will required it, but for the first time in a very long time, he wasn't coming home to an empty house.

He was coming home to Leila, and it felt damned good.

Too good?

Maybe.

But he'd hold onto all the good he could find right now.

CHAPTER 19

LEILA STARED after Dash's truck as he drove away, emotions swirling inside her.

He was such a good man. His commitment to his new kids was unwavering, even though his life had been torn apart by all the events that had led to him becoming a father.

He'd admitted he was terrified.

What man did that? Especially a bad boy rebel who had spent time in prison?

His last kiss, that magical kiss, had nearly melted her heart.

She'd had a crush on him when she'd barely known him.

She'd had a blast the last two days with the great sex and all the laughter.

But in this farewell, things had changed.

Because she was starting to fall for him. For real.

For this man who was going to be a *dad*.

She'd never seen herself as a mother. It had never been her plan or her vision.

If she fell for Dash, he came with kids.

She'd have to stay in Birch Crossing.

She'd have to live in Bea's old house, and see her old home

across the road every single day, forcing her to relive all the memories from her childhood that she'd fought so hard to leave behind.

She'd have to live the life that she'd left town to avoid.

"Oh, Dash," she whispered, regret heavy in her heart. "I can't do that. Not even for you."

Maybe it was time. Time for her to break her ties to this town. Time to break her ties to Dash, before she was tempted to give up her life and move to the town that had nearly broken her soul the first time she'd lived here.

Maybe she'd never move on until she was no longer tied to Dash.

She didn't want a divorce.

But maybe that was exactly why she needed to get one.

The tears were falling as she turned and walked back to her car.

———

THE KNITTING WELL was a little store that was attached to the beautiful, huge, old home of Chloe and Blue. The store had its own entrance, a cute stoop with pots of pink geraniums and a sculpture of a bunny. Across the stones was a beautiful painting of women and girls, holding hands and laughing on the shore of a lake. It was signed by Emma.

Leila stared at the painting, and to her surprise, a little lump formed in her throat. She knew that Chloe and Blue ran a foster home for girls, and that they'd adopted several girls from the program, but somehow, seeing the painting of female bonding made something inside her get emotional.

She barely remembered her mother, and Maura had been the only real girlfriend she'd ever had, so long ago.

The sound of women's laughter echoed out from the store, and Leila looked up. She could see movement behind the glass panes in the door, and she could tell there were quite a few women inside.

She barely knew the women, and she didn't knit, but she didn't turn away. Something inside her was calling to her, telling her she needed to go in there.

So, she ignored the part of her that told her to hide, and instead, she jogged up the steps and opened the door, and then started laughing almost right away.

Eppie was standing on a stool, and she was draped in knitted scarves of assorted colors, patterns, and sizes. There were six or seven other women present, and they were standing around her, tossing more scarves on her, turning Eppie basically into a scarf Christmas tree. Some of the woman looked to be Eppie's age, but Chloe, Emma, and Clare were also there. Everyone was laughing hysterically, and piling more knitted items onto Eppie.

It looked so silly and ridiculous, and also such warm-hearted fun.

Eppie looked over at the door and waved at her. "Leila's here! Leila, come on in!"

The customers all turned toward her, and unleashed a round of friendly, jovial greetings.

Leila stepped inside, still smiling. "What's happening here? Mummifying Eppie before she even goes?"

"Burn your words," Eppie shouted. "I'm never going to go!"

Chloe grinned. "We're making our Christmas brochure. We're experimenting with live human models today. Help decorate Eppie!" She tossed a handful of scarves at Leila.

Leila immediately set her purse and notebook on a shelf, and joined in, laughing as Eppie twirled around. It was silly, fun, and the women made her laugh.

She quickly discovered, however, that the women, especially Eppie, were also secretive, plotting, and subversive. By the time they finished the photo shoot an hour later, they'd dragged every detail of the situation with Dash from her.

"Well," Eppie put down her arms. "It's pretty clear what has to happen."

Leila raised her brows. "What's that?"

"You need to march your butt into Dash's workshop, take some great pictures of his work, and then sell it for huge amounts of money."

Alarm prickled through Leila at the spark in Eppie's eyes. "He made it very clear that selling his work was not acceptable."

"Men don't always know what's best for them," Eppie said. "Am I right, ladies?"

There was a murmur of assent that made Leila even more alarmed.

"You guys," she said. "I'm not going to violate his trust—"

"What trust?" Eppie said. "He left you at your own house which you have every right to be in. He can't stop you from visiting his workshop."

"I'm not selling it—"

"Could you?" Clare was sitting on a chair, her toddler on her lap. "Do you have the contacts and the skills?"

Leila thought about it. "I do have some former clients who would probably be interested," she admitted. "But we'd need to draw up a contract and—"

"I'm a lawyer. I can do that," Clare said.

"I can add his work to my website," Emma said. "I created a small gallery business so I could sell my paintings, and I include other local artists. I'll process all payment through that. It would take me only a few minutes to add a page for him."

Leila looked around the room at all the eager faces. "Absolutely not," she said.

Judith, Eppie's best friend, who Leila vaguely remembered as being friends with Bea waved her coffee mug in Leila's direction. "No one in this town wants a freebie from him. He just thinks they do. Gotta straighten him out."

"You're his wife," Eppie said. "That gives you the freedom to do the things that are right for him."

"I literally told you I was going to have to divorce him," Leila said.

"That's panic talking," Eppie said. "Go take some pictures. Get his stuff online. Earn him some money before he gets back."

Leila looked around at the small store. "I can't betray his trust," she said again.

Clare sat down next to Leila. "When I was doing Bea's will for her, she told me that the reason she wanted to leave the house to Dash was because he had the biggest heart she'd ever met. She said no one saw it, because he put on this image of being a troublemaker, but she saw it. She said he'd give his time and money away until he was broke if it would help someone else, so she gave him the house."

Leila looked over at her. "He is a good man," she agreed softly.

"The best. And sometimes, the nicest people need help being a little mercenary."

Leila bit her lip. "I can't—"

"What if Dash got to raise his girls working from home? In his workshop? Doing what he loves for great money?" Clare asked. "Griffin supported me moving from being a lawyer to making cupcakes, and it was the best choice I've ever made."

Leila raised her brows. "You still do legal work."

"Only for friends and people I want to help," Clare said. "Dash can still find ways to help others, but he can do it without sacrificing himself. Being a dad is tough, and he has no idea how tough. He'll need help."

"Your help," Eppie said.

Leila looked around the room. "I'm not staying with him.

I'm not raising the girls." She didn't miss the look that passed between Clare and Eppie. "What?"

"You need to put his art up for sale." Eppie looked around the room. "Who agrees that Leila needs to put Dash's work up for sale and show him how much money he can make doing what he loves?"

Everyone in the room raised their hands, except for Chloe.

Eppie glared at her. "Chloe! Raise your hand!"

Chloe was folding the scarves that Eppie had been wearing. "Dash has lost a lot," she said. "His family betrayed him. From what Leila said, I think he trusts her. If she does it behind his back, their relationship will never recover."

Leila's heart tightened. "That's what I think, too," she said, relieved that Chloe understood.

She looked at Leila. "I know what it's like to be left with nothing. Whether you like it or not, Leila, you're the only foundation he has right now. I think you should sell his work, but I believe you need to get his permission first."

"I tried—"

"You need to try again," Chloe said. "I think it's the right thing to do, but I also think you can't go behind his back."

Eppie inclined her head. "Chloe has a point," she acknowledged. "Dash has been through a lot. I got excited about helping him out of his stubbornness, but I think she's right."

Clare nodded. "Call him. Talk him into it. We'll help you however we can with selling it."

Leila looked around. "Now? He's a little busy—"

"He's driving to New York. He's not busy at all," Judith said.

"I'll start working on my website," Emma said. "Text me when you get to his workshop and send me pictures. We'll figure it out."

The rest of the group chimed in with ideas, chattering excitedly. It was overwhelming, and Leila quickly stood up.

"All right. I'm going." She said goodbye to everyone, and then hurried out to her car.

She got in, then sat there, trying to process, trying to feel what was the right choice.

Did she have the right to force Dash into a business he didn't want, just because she wanted him to have enough money to buy her out?

Maybe he didn't even have anything to sell right now. Maybe there was nothing to discuss.

Yes, she needed to figure that out first.

She started her car and headed home, a part of her really, really hoping that she wasn't going to find anything amazing in his workshop.

CHAPTER 20

She didn't get her wish.

Leila stood in Dash's workshop, stunned by the piles of completed projects stacked against the back wall. There were fireplace screens, railings, mailboxes, light posts, and dozens of smaller art pieces, things that people could hang on walls or use as signs.

Every piece was gorgeously crafted in intricate details she hadn't even realized was possible to do with iron.

She picked up a twelve-inch square piece of flat iron, into which he'd carved a sunset above a mountain that was reflecting on a lake. He hadn't painted it, so the entire project was in black, but it was so extraordinary that she could almost see the colors of the sunset.

Another one had a family of raccoons, and the words "Welcome" were sculpted across the bottom.

There were dozens of pieces, and they were the work of a true artist.

She sat down on a stool, stunned as she looked at the array. There were so many items that she was sure he didn't have homes for all of them. He just made them and set them in the shadows.

His work deserved more than a page on Emma's website. So much more.

She knew Maura had been an artist, and her wife had owned an art gallery. Dash had told her that was how they'd met. But despite Dash's words, his sister wasn't the only artist in the family.

Why had he lied to her that he did everything for the locals? Because it was clear he spent a lot of time creating items that would never have a home other than the back of his shop.

She needed answers, answers he hadn't wanted to give her. Answers he didn't owe her, or anyone at the Knitting Well, or anyone else.

Dash deserved to keep his secrets…didn't he?

————

DASH FLEXED his legs as he headed back to his truck. Several hours in, several hours to go.

He missed Leila.

He missed the fun they'd had this week.

He missed being home.

But this was his last trip to New York. He didn't have to go back again. If Frank and Vivian wanted to see the girls, they could drive up to Maine. The judge had given them a week to say good-bye to the girls before turning them over to Dash, but Dash's lawyer had convinced the judge that visits from the grandparents would better serve the girls if they were in their new home, once they'd made the transition.

Last trip.

Last few hours until his life changed forever. Again.

He swung into his truck and set his coffee in the console. He texted Frank and Vivian. *My ETA is around three to be there to pick up the girls.*

Both of them ignored his text, as always.

They hated that he was taking the girls, but they always met their court duty of allowing him to visit.

He started up the truck and got back on the highway. The road stretched long, and it gave him too much time to think about things.

Like the fact he didn't want to let Leila go.

He knew she didn't want to be a mom. But he hadn't wanted to be a dad, and now he was looking forward to it. Scared shitless, but still excited and committed.

What if Leila changed her mind when she met the girls? Could he even ask that of her?

Ask her to take on two kids? No. He couldn't do that.

But he wanted to. He—

His phone rang, and the screen on his truck told him it was Leila. Adrenaline leapt through him, and he immediately answered it. "Hey, Leila. What's up?"

"Hi. How's the drive?"

He frowned at the edge in her voice. "What's wrong?"

She laughed softly. "Your daughters are going to be in such trouble. You're much too observant for anyone's well-being."

He grinned, his tension already easing at the sound of her voice. "When you're in prison, you learn to read subtext very well. It's a survival skill."

"You're saying prison prepares you for fatherhood?" There was laughter in her voice, which made him laugh.

"Exactly. If only you'd spent some time in prison, you'd be all set to be a mom."

"Damn. I'll keep that in mind and engage in a little grand theft auto if my biological clock starts ticking."

Dash had a sudden vision of Leila and the girls at the dinner table. Of Leila's laughter and warmth easing their tension after a tough day at school. "You'd be a great mom even without prison."

There was a brief pause, and he swore, regretting if she felt like he was pressuring her.

"Thanks," she said, her voice a little quieter. "Honestly, I wouldn't know how to be a great mom, but it's good to know at least one person sees potential in me."

"Lots of potential," he said. "Hell, if I can be a dad, I think anyone can manage."

"Those girls are lucky to have you," she said. "I was just at the Knitting Well, and everyone was talking about what a good person you are, and what a huge heart you have."

He blinked, surprised by her comment. "You guys were talking about me?"

"Of course we were. Women talk about their husbands, so you're on the hook when I'm with the gals."

He liked that, he realized. He liked that a lot. "I didn't realize that. I'll have to up my game."

"Clare said that Bea left you the house because you were a good guy, but you hid it from everyone behind your 'I'm an ex-con' bravado."

His amusement faded. "Clare said that to everyone?"

"Yep."

"I am an ex-con. It's not bravado. It was a stupid move that I have to carry with me."

Leila was quiet for a moment. "Is that why you want to give away your art? Because you're trying to make up for what you did that got you sent to prison?"

"My art?" He switched lanes, tensing at the chance in topics. "I don't make art."

"Actually, Dash, I have to disagree. I'm sitting in your workshop right now, staring at a cornucopia of pieces that were created by an extremely talented artist. Not an iron worker. An *artist.*"

Dash gripped the steering wheel. "I didn't give you permission to go in there."

"I own half of it, Dash. You can't ban me from it."

He swore under his breath and hit his palm against the dashboard. "Leila—"

"There is so much in here, Dash. You can't possibly give it all away to the locals you say you want to help. What are you going to do with it?"

"It's practice. Not for sale. Not for giving away. It's just... stuff I do."

"Why do you hide it?"

He ground his jaw. "Let it go, Leila."

"You're a dad now, Dash. Your life isn't simply about you. And you have access to resources that could support your girls financially. Do you have the right to not use it to benefit them?"

Anger coiled through him. "Don't play that card on me."

"It's not a card. It's the truth. Why wouldn't you sell it, Dash?"

"Because it's crap!"

"It's not crap!" she shot back. "Why are you so blind, Dash? You're an amazing artist, just like Maura was. Who is running Sophia's art gallery? Did you inherit that? Why don't you ask whoever is running it to take a look at your art? See if they can sell it?"

"No." He was so amped up with resistance that he could barely think. "It's not art."

"What if it is? What's the harm in asking?"

"Because I own the damned gallery now. What's Otto going to say? No? He'll take the art, and it'll bankrupt the business. He's only keeping it open to sell the rest of Maura's paintings." He paused, his gut clenching. Fuck. He didn't want to sell his sister's art. They were Ashley and Aimee's legacy.

"Have him sell your work instead, so the girls can have their mother's."

Of course Leila had known exactly what he was thinking. "He can't sell my work."

"How do you know until you try? What's the harm in trying?"

He hit the steering wheel again. "Maura was the one with the talent. Not me."

She paused. "Is that what your parents told you, Dash? Because they told Maura she wasn't talented at art either, if I remember correctly. But she ignored them and became a success."

The roadside was whizzing past him relentlessly. His gut was clenched. "My parents were bastards."

"I know. So were mine." She sighed. "What if I text you a few pictures of your work? Then you can send them to Otto. You don't need to tell him you did it. Just tell him you were thinking of keeping the gallery open, and featuring New England artists. Ask him if your art would sell. What's the harm?"

What's the harm? It was a good question. "I don't know," he said finally. "I don't know why I don't want to do it, but I don't."

"Will you do it for the girls?"

He gripped the steering wheel, resistance flooding him. But at the same time, there was something else trying to come alive inside him. Hope? Hope that he could be more than what he'd chosen to be for so long? It was fragile, barely there, but it felt like oxygen.

"Dash." Leila's voice was gentle. "It's time to be brave. For them."

He stared grimly though the windshield, thinking about what she said. Knowing in his gut that she was right. "I have to, don't I?" he finally said.

"You don't have to do anything, Dash. But I think you should try it."

He wanted to say no but this was Leila. She believed in him. And he did want to save Maura's art. And the idea, the whisper of the possibility, that he didn't have to work construction, that he could work in his studio and support his family from that...even the idea of it was stunning. He didn't believe it, but even the possibility was too much to ignore. "All right," he said. "I'll text the two of you together and introduce you. Then you take over. I don't want to be involved."

"All right. I'll handle it." She paused. "Thanks for trusting me, Dash."

The miles were hurtling past, taking him further from Leila and closer to the girls. He did trust her, he realized. He trusted her in a way he'd never trusted anyone except Maura, and then Sophia. "I know you don't want to be a mom," he said. "I get that. But I'd like to ask you out on a date when I get back. One night, when the girls are asleep, we'll get Eppie to babysit, and I'd like to take you out."

She was quiet for a moment. "Dash—"

"You want me to try with my art? I'm calling you out, Leila. Don't hide. I know we have something. Let's see what it is."

Again silence.

"We stayed married for a reason," Dash said. "Let's find out what it really is. Go out with me, Leila. A drink. Dinner. Whatever it is. Be brave enough to try." He knew he was pushing her. He knew maybe it was unfair. But he'd had so little in his life worth fighting for, and he knew Leila was worth it.

"You want to date your wife?" she finally asked.

He grinned. "I do."

She was quiet again, then she sighed. "Honestly, Dash, I would like that very much."

Excitement leapt through him. "Great, I'll—"

"I thought about that after you left. If something happened between us, I'd have to stay in Birch Crossing. I couldn't ask you and the girls to leave. Which means I'd have to look at my old house every day. I'd have to relive the life I ran away from. I don't like the memories of that time, Dash. I don't like who I was back then. I don't want to be back in the world that almost destroyed me, and I'd have to stay there if you and I became a real thing." She paused. "And that doesn't even address being a mom."

His excitement faded into shadows and weight, and he paused for a moment, trying to figure out how to reclaim control of the conversation. "You're getting ahead of things, Leila. I just wanted to start with a date."

"I know, but I have to look ahead. I'm falling for you, Dash. Falling hard. And I need to look ahead and see what that could mean before I go any further. I don't want to hurt you if we start something and I decided I can't do it."

He lightly bumped his fist against the steering wheel in triumph. *She was falling for him.* It wasn't just him who was finding himself falling hard. It was mutual. He could work with that. "I get that," he said, weighing his words. He didn't want to scare her, and he had thirty days guaranteed with her. But he wanted to make sure that the door he wanted open was open. "But you need to remember that I've been through hell and back and survived. If we try something and you decide to leave, I'll handle it. No kid gloves for me, Leila."

She laughed softly. "You're a tough guy, huh?"

"Yeah. I am. For what it is."

"Well, I'm not sure I'm that tough. I actually decided today that maybe we should get a divorce. Cut the ties."

Coldness clamped his gut, and his hands tightened around the steering wheel. *Holy shit.* Her words cut like ice through his gut. "I know I suggested that," he said carefully, fighting to modulate his tone. "But I have a better idea."

"What's that?"

"Be roommates for the next month and see what we feel like at the end."

"Roommates?" She sounded skeptical. "No sex?"

"Do roommates have sex?" He kept his tone light, easy, trying to get her off her heaviness.

She laughed. "Sometimes."

"Okay, then, sometimes sex."

"You're impossible." But she was laughing now. "I have to protect myself from you, Dash. You're winning me over, and I don't want to be won."

"I'll be an ass, then. I'm sure I can manage that. Just to give you space from my charm."

"Perfect. I've always wanted to be married to an ass. I can't wait."

"It's a deal then." He saw a rest stop ahead and put on his blinker. "I'm going to pull over now and text you and Otto, who manages Sophia's art gallery. Get the iron art thing started. I would like to save Maura's paintings for the girls. If there's a miracle possible, I'll take it." He'd gotten the first one of his life when the judge had ruled in his favor with the girls. And then when Leila had showed up at his front door this week when he'd been at his darkest, spiraling under the pressure of being the father that the twins needed, mixed with the weight of death—Bea, Maura, Sophia.

Maybe he deserved one more.

"Awesome. I'm on it." She paused. "I do miss you, Dash."

He grinned as he pulled into the truck stop. "I miss you, too, Leila."

She sighed. "That's so aggravating. You can't make it easy for me to just walk away, can you?"

"Back at ya, sweetheart." He parked the truck and pulled up Otto's phone number. "Texting now." He paused. "I think you're crazy that this can work, but I hope you're right." Hell, with each passing moment, hope was growing stronger. He did want this. He fucking wanted it badly. Now that he'd acknowledged it, the desire was gripping him like a vise.

"I'm so glad you're trying, Dash." Leila did sound pleased. "We'll make it happen."

"I love that confidence. You have my full support." He paused, wanting to say more, but feeling like they'd gotten the conversation to a good spot, and he needed to exit before Leila started backpedaling. "I'll talk to you later. Going to text now."

"All right. I'm on it. See you soon."

"Yeah. I'll see you when I get home." He hung up, then took a breath. Things were getting so damned complicated with Leila. What the hell were they doing?

He didn't even know. He just knew he wasn't willing to walk away yet. No matter how much it burned him.

He'd been burned plenty in his life. What was another scar?

CHAPTER 21

AN HOUR LATER, Leila sat in Dash's studio, staring at the text message she'd just gotten from Otto.

No market for that in the city. No one will want it. Sorry.

Her stomach hurt. Dash had trusted her with putting his art out there, and it had taken less than an hour to get it shut down. She'd sent Otto pictures of forty-six different things, and none of them had won him over.

Crap.

What was she going to do now? She'd heard the hope in Dash's voice. She'd gotten him to believe, and she'd failed him almost instantly.

She shoved her phone in her pocket and stared at the array of iron creations she'd spread out for taking the photos. Was she wrong that it was special? And if she was, then what?

Her phone rang. Crap. Was it Dash asking her how it had gone with Otto? She pulled out her phone and saw it was Gordon. "Hi," she said.

"You never called back with ideas."

"I had one." She filled him in on what she'd done with Dash's iron art, including Otto's response.

"Send me pictures," Gordon said. "I want to see if you're delusional."

"Okay. Hang on." She texted him a bunch, then waited for him to scroll through.

He didn't say anything, but she could hear him breathing.

"Gordon? What do you think?"

"I think the lighting is crap. It's difficult to get a sense of any of them. No good art dealer is going to make a move on photos that look like an amateur took them. You can tell they're in a barn. Hell, Leila, you're in marketing. Where's your brain? You're better than this. You're the one who taught me how to market myself to get better roles."

Leila rubbed her head, suddenly tired. "I was rushing."

"Well, un-rush. What would you do if you were still working for Robbie?"

"I'd tell Dash that no art collector in New York City is going to buy sculptures of lake items," she admitted.

"Who would buy them?"

She paused to think about it. "I would."

"Who else? Who else with money?"

She rubbed her forehead again. "I don't know. Rich people who have lake homes."

"Bingo. Some of those live in New York, and some of them have houses on lakes all around the region. Find those. It's like you told me, not everyone is going to love me, and that's fine. I just needed to find the part that no one else but me could do, and the director who would see it."

Find those people. How? She could talk to builders. Real estate agents. Interior decorators. And then what? "Do you think I'm wrong about the quality of his work?"

"I think there's a market for anything."

"So you don't like them?"

"They're not my style," Gordon said. "But that doesn't mean they aren't someone's. But you might keep working on your list of ideas, because that clock is ticking."

"Yeah." She rubbed her jaw. "What do you think of me and Dash? Am I crazy to think of it?"

Gordon was quiet for a moment, then he said, "I think you've had this image of him as being your savior for a very long time. I don't think you have a clear idea of who he is to you, and I think you should think long and hard about why you are even thinking about pursuing something long-term with him. You're on the rebound, you're in the town that tore up your sweet little heart, and you're having amazing sex with a hot guy. That can distract a girl from what's really going on."

"What do *you* think is really going on?"

"I think you need to figure it out," Gordon said. "You're the only one who knows."

"What if I don't know?"

"Then you need to look harder, at the things you don't want to see."

———

DASH PULLED into the parking garage of Sophia's parents' condo building. The building was so nice that even the garage was gorgeous.

He paused at the attendant. "Dash Stratton to visit Frank and Vivian Wilson."

The attendant checked his list. "I'm sorry, you're not on the list today."

Dash ground his jaw in frustration. They'd agreed to let him park in the garage today so it would be easier for him to load his truck with all the baby gear. He was planning to get the girls out of the city, and stop at a hotel on the way home.

"Hang on." He pulled out his phone and called Frank.

It went right to voicemail.

He tried Vivian's cell.

Right to voicemail.

He called their home phone.

They didn't answer.

Suspicion settled deep in his gut. He hung up the phone, and paused, tapping the phone on his thigh. "Are Frank and Vivian in town this weekend?"

The attendant looked at him blankly. "I'm afraid I'm not at liberty to discuss our residents."

Dash looked at the attendant's name tag. Tim. Tim was in his early twenties, clean-cut, and looked like he was working in that building because he wasn't tough enough to handle anything actually challenging. "My name is Dash Stratton. One week ago, I was legally named the father of Aimee and Ashley. At three o'clock today, which was one minute ago, custody goes to me. If they took those babies somewhere, it's kidnapping, and anyone who helps them or protects them can go to prison for kidnapping."

Kidnapping. Dash hoped he was overreacting. But something in his gut was telling him this situation wasn't right.

Tim's face paled. "They left this morning with them," he blurted out. "They had a lot of luggage."

Mother fucker. Fierce protectiveness surged through Dash, a deep, unrelenting fury. What the hell? He hadn't even remotely suspected they'd take off with the girls. They had deep pockets, and they had the money to disappear. *Shit. Shit. Shit.* "Where did they go?" His voice was like ice.

"I don't know." Tim held up his hands. "I swear I don't know."

Dash believed him. "What time did they leave?"

"It was right after I came on duty, so a little after five this morning. They had the babies with them."

Son of a bitch. Deep focus settled on Dash, a laser focus on what mattered. "This is what's going to happen. You're going to let me into this garage so I can park. By the time I'm done, your boss is going to meet me at the elevator, and we're going up to their condo to search it. You're also going to call the police and report a kidnapping, including their car info and license plate. I'm going to make some calls. Got it?"

Tim looked scared, which Dash regretted, but if it got action rolling for getting the twins back safely, then it was worth it.

"Got it." Tim punched the button and the gate started to go up. The minute the gate was up, he took off running for the elevator.

Dash pulled into the garage and created a spot right in front of the elevator lobby even as he dialed one of the men he'd seen this morning at Wright's.

Blue answered on the first ring. "What's up?"

"Frank and Vivian took the girls this morning," he said without preamble. "They have an eight-hour head start. Deep pockets."

"Those bastards." Blue swore. "Harlan and I can find anyone. Stay by your phone. I'm going to make some calls. We got this. Stay focused."

"I'm going to search their apartment."

"Text me the address. I'll have someone meet you there to help."

"Got it."

"Harlan and I never lose," Blue said. "They have no chance. We'll get them."

"Yeah, all right." Dash hung up. His heart was racing, and fear was clawing at his gut, fear he'd never felt before. His kids. *His babies were missing.*

Dash's hands were shaking. He'd never been so fucking scared in his life.

Gone was all his hesitation about being a dad. He was coming for them, and he would never, ever leave them unprotected again.

He got out of the truck and strode for the glass doors that kept him away from the elevator. He felt like he couldn't breathe. He'd gotten in so many fights in his life. He'd emerged from prison with the kind of confidence and toughness he'd never wanted to have.

And yet standing there, in that clean lobby, he was absolutely fucking terrified.

He stood there.

Waiting for the manager.

Waiting for Blue to call back.

Unable to do anything.

It was only seconds Dash had been waiting but it was too long, so he pulled out his phone and called the only person he wanted to talk to right now. The minute she answered, he spoke, "Leila. They kidnapped the twins. Blue and Harlan are on it. I'm waiting to get into their condo to see what I can find. But they could be anywhere. I—" He stopped. He didn't know what to say.

"Oh my God, Dash. I'm so sorry."

He heard the alarm in her voice, and he swore. "Shit," he said, feeling like an ass for calling her. "Sorry. I shouldn't have dragged you into this. Forget it—"

"Dash," she interrupted. "They took those babies because they love them. They won't hurt them. You know that, right?"

He closed his eyes, thinking, trying to think. "Yeah," he finally said. "Yeah, I think you're right." They wouldn't hurt them to spite Dash. They just wanted to raise them.

"Which means you have time," Leila said. "The girls are safe."

"It doesn't feel like it."

"Because you watch too many terrible movies and TV shows."

He laughed softly. "I don't watch anything. I like to do things, not sit around and watch."

"Well, great, then. Imagine if you did? You'd be even more upset."

"More upset?" He gripped the phone, feeling like she was his lifeline to his sanity. "I'm not sure that's possible."

"You're having a coherent conversation with me. You managed to call Blue and Harlan. You're doing great."

He closed his eyes. "All right."

"I'm already in my car. I'm coming down there."

"No. Don't. It's too dangerous."

"I'm married to an ex-con. I live for danger. Text me the address of where you are now, and if you go somewhere else, text me that address. You don't need to call if you're in the middle of something. Just keep me updated with where you are."

He saw the manager coming at a fast walk. "I gotta go."

"Text me the address right now."

"Yeah, okay," he paused. "Thank you."

"You got it. Now text me. I'll see you soon." She hung up on him, setting him free to handle the moment.

He quickly dropped a pin to show her where he was, then shoved his phone in his pocket as a woman in a suit pushed open the door. "Mr. Stratton. My name is Leslie Ottom. Please come in."

He stepped inside, not sure what kind of reception he would get. Would Leslie defend her residents and try to avoid a scene? Or would she do what was right? "Did you call the police?"

"I need to see the paperwork that you are their legal father before I can do anything. Did you bring it?"

He nodded. "It's in my glove box." He'd stashed it there the first time he'd come down to see the twins, unsure whether Frank and Vivian would try to block him. They never had, until now, but he'd kept it there. He jogged back to his truck, grabbed the envelope, and then showed it to her.

Emotion flickered across her face, and her jaw tightened as she read it, but she maintained her professionalism. "Very well. Yes, I've called the police. They're on their way here."

"Great." He decided to keep the papers with him, just in case he needed to prove it again.

"We'll head up to their condo now and wait for them," Leslie said. "Legally, I can't let you into apartment 21C, but the police will probably be able to get by that." She held out a key, then dropped it with a clatter to the marble floor. "Crap. I don't know where the key is. I need to go back to the office and get a new one. I'll meet you at the apartment."

Dash grinned. Frank and Vivian had made no friends, and he was grateful for that. "21C. I'll meet you there." He snatched the key off the floor, along with the elevator key card that was on the same key ring, and then he sprinted for the elevator.

He punched the button, waited too damn long, and then the doors finally opened.

He leapt inside, hit that button, and then waited again.

Every minute he waited was another minute that Frank and Vivian could be getting further away...and harder to find.

He slammed his fist against the wall of the elevator. "I'm coming, girls. I swear to you, I'm coming."

CHAPTER 22

Leila gripped the steering wheel, tears streaming down her cheeks as she drove to New York.

All she could think of was that day when her stepfather had found out that she was planning to marry Dash on her eighteenth birthday, a marriage that would strip him of his right to manage her inheritance from her mother.

It hadn't been much money, just enough to get her started in her new life, away from him, but back then, it had meant freedom, and that had been everything.

Leila still remembered him coming for her, planning to kidnap her so she couldn't get away from him.

She remembered how scared she'd been, how she'd fought him, how she'd climbed out the window and run for Bea's house. Bea hadn't been home that night, so Leila had hidden under the front porch for hours. Afraid to come out. Afraid to go anywhere.

No one had known that she'd spent the night there.

Not even Bea.

Leila never told anyone, but now, seeing someone trying to stop Dash from saving someone else, two baby girls, was making her remember that time when he'd been trying to save her.

The darkness under the porch.

Shivering.

Afraid of every pair of headlights that went by, certain that it was her stepfather, coming for her, afraid that he'd known Bea's house was where Leila would go.

She lifted her chin. "No," she said. "I'm not that girl anymore."

But she couldn't keep her mind out of the past. She could feel the clamminess and dirt on her skin. The shivers deep down in her belly from being so cold. The racing of her heart. The sounds of the night animals that were scarier than comforting.

The feeling of helplessness where the only way out was Dash.

She blinked, startled by the thought. Yes, she had thought that. That her only chance to escape was her best friend's brother. That she couldn't save herself.

Wow.

Leila was stunned by the realization of how she'd thought when she was seventeen.

She couldn't save herself.

That was why she couldn't stay with Dash now. Because it would be the same thing, running to someone else to save her. Not from her abusive stepfather this time, but from her own pain and failure. From the mess she'd made of her own life, all by herself.

"No!" She shouted the words aloud, anger tearing through her. "I'm not weak! I don't need anyone else to save me!" Not Gordon. Not Dash. Not Bea. And there was no freaking way she needed to take a house from two baby girls to get the money to fix her life.

She was more than that. She didn't know how, but she was.

She didn't want saving.

She didn't want Dash the protector.

She didn't want to be in an eight-year relationship with a man who was cheating on her, stealing from her, and seeing her as nothing more than a pile of sand in his life that he could kick over whenever he was finished with it, like Robbie had.

"No!" She yelled again. "No!" And again, and again, until her throat hurt, until years of not having a voice or feeling her own power finally fell away, replaced by a raw, aching void that she didn't know how to fill.

A glorious, empty void that was hers, a place to become who she needed to be, who she knew she could be. Powerful. Confident. Independent.

Scared? Yep.

But that was okay.

She was okay with being scared, because that was the first step to feeling safe in her life, safe because she could count on herself.

And the first thing she was going to do? Be the strength for someone else, for Dash. Not to win him over, but because standing by his side made her look directly into her own past that had kept a terrifying grip on her for so long. "No more," she shouted. "No freaking more!"

Then she hit the gas and felt free, gloriously, terrifyingly free, for the first time in her entire life.

———

DASH STOOD by the window in his daughters' room, looking out at the city.

It had been almost six hours since he'd arrived to find them missing.

The cops had been searching. Blue and Harlan were still working their contacts. He'd called every single friend of

Maura and Sophia he had phone numbers for, which had taken him down a dark path wrought with reminders of their deaths, but he'd done it anyway, facing every emotion that tried to take him down.

Everyone had tried everything, but Frank and Vivian were still in the wind.

Wherever they'd gone, they'd probably reached their destination before the Amber Alert had gone out, and were laying low. He knew they'd have to come out of hiding eventually, but when?

Had they made it out of the country? Harlan, Blue, and the cops were certain they hadn't taken a flight, but anything was possible.

He braced his hands on the window frame, his mind reeling. "I'm sorry, Maura," he finally said. "I let you guys down." He bowed his head, fighting against the emotion. He'd been an idiot to ask Otto to sell her paintings, to believe that was his only choice—

He grabbed his phone and texted Otto. *Don't sell Maura's paintings. Cancel any sales you have made that you haven't delivered the painting yet.*

Leila told me that already. Covered.

Dash let out his breath. *Great.* He paused, his fingers hovering over the keys. Did he want to know what had happened with his work?

Sorry about the iron work. Can't place that in New York. Otto gave him the info without Dash asking.

Dash gritted his jaw, surprised by the wash of disappointment. For the money it would have brought? Or had Leila gotten him to start to believe he had something worth giving? *No problem.*

I did find another artist that I like. Have you changed your mind about closing the studio? Just wondered because of the iron thing. This artist is a contemporary artist, not that local Maine artist thing Leila was talking about.

Dash put his phone down and looked around the room. The two cribs with their pink sheets and matching blankets. The room was full of toys and dolls, books, kid things. He recognized some of it from when the girls been at Maura and Sophia's. He'd helped Maura and Sophia pick out the cribs, not because they'd needed his advice, but because he liked hanging out with them.

On the walls were some paintings Maura had done for them, of butterflies, puppies, and hearts. Art was the legacy that Maura and Sophia had left for them. Didn't he owe it to them to let art continue to be a part of their lives?

He turned his phone over and typed a reply to Otto. *You think you can make a successful profit? I don't have art experience like Maura and Sophia did to help you out.*

His phone rang, and he grinned when he saw it was Otto. "Hi."

"Dash, sweetheart, I was born for this. Sophia and Maura were my special girls, and I will take care of Aimee and Ashley's legacy like they were my own babies. You give me the green light, and I will make this gallery come to life. Are we in?"

Dash took a breath. "I don't have any cash reserves. I have nothing to pay your salary with or the rent or any of that right now."

"Well, babycakes, I have some money saved up. What do you say we become partners?"

"Partners?" He'd known Otto for a long time, and he trusted him. He loved the idea. "I'll give you twenty percent."

"Fifty-fifty. I'm the brains behind this."

"Thirty."

"I'll take one hundred percent. Buy you out completely."

"No," he said instantly. "This is their legacy. It stays in the family."

Otto laughed. "You're such a boss. I love it."

"Why don't you send me an offer? How much are you

STEPHANIE ROWE

willing to put in? We'll figure it out. But the girls always have to maintain control. I'm not going to budge on that."

"Yes! Perfect! I'll put something together and go find some new artists! This is going to be fabulous! Talk to you later—"

"Wait!" Dash interrupted.

"What's up, sparky?"

"Frank and Vivian took the girls somewhere. Do you know where they might go?"

"You mean like a museum?"

"No. To hide them from me." He hadn't thought to call Otto, because he was Sophia's employee, not someone who would know Frank and Vivian personally.

"What? They took the girls? Those little shits! Go get them back! Sophia and Maura made it very clear to everyone who knew them that you were the one who is supposed to raise them!"

"I know. I'm working on it."

"Go find them," Otto snapped. "Now!"

Dash ground his jaw. "I'm working on it."

"Well, work harder!" Otto hung up, leaving Dash holding the phone.

Work harder? What was he missing?

There was a light tap at the door. "Dash?"

He spun around at the sound of Leila's voice. She was standing in the doorway wearing an old gray sweatshirt, denim shorts, and sneakers. "Fuck." It was all he could say, the only word that seemed to sum up everything inside him.

Her face softened. "Dash." She ran across the room and threw her arms around him.

He grabbed her and pulled her against him, burying his face in her hair. He clung to her, breathing in the feel of her body against his, the scent of her hair, the warmth of her breath against his skin.

She held on tight. "It'll be all right, Dash," she whispered. "We'll find them."

"I know." His throat was clogged, and he had to fight to hold onto his emotions. "Thanks for coming."

"Of course."

Words faded into unnecessary, and they stood there for what felt like an eternity, leaning into each other. He felt like he couldn't let go, like Leila was his anchor that was keeping his head on straight.

She held onto him, not pulling away, being his strength, which was hilarious and awesome at the same time. "What can we do?" she asked.

What can we do? It was the same question he'd asked himself. He took a breath, and then released her. "I don't know." He touched her face. "God, it's good to see you."

She smiled, stood on her tiptoes, and kissed him. "I'm here for you, Dash. It's my turn to help you, and we can do it."

He brushed his hand over her cheeks. "Just you being here helps. Makes me think more clearly."

"Good." She patted his cheek, a brisk pat that was clearly a call to action, not a placating soothing touch. "Let's do this. What have you not thought of?"

He grinned. "I literally just asked myself that question when you walked in."

"Awesome. We're simpatico, then." She set her purse down on the windowsill, then looked around the room. He saw her face soften, and sudden emotion flood her face. "Wow," she said softly. "Being in their room makes it terrifyingly real."

"Yeah."

She walked over to the nearest crib and looked inside. She picked up a little blanket. "That looks handmade. Did Maura or Sophia knit?"

"No. Vivian does."

"Vivian made this?" She unfolded it, and Dash saw that it had Sophia's initials on it. "She made it so they'd remember their moms."

"One of their moms," he said. "They never accepted Maura."

"No?" She held up another one, and that one had his sister's initial on it.

Dash's throat clogged, and he walked over and took it from her, tracing his finger over the M. Vivian had made one for Maura?

"And this?" Leila walked over to the pink bookcase and picked up a picture frame. "I assume this is Sophia with Maura in this picture?"

Dash walked over and took the photograph. It was a picture of Maura and Sophia on their wedding day. They'd gotten married at a beautiful spot on a lake in upstate New York. Frank and Vivian had refused to come. "This photograph was on the mantle in Sophia and Maura's apartment," he said. "I didn't see it when I cleaned out their apartment."

"And now it's on a bookshelf in Aimee and Ashley's room, so that the girls never forget their moms."

"Yeah." Dash traced his finger over Maura's face. "They were so happy that day," he said quietly. "My parents weren't invited, and Sophia's parents didn't come. I was their only family, but they still were so happy. They decided that no one could stop them from their happiness, and they lived that commitment every day."

Leila looked at him, her eyes glistening with tears. "Dash, I know that Sophia's parents weren't good to them. But they are parents who rejected their daughter, and then, before they could fix it, she died. All they have left of her are their grand-babies, and they know that they burned bridges with you. Once you take them, all ties to their daughter will be gone."

He looked over at her. "I'm not going to feel sorry for them."

"No, that's not what I'm saying." She gestured at the room. "This was clearly put together with love. They do love the girls, right?"

"Yeah." Of that, he didn't doubt.

"What if, when Frank and Vivian got up this morning, the thought of losing the girls was more than they could bear? The loss was simply too much, on top of losing Sophia twice, first because of their own rejection, and secondly, because of the car accident. What if they grabbed the twins and held on because they were too scared to let go?"

Dash rubbed his jaw and sighed. "I get that," he admitted. "I hate to give them any leeway, but I get it."

Leila picked up a pink, stuffed unicorn. "If their only focus was to try to hold onto the memories of their daughter and hide from the pain, where would they go? Sophia and Maura's old apartment?"

He shook his head. "I already cleaned that out and turned the keys in."

"Is there a place that meant something to them? Did they have a summer house where Sophia would go with them as a kid?"

Dash shrugged. "I don't know. They were never a part of Maura and Sophia's life."

Leila's gaze went to the photograph in Dash's hands. "What about where they got married? The most important moment of Sophia's life, and they missed it. Would they go there?"

Dash looked down at the picture in his hands. "You think they went to the wedding site?"

"If we go on the assumption that they're being driven by their emotions, it's possible." She paused. "Places are power-ful. I'm realizing that now, just how much that is."

He raised his brows. "Because you're back in Birch Crossing?"

She nodded. "It's a lot."

Empathy tightened his chest at the depth of emotion on her face. "I know." He pulled out his phone. "I'm going to call the place." He found the number online and then called the front desk, leaving it on speaker phone so Leila could hear.

Someone answered promptly. "Ocean Bluffs Resort. May I help you?"

Dash cleared his throat. "I'm looking for Frank and Vivian Reardon. Can you connect me to their room?"

"Certainly. Please hold."

Stunned relief rushed through Dash, and he hung up before they were able to connect him to the room, his heart pounding. "They're there," he said. Holy crap. It was all right. "It's going to be all right."

Leila smiled. "Yep. They're safe."

"Fuck." He looked at Leila, emotions warring in his chest. "They're there," he said. "Like you said." *They were there.* "We know where they are."

She nodded. "Do you want to call the police?"

His instinct was to say yes, to send the cops and Blue and Harlan after them. But Leila's observation gnawed at him. "They checked in under their own names."

She nodded. "Either they're really terrible kidnappers—"

"Or they weren't really trying to kidnap them."

"They're just trying to cope."

He swore under his breath. "I don't want to see them as people," he said. "They weren't good to Sophia and Maura. They don't deserve kindness."

"Do they deserve prison?"

Fuck. "I don't know."

"Why don't we go talk to them and see?"

He stared at her. "Talk to them? They rejected my sister. And their daughter. And their granddaughters."

"I know. But maybe they realized too late what a mistake that was."

He paced across the room and braced his hands on the windowsill, staring out across the skyline. "I want to hate them," he said simply.

178

"I know." Leila walked up behind him, wrapped her arms around his waist, and rested her cheek against his back. "But right now, what you really want is to get Aimee and Ashley home safely without trauma to them."

He swore again. "You're right." He hit his palm on the windowsill. "I'm calling Blue and Harlan to watch them in case they move again."

She nodded approvingly. "And then?"

"We're going to get them. You and me, because if I go by myself, I might wind up back in prison."

Her eyes widened. "I think you're kidding."

"I don't know," he said honestly. "They took my kids. I don't know how I'm going to react when I see them. But you level me out in a way that no one else ever has, so you're coming with me."

She smiled. "All right."

Relief rushed through him. He'd been afraid Leila would decline to join him. He didn't know if it crossed the line that she was trying to hold between them, but he didn't care.

He needed her right now, and he wasn't above asking for it.

He took a breath. "Let's go get them. We'll be there by midnight."

CHAPTER 23

THEY WERE an hour into the drive when Blue called. Dash hit the send button on his dashboard screen. "Tell me something good."

"I have a couple buddies at the resort," he said. "Frank and Vivian have the girls in their hotel room, and it's good. The girls are fine, and everyone is asleep."

Relief rushed through him, and Leila fist-pumped over her head in the sign of victory. "Did they see the girls?"

"Yep. They went into the hotel room and checked on everything. It looks like a family vacation. It's fine, and they're there for the night."

Leila laughed, relief evident in her voice. "I wouldn't want you for an enemy, would I, Blue? Sending your friends into a hotel room while everyone is asleep to check on them?"

Blue chuckled. "I'm not that guy anymore, Leila. I'm just a dad in a small town."

"You're both, and everyone knows it." Dash let out his breath, and the tension that had been gripping him for so long finally began to release. "Your friends will stay and watch?"

"You bet. They'll testify to the police if you decide to call them in."

"Got it. Thanks." The weight that had been consuming Dash finally abated, and he took a deep breath. His daughters were located, safe, and protected. "We'll be there a little before midnight."

"Yeah…about that. Want a recommendation?"

Dash frowned. "Yeah, sure. What's up?"

"Don't go in the room tonight. Everyone is asleep. Wait until morning. I can have my boys let you know when they get up."

"You're serious?"

"Yeah." Blue paused. "As you know, Harlan and I special-ized in rescuing kidnapped kids. The trauma is real, and it can last forever. Right now, the girls don't know anything is wrong. They're happy with their grandparents. If you barge in there in the middle of the night, Frank and Vivian will freak out, the girls will understand that, and it will affect them."

Dash gripped the steering wheel. "You want me to *wait?*"

"Sometimes Harlan and I waited for days for the right moment for an extraction. It's hard as hell when you know the kids are suffering, but Aimee and Ashley aren't suffering. Put their well-being before yours, get a room in the resort, and cool your jets until morning. Then consider how you're going to walk in that door."

"But what if they try to leave and I have to stop them? That's conflict."

"Their belongings are all over the place. It'll take a couple hours to pack everything up and go. They're not going anywhere. Honestly, my guess is that they're just waiting to be found. They aren't hardened criminals, Dash. Think about the girls. Not what you want. What's best for them."

Dash looked over at Leila and raised his brows.

She gave him a little nod, telling him she agreed with Blue.

He swore under his breath. "I don't like it."

"I know you don't, but I have great people watching them. The instant Frank and Vivian wake up, you'll know, before they even get out of bed. There's no chance of them leaving. Go get a room and get some sleep. Beginning tomorrow morning, you won't be getting much sleep for the next eighteen years, so enjoy it." There was humor in Blue's tone, which took some of the edge away from Dash.

"You're really not worried about leaving them there tonight?"

"My team installed a few cameras. They'll be watching those kids every second. If *anything* happens that's not good for the girls, I'll call you."

"I want the link to watch the cameras."

"Nope. That's not going to serve you. Get some sleep. Leave it to me. Got it?"

Dash ground his jaw. "I don't—"

Leila put her hand on his arm, drawing his focus back to her. He glanced over at her, and she smiled. "Haven't you heard the stories about Blue and Harlan?"

He inclined his head. "Some of them, yeah."

"You do realize that if Frank and Vivian needed to 'disappear' to protect those girls, they would be gone when you walked in there in the morning, right?"

Blue cleared his throat. "We don't abduct people. We save them."

But Dash met Leila's gaze, and he knew she was right. Blue and his team were protectors of innocents. Those girls were the safest they'd ever be in their entire lives right now, and they would continue to be until he walked in there.

"Frank and Vivian love them," Leila said softly. "The girls feel safe."

"I'll text you some photos," Blue said. "We'll update you every thirty minutes."

Dash knew Leila was right. Blue was right. "Okay. Morning, it is."

"Good call," Blue said. "I'll book you a room. I'm headed down there, and I'll be with you in the morning when you go in there. Just in case."

"All right." Dash paused. "Thanks, Blue."

"My pleasure. I miss the action. It's fun to be involved again. See ya." He disconnected.

Leila laughed softly. "He thinks this is fun? He's a little crazy."

"Yeah, he is. So's Harlan." Dash flexed his hands as he drove. "You think it's the right call to wait?"

"I do." When his phone dinged, she picked it up. "I'll check the pictures."

CHAPTER 24

LEILA HAD INTENDED to check the photos simply so she could reassure Dash that the twins were safe, since he was driving and couldn't look.

But when she opened the picture and saw the grainy, black and white photo of the two little girls sleeping together in a little play pen, her heart stuttered.

The girls were hugging each other in their sleep, and their little sleeping area was filled with lots of stuffed animals, and blankets. The girls were sound asleep, their little faces clearly visible in the black and white image.

They were so little. Babies. Real little people who were completely dependent on the adults in their lives to take care of them. Sudden tears filled Leila's eyes, and she touched the screen, wanting to hug them.

"What's wrong?" Dash sounded alarmed.

"Oh, nothing. They look adorable." She wiped her cheeks, trying to hold her emotions in. "They have a bunch of stuffed animals. It's as he said."

Dash glanced over at her. "Then why are you crying?"

Emotions clogged her throat, and she clenched her hands in her lap. "I was ten when my mom died," she said, unable to keep the memories at bay. "I was shattered, and then when I found out my stepdad was my guardian, it was awful. This terrible man had complete control over me and my life."

Dash reached across the seat and wrapped his hands around her clenched ones. "I know," he said softly.

She looked down at his hand, so strong, so warm. "When I saw the pictures of the girls just now, all I could think about was that their moms are gone, like mine was. I felt that loss, that terrible loss that I had when I was ten, and that sinking feeling when I realized what that meant for me. I just..." She swallowed. "Aimee and Ashley looked so peaceful and happy. I know they're too young to understand, and at some point, they'll experience the loss of their moms, but right now, they're happy." The tears began to stream down her cheeks. "My mom was amazing. I missed her for so long, and I still do sometimes."

Dash put on his blinker and pulled off the highway into a rest area. He parked the truck, turned off the ignition, then got out.

Leila watched as he jogged around the front of the truck, opened her car door, and unhooked her seatbelt. "What are you—"

He pulled her into his arms.

He said nothing, but the tenderness of his hug broke the dam that she'd been trying to hold back since returning to Birch Crossing. She turned in her seat, and her knees went on either side of his hips. He leaned into the truck, and held her while she cried. "I feel so stupid," she muttered, as she tried to pull herself together. "Your kids are in a hotel room, and I'm the one who's crying."

"You're not the only one."

Surprised, she looked up and saw his eyes were glistening. "You're crying?"

"Don't tell anyone." He framed her face with his hands

and kissed her for a moment, and then pulled back. "The day has been emotional as hell."

She wrapped her hands around his wrists. "I'm sorry today happened."

He shook his head. "I'm grateful they're safe. And it's because of you, your vision." He traced his thumb over her lower lip. "Is that what I'm going to need to do in order to be a dad? Be all empathetic like that? Because it's not my thing."

She laughed through her tears. "You're literally crying as you said that. I think it might be your thing."

"A one-time thing." He thumbed the tears from her cheeks. "I'm having to relive the loss of my sister as well. The past is haunting both of us."

She nodded. "Yes." She sighed. "Where's the fun we were having?"

"It'll be back," he said. "We're resilient."

"Yes." She took a deep breath. "I didn't want to come back to Birch Crossing," she said. "I felt like such a failure when Robbie and I broke up. All this time has passed, and yes, I felt like I came back a failure, the same person as when I left."

"No chance of that," Dash said, his voice gruff. "You're an amazing woman who has been my strength today. Thank you for that."

She lifted her chin. "I did some good work in that apartment, didn't I?"

"Yes." He traced her jaw, a touch that felt so good. "I'm sorry about your mom, Leila. I really am."

This time, the thought of her mother didn't feel so overwhelming. The pain of that memory had started to recede, chased away by Dash's touch, his presence, his simply being there. "Ashley and Aimee are lucky to have you," she said. "You'll make it okay for them."

He grimaced. "I'm not going to lie. It feels like a huge challenge to fill the hole that Maura and Sophia left, but I'll give them everything I can."

She took a deep breath. "I would have given anything to have a man like you watching over me. *Anything*."

He grinned. "You got me as your husband."

She rolled her eyes. "Obviously, I know that. I was talking about when I was younger. As my dad."

"Oh, God." He feigned a look of horror. "Can you imagine if I'd taken over as your dad? That would have been so weird, you know, since we got married, and especially with all the sex we've been having."

She burst out laughing, a desperate, welcome relief from the weight that had been crushing her. "You're a lunatic."

He laughed. "See? We're resilient. We're making jokes."

Her laughter faded, and emotions tangled around her chest. "You're good for me," she said. "You somehow lighten my heart, no matter what I'm feeling."

His face became serious. "You do the same for me."

Silence fell between them, a complex silence thick with a tension she didn't quite understand. All she knew was that as she sat there in his truck, looking at him, she knew she'd been wrong. She wasn't *starting* to fall for him. She'd fallen completely.

Maybe it was because she'd come to Birch Crossing wrapped up in dreams and fantasies of this man who'd rescued her so long ago. In fact, there was most likely an element of that history, but it was because there was no way to eliminate that factor, because it was who she was.

But she knew her falling for him was also because of the way he lit up her heart now. It was because of the way he loved his daughters and fully committed to go all in on them. It was because he made her laugh, held her when she cried, and was willing to get tough, and also, not barge into a hotel room at midnight because it was best for his kids.

"Leila—" He paused.

She looked at him. "What?" Emotions were etched on his

face, and her heart started racing. What had he been about to say?

He tucked a lock of her hair behind her ear, searching her face. "We'll talk later. Let's get on the road. I want to be up early and ready to go."

Disappointment fluttered through her, but she nodded. The day was too much already. It wasn't the time or place for making statements she'd never be able to take back. Statements like she was falling head over heels in love with this man who she'd married so long ago.

CHAPTER 25

SHORTLY AFTER MIDNIGHT, Dash sprawled against the pillows on the hotel bed, scrolling through the pictures that Blue had sent, that his pals had taken. Aimee and Ashley looked so vulnerable, so tiny, all tucked up in their little playpen, sleeping.

Fragile, tiny human beings who would be one-hundred percent reliant on him for everything.

Dash thought of Leila as a little girl, and how her world had been rocked when her mom had died.

He had so much to make up for with Aimee and Ashley. He knew Sophia and Maura had chosen him, but as he looked at the pictures, the raw magnitude of the responsibility settled on him with a chokehold he couldn't shake.

He leaned back against the pillows, his gut heavy and weighted as Leila came in from the bathroom, wearing his tee shirt, because she'd left Birch Crossing in such a hurry that she hadn't brought anything with her.

He smiled as she climbed onto the bed next to him. "You're gorgeous. Will you marry me?"

She laughed as she tucked up next to him and rested her chin on his shoulder. "Will that joke ever get old?"

"Never." He put his arm around her and took a deep breath, breathing in the feel of her body against his. "Thanks for coming with me."

"Of course." She put her hand on his chest. "How are you doing?"

With anyone else, he'd simply blow off the question with a platitude. But with Leila, he couldn't do it. He needed her right now. He needed her help. "I am terrified I'm going to fuck it up," he said. "I know that everyone says parenting is imperfect and you make a million mistakes. I get that. But looking at those pictures...they're so damned vulnerable. I wasn't meant to be a dad. They deserve better."

"Better?" Leila sat up. "Seriously?"

He looked over at her. "I was in *prison*, Leila. I'm such a fuck up that my own parents kicked me out when I was eighteen. That's why I stayed in Birch Crossing at the end of that summer. Because my parents told me I couldn't go back home to New York with them."

Leila got to her knees, faced him, then slung her leg across him, and then sat on his thighs, her knees on either side of his hips. "Shut up, Dash."

He raised his brows. "Really?"

"Yes. Look, I've had enough of this crap with you."

Darkness settled on him. "Is that so?"

"Yes. You keep talking about how you're not enough for Ashley and Aimee. What will it take for you to realize that you are? You're a freaking hero, Dash. You're kind, warm, funny, and a protector. You're driven by one thing, and that's love. You took care of Bea and Roger, you took care of me, a helpless teenager who was your little sister's friend. You're a great man, Dash."

He wanted to believe it. He did. "You're not objective. You're obsessed with me, remember?"

"No. I'm not obsessed. I love you, and I wouldn't love you if you weren't worthy, because I'm cynical, scared, jaded, and categorically opposed to falling in love with anyone ever again, especially my husband, because that is so complicated I can barely wrap my head around it."

His heart started racing. "You love me?"

She managed a smile. "I do. I really tried not to, for many reasons. But I do. You're irresistible." She paused, and her smile faded. "It scares the daylights out of me to love you," she admitted. "I don't want to get hurt again, but love doesn't always care, right?"

He sat up, framed her face with his hands and kissed her. His heart was dancing, singing, gallivanting. *She loved him. Loved him. HIM.* He knew he didn't deserve it, but he wasn't going to turn it down. "I need you, Leila," he whispered.

"I know." She managed a smile. "I don't want to need you, but it's going to take some work."

He felt her resistance. She didn't want to love him. She didn't want to need him. She didn't want their marriage to become real. But he understood now. It was about fear. She was scared, of the past, of the future, of a life she didn't know she could handle.

He knew he had to be careful not to push her away or freak her out, but now that he knew she loved him, he knew something else for sure: he was going to do everything possible to make her realize that staying with him and the girls in Birch Crossing was the life that would make her truly happy.

He and his girls, and all of Birch Crossing, were the life of her heart.

If she didn't figure it out, then he was the one who was going to be lost, because he loved her, too.

———

LEILA'S HEART turned over when Dash kissed her after her declaration of love. His kiss was so tender, so beautiful, she knew it was his way of telling her that he loved her, too.

She was so glad he hadn't said it. She'd told him only because he'd needed to see himself the way she saw him. She hadn't told him to turn the relationship into a forever she didn't want.

But the way he was kissing her made her feel safe for having said it.

It was the perfect response, a response that wrapped her up in love and security without forcing a conversation she didn't want to have.

His hands went to her bare thighs, then slid upward to her hips while he continued to kiss her. Her heart started to dance as she felt his palms wrapped around her. She loved the feel of him touching her.

His arms locked around her lower back and he pulled her against him, their kisses mounting in intensity.

She was still on his lap, so she was higher than he was. She braced her hands on his shoulders and bent down, kissing him back, loving the feeling of power that her position gave her.

"I need you," he whispered. "You ground me."

She smiled. "Why can't I ever resist you?"

"Why resist? You know I'm your destiny." He grasped the hem of her shirt, pulled it over her head, and tossed it aside. "God, you're beautiful."

Her heart swelled at the awe in his tone. "You mean that."

"Hell, yeah." His gaze roamed her body, and his hands did the same, traveling from her hips to her ribs, to her breasts. The way he looked at her made her feel like the most gorgeous woman in the world. "I could make love to you every day for the rest of my life, and it wouldn't be close to enough."

Tears filled her eyes. "Don't say beautiful things like that," she whispered.

"It's the truth. You need to know how amazing you are."

He lifted her up, and in a couple swift moves, he'd shed his boxers and her underwear before setting her back on his lap.

Only now, there was nothing between them. Just vulnerability, trust, and bare skin. She loved the feeling of her inner thighs against his skin. She leaned forward and pressed her palms to his muscled chest. "You're like a Greek god with this body of yours."

He grinned. "Thanks. I love how you look at me. It's such a turn-on."

She raised her brows. "You're the turn-on. With those biceps and gorgeous eyes. And the way your hands keep caressing my breasts with utmost skill and precision. You're the one who's on fire."

"Nah. You're the hot one." He sat up and took her left nipple into his mouth, his tongue and lips doing magical things to the pink nub.

"Oh, wow." She tipped her head back and closed her eyes, basking in the sensations he was evoking in her. "You definitely win. I'm just sitting here and you're unleashing these master life skills on me. I'm the luckiest girl ever right now."

He laughed softly as he switched his magic to her other breast. "You bring out the best in me. I'm inspired. You're like this amazing piece of art that unlocks the brightest part of my soul."

She opened her eyes and pulled back. "I can't believe you just said that. That was literally the most beautiful thing I've ever heard."

"Fits, then, because you're the most incredible human being I've ever met." He pulled her in for a kiss before she could respond, a kiss that overwhelmed her with its intensity. He didn't let up, he didn't give her a moment to breathe.

It was as if he were trying to keep her from thinking, from doing anything but surrendering to him and the moment.

The moment she thought it, he shifted her hips, and slid inside her, and she lost all focus on trying to analyze his words or his motivation. He became her entire world in that moment. She surrendered to him and the desire he was unleashing within her. He gripped her hips and began to shift her, rocking her back and forth.

The action was electrifying, and she took over the movement, testing different angles, basking in the moments when he gasped and his muscles went taut. She moved fast and slow, taunting them both, bringing them to the edge, until they were breathless.

He gave her a look. "I'm taking over."

She raised her brows. "You can't. I'm in charge here."

"Are you?" He gave her wicked look, and then he moved his hand between her legs. She gasped as his fingers found the perfect spot, tearing all self-control from her. The orgasm was so fast, so consuming, that she screamed his name and clung to his shoulders, fighting not to fall.

"*Leila.*" He surrendered, and his body bucked beneath her, his hands on her hips, holding them together as the final orgasms rocked them both. It wasn't until they were both finished, sated, and exhausted that he let her go.

She tumbled beside him onto the bed, laughing and crying. "I'm ruined for life," she moaned. "Literally. Nothing will ever be like that again."

He pulled her against him, nuzzling the back of her neck. "I take that as a challenge."

"Of course you do. You're a man."

"Not a man. Your man. Your husband. My job is to rock your world every day for the rest of our lives. I'm fully confident I can handle it."

She closed her eyes, basking in the feel of his body against hers, in the warmth of his arms around her belly, holding her right. "You have kids, Dash," she said, her heart aching for the future they couldn't have. "It won't stay like this."

"Nothing ever stays the same," he agreed. "But why can't change be even better than where we are now?"

"Because that was the best."

"The best so far." He kissed the back of her neck. "Leila, I don't want to freak you out, but I need to tell you something."

Her heart started pounding. His tone was serious, and it scared her. "I don't think you should say it."

"I'm going to anyway." He turned her over so she was facing him. His eyes were dark and intense. "I think you'd make an amazing mom, Leila, but I don't want the fact I have kids to freak you out or make you feel pressure."

She bit her lip. "Dash—"

He put his index finger over her lip. "I'm not finished. Let me finish?"

She didn't want him to finish. She was scared of what was coming. But this was Dash. How could she say no? She couldn't. So she nodded silently.

"I love you, Leila."

Tears filled her eyes, and her throat clogged up, but his finger was still on her lips, so, she was spared from having to say anything.

"I want to make this marriage real. I want forever with you. I want to solve problems with the girls together. I want to help you work through your past with Birch Crossing and your mom and your stepdad. I want to help your heart heal, and I want to fill it with so much love and worthiness that you wake up every morning with music in your heart and a dance in your spirit."

The tears trickled down her cheeks now. His words were precious, a treasure, and she wanted so much to throw herself into his arms and never leave.

"I'm asking you to be my wife," he said. "But I don't want an answer today. We have to live together for thirty days when we get back. Tell me on the last day. Take that time to see how it feels to be a mom, to live in Birch Crossing, to wake up every morning with me whispering how much I love you, and to fall asleep every night in my arms. I'm not going to bring this up again, until that clock expires." He paused. "Except I'll tell you that I love you. I have to do that. Other than that...this is tabled. But know that I will still want it, and I'm waiting for you to know how you feel. Okay? Just nod yes or no. No answers now. Just understanding."

His finger was still on her lips, which made her want to laugh. "You think you can stop me from talking by putting your finger on my mouth?"

He smiled, but it was the kindest, most tender smile he'd ever given her. "I don't think anything can stop you from talking," he said. "I was surprised it lasted that long."

"I didn't really want to give you a response," she admitted.

"I know." He kissed her lightly. "I know you're scared," he said. "I am, too, and I've had six months to get used to the idea of being a dad."

"I'm new to you, though. You haven't had me for long."

"Fifteen years is not nearly long enough," he agreed.

She laughed. "You've had me for only a few days." She knew she was avoiding the topic, and she was grateful that he was letting her.

"Fifteen years and a few days. These last few days were different. Our relationship changed. And I'd say it was a good change."

She poked him in the chest. "You said you weren't going to bring it up again."

He held up his hands in innocence. "It was a random comment about change. That's all. I meant nothing by it."

She rolled her eyes. "Liar."

He grinned. "I love you, Leila. I think I always have."

She sighed. "This is exactly how I imagined it would be. You being all hot and sexy and declaring your undying love for me, and wanting to make our marriage real."

His smile faded. "Take your time, Leila. No answers now. Just one day at a time. All I ask is that you give it the full thirty days. Will you do that? I believe we have enough to build on that it's worth giving it a try."

She took a breath. "I don't think I can give you the answer you want. I have to be honest."

"Do you love me?"

She nodded. "I do. With all my heart."

Yes. "Then I'm willing to put myself out there." He traced his finger down her jaw. "Let's get some sleep. It's a long day ahead of us."

She nodded. "How are you going to handle it in the morning? With Frank and Vivian?"

Tension settled back in his body. "I want to call the cops and have them arrested."

She felt his hesitation. "But?"

He looked at her. "I don't know. I really don't know how the morning is going to go. I have a side to me that isn't pretty, and I'm afraid it's going to come out." He paused. "I'm worried I'm going to show up as the man that they told the judge I was, that they used to try to convince the court I wasn't fit to raise the girls. I'm afraid I'm going to be that man when I walk in that door. And then they'll be right, that I don't deserve them."

Leila's heart tightened. "I'm sure you have that man still inside you, but what you didn't have before was a reason good enough to be someone else. Now you do."

He searched her face. "A reason is enough?"

"If it's a good reason for you."

He shook his head and pulled her into his arms. "It's a good enough reason, but I don't know if it's enough to stop me."

"You're a good man, Dash." She snuggled against his chest and closed her eyes. "You'll be who you want to be."

"I want to be both," he said softly. "I want to kick their asses, and I want to be what those girls need. I can't do both."

"No," she agreed. "You can't."

CHAPTER 26

EARLY THE NEXT MORNING, Dash sat on the armchair by the window, his forearms braced on his thighs, his head low, talking to himself, trying to calm himself down. His body was so tense that his muscles ached.

Dawn was stretching its orange glow across the sky.

He knew the twins would be awake any minute. At any second, he'd get a text from Blue that it was go time.

What the fuck was he going to do?

He'd been up for hours. Sleep had given him an hour, maybe two of rest.

And the rest of the night, he'd been sitting in the chair, watching Leila sleep, scrolling through each new set of pictures that Blue texted every thirty minutes. The girls were fine, sleeping peacefully. Frank and Vivian, also asleep. Everyone at rest.

Except for him.

Leila came out of the bathroom, dressed in the same clothes she'd been wearing yesterday. Her hair was wet from the shower, tucked up in a bun, her face clean of any makeup. She looked so beautiful she took his breath away.

She raised her brows. "The vibe coming off you feels slightly terrifying."

He grimaced. "I'm trying to pull my shit together, but I feel like how I felt every morning when I woke up in prison. On edge. On full alert. Ready to fight. Ready to do whatever I have to do to survive another day."

Leila walked over and knelt on the floor in front of him. She put her hands on his wrists. "You look ready to shiv someone."

He was so stressed he could barely feel her touch. It was nothing more than a breath of warm air drifting across his skin. "I am."

She shook her head. "No, you're not. Why did you wind up in prison? You never told me."

"I stabbed a guy."

Her eyes widened. "The tone in your voice is very confrontational. I'm not going to play. I know you're a good man. What happened? The whole story, Dash."

He stared at her hands on his wrists, still not really able to feel her touch. "I was outside a bar. Leaving. Maybe a little drunk. A guy I knew was in the alley with his girlfriend. He was..." He paused. "He was saying things to her that no woman should ever have to experience. So I told him to shut up, and I offered her a ride."

Leila's fingers drew little circles on the insides of his wrist. "Then what?"

"He got pissed. Told me to stay out of it."

"But you couldn't."

He looked over at her. "I couldn't," he agreed. "I walked over to him and I told him that he was an asshole, and he didn't deserve her or anyone. I told her she could do better, and to walk away."

Leila grinned. "I love that. Did she leave?"

"Yeah. But when she started to head toward her car, he went after her." Dash continued to stare at Leila's hands on his wrists. "I saw his face. He was going to hurt her. So I punched him before he could get to her."

Leila smiled. "I bet you did. When did the knife come out?"

"He pulled it. I grabbed him to try to disarm him, but the knife slipped and I stabbed him. Almost killed him." He shrugged. "I didn't mean to stab him, but it happened."

"And you got prison and he got to walk away?"

"Yeah." He finally looked at her. "Turns out, you can't use violence to stop verbal abuse. Who knew, right?"

She smiled, and on her face was only understanding and kindness, not judgment. "You sacrificed yourself to protect her."

"I didn't know I was sacrificing myself at the time." He finally turned his hands over and took her hands in his. "If I had to do it again, I'd still step in to protect her, but I'd like to think I wouldn't throw the first punch, that I'd keep it from escalating to a physical altercation. Prison sucked. But when I saw him reaching for her, something inside me snapped." He grimly admitted the truth that had been weighing on him all that time. "If I had a do-over, I might hit him again, even knowing what was coming for me if I did."

Leila squeezed his hands. "You're a hero, Dash. It's who you are in your soul. Back then, you were an angry, pissed-off rebel with nothing to lose. Today? You're still a protector, still a hero, but you have a focus that's different. You'd never put getting your daughters back home with you at risk. Never. No matter what. You're the same man, but you're also not at all."

He ground his jaw and looked up at her. "What if, when I see Frank's face, or I see my girls in his arms, my mind goes blank, like it did back then? What if I don't think? What if I just act and throw that punch? I'll lose everything."

She shook her head. "You won't hit him."

"What if I do?" He could feel sweat dripping down his

back. "I'm so fucking tense right now I feel like I'm going to snap."

Leila took his face in her hands. "Look at me, Dash Stratton. Look at me and listen to what I have to say."

He met her gaze.

"Give yourself credit for who you are. Believe in yourself."

"Believe in myself?" He raised his brows. "That's your advice?"

"Yep. That's all it takes. Believe you're worthy of being their dad, and then go act like the man you want to be."

He stared at her, and somewhere, deep in his gut, resolution settled. Determination. Focus. *Believe in yourself. Believe in yourself.*

There was a light knock at the door. "Hi guys, it's Blue. It's game time."

Adrenaline spiked through Dash, and he met Leila's gaze for a brief second. "Game time," he said.

She nodded. "You're ready."

He ground his jaw. "Maybe." He squeezed her hands, then stood up. He pulled her to her feet, gave her a long look, then headed toward the door.

He didn't kiss her, because maybe, he didn't deserve that. He'd find out shortly.

CHAPTER 27

DASH STOOD RESTLESSLY, shifting his weight back and forth as he, Leila, and Blue stood outside Room 312. He could hear sounds through the door, movement, low voices, but nothing discernible.

His heart was racing, and he leaned in, so he could hear.

The sound of little girl laughter leaked through the door, a shriek of delight and then the hysterical laughing. His heart turned over, and he closed his eyes, listening to the joy coming at him. He could hear Vivian singing something, and more shrieks of laughter.

There was pure joy and love coming through the door.

"The girls sound really happy." He looked at Leila, sudden doubt gut-punching him. "Maybe I should leave them with Frank and Vivian."

Leila raised her brows. "Is that what you want? Is that what Maura and Sophia wanted?"

Resistance flooded him. "No."

"Then go in there and find a better solution." She knocked on the door. "Hello," she called out cheerfully. "Housekeeping. I have fresh towels."

Dash glared at her. "I wasn't ready."

"No one ever is."

The door opened, and Dash found himself face to face with Frank, who was holding Aimee in his arms.

The gray-haired man's eyes widened, and panic flickered in them. Behind him, Vivian sucked in her breath, and froze. Both grandparents stared at him in silence, fear on their faces. Dash went still, unsure what to do.

Aimee jabbered gibberish at Dash, then held out her arms to him. He looked at the little girl, her big smile, her adorable as hell pigtails, and then all the tension inside him vanished. "Hey, Aimee," he said, reaching out for her. "How's my little girl?"

Frank handed her over, and then backed away.

The minute Dash held his daughter in his arms, he knew everything was going to be okay. He grinned down at her and then made the face that always got her to laugh. As soon as he did it, she burst out in delighted giggles and patted his jaw.

Ashley held out her arms and started babbling, so Dash walked over to her. Vivian handed the baby over, and Dash took a deep breath, everything settling inside him when she snuggled against his chest beside Aimee.

He walked over to the bed and sat down, chatting back to them in the same happy tone they were using with them. "You get to call me Daddy, now," he said, keeping his voice singsong and silly, using that tone that always got them giggling. "Can you say, 'Daddy is the greatest?'"

Daddy.

That word had scared him for the last six months, but suddenly, it was perfection. He loved it. It was who he was. His identity. His purpose.

Daddy.

He smiled at his daughters, his heart dancing with light-ness he never thought he'd feel. "I don't cook well, but Eppie promised to get me up to speed. I've been practicing. I can make pancakes that almost look like a princess. And Clare promised to help me up my braiding game."

Movement from Frank caught his eye, and he looked quickly over at him, his body tensing, ready to protect the girls.

But Frank was simply standing beside his wife. Fear was etched on his face, but when he turned to look at his wife, Dash saw utter, agonizing sadness on Vivian's face. The pain was visceral and real, the kind that tore away at a soul until there was nothing left.

Dash glanced at Leila. She was watching Vivian, and she, like Vivian, had an expression of sadness on her face as well. Sadness for Vivian's pain.

Fuck.

"My name is Leila." She stepped inside the room. "I'm Dash's long-lost wife, and one of Maura's best friends from when we were little."

His wife? She'd introduced herself as his *wife*?

Knowing how she felt about being married long term, Leila's claiming of him was stunning. Unexpected. And he *loved* it.

Frank and Vivian's gazes swiveled to Leila, in evident confusion. "His wife?" Frank asked.

"Yes." Leila walked right in. "My mom died when I was ten, and my stepfather was an abusive bastard with full custody of me. Dash knew me only as the best friend of his little sister, but he married me on my eighteenth birthday to break my stepfather's legal hold on me. We've been married ever since. He's a protector. He's funny. And he's got the most tremendous heart of anyone I have ever met."

Dash's chest seemed to fill with emotion as Leila smiled at the girls. "Hi cuties," she said, genuine warmth evident in her voice. "You've got a much better new dad than I had. You're going to be okay."

Blue cleared his throat. "Hi." He waved at the room as he

walked in and shut the door behind him. "I'm Blue Carboni. I'm a friend of the family, and I'm just here to provide witness if that's needed. Don't mind me." He sat down at the breakfast table, leaned back, and folded his arms over his chest.

The threat of Blue's presence was obvious, and Dash saw the resignation on the faces of Frank and Vivian. There was no escaping for them. No happy ending, and they knew it.

Silence fell over the room, with the exception of the girls, who were chatting happily and tugging at his whiskers.

Dash's heart tightened as he looked down at them again. His girls. *His daughters*. Suddenly, the magnitude of the moment settled on him. These were *his daughters*. Forever his to love, to protect, to teach, to empower. Little tiny human beings that were completely reliant on him.

And he'd have to figure it out as he went.

He shot a look at Leila, suddenly wanting her with him. She was the one who believed in him, even more than he did. "Come meet them, Leila."

Leila hesitated, then, to his relief, she walked across the room and sat down next to him on the bed. "Hi— Oomph." She grunted with laughter as Aimee launched herself at Leila.

The little girl grabbed Leila's necklace, but she quickly protected it with warmth and gentleness.

Dash grinned watching Leila with Aimee. She didn't look awkward at all. In fact, she was smiling and seemed completely at ease with her. He looked at Blue, and the men exchanged smiles. All Dash's tension eased now that Leila was beside him.

She made his soul lighter.

She made him laugh and see hope and possibility.

She made him believe that he could be the man Maura and Sophia expected him to be.

Hell, he loved her. Completely. She was his light, and he knew it. She was the girls' light, too, and he was certain of that.

At that point, Frank shifted, drawing Dash's gaze toward him. The two grandparents were standing side by side in the little kitchenette. Their shoulders were tucked, as if they were trying to make themselves small. They looked scared. And sad. The minute Dash looked at them again, he felt their sadness wrap around him, like a great weight in the room.

Hell.

He glanced at Leila, and she looked at him over Aimee's head. She raised her brows at him, communicating in clear, unspoken terms. He had to be more than what he wanted to be right then.

Double hell.

He gritted his teeth and addressed Frank and Vivian. "What do you have to say?"

They looked at each other, and Frank put his arm around Vivian. "Are you going to call the police?"

"I don't know yet. Why did you take them away?" His arm tightened reflexively around Ashley as he said it, as if Frank and Vivian could take them again.

Frank looked at his wife again, and then he sighed. "They're all we have left of Sophia."

"You cut her off," Dash snapped. "You rejected her and my sister. You didn't go to the wedding, or to Ashley and Aimee's birth—"

Leila put her hand on Dash's arm, and he took a breath, watching as tears glistened on Vivian's cheeks.

"I know," Vivian said. "We regretted it, but we didn't know how to fix it. We called Sophia so many times, and she refused to answer the phone or call back."

"Because she was protecting my sister," Dash said. "She loved Maura, and she would never welcome you back if you couldn't love the woman she loved."

"We were wrong," Frank said. "We were wrong! We knew it, but we couldn't fix it!"

"We had decided to drive down there to see them," Vivian

said. "We were packing our bags that day and we were going to go there and stay until they forgave us. And then..." Her voice trailed off. "It was too late," she whispered. 'We were too late."

Dash gritted his jaw. "Why then? So you could see the grandkids? They were married for six years before they had the girls. What were you doing all that time? You had so much time."

Again, Leila put her hand on his arm, and he looked down. Ashley and Aimee were staring at him with wide eyes, both of them silent. He looked into their little faces, and he thought of how Maura and Sophia had chosen him. How they'd believed in him. How they'd trusted him with their greatest treasures.

Suddenly, emotions clogged his throat. He pressed a kiss to Ashley's head, and then he looked at Frank and Vivian. "Maura and Sophia chose me," he said. "Do you know why?"

Dash expected some comment about how it had been to spite Frank and Vivian, or to punish them.

But Frank surprised him. "They picked you because you're the best choice," he said. "We've been watching you for the last six months every weekend when you came by, and you're amazing with them. We didn't want to see it, but it's the truth."

Dash took a breath, the anger draining away at Frank's response.

"We kept going with the lawsuit because of me," Vivian said. "Frank wanted to stop, to honor Sophia's wish, but I couldn't. I knew we'd burned our bridge. I saw the hate in your eyes when you looked at us, and I knew that we'd never see them again if you got the girls. I know it's what we deserve, but I couldn't live with it. I couldn't give up without trying." She touched Frank's arm. "I made Frank leave yesterday morning. It's not him. It's me. My baby girl," she said, tears filling her words. "I lost her twice, and it's too late now."

Dash closed his eyes as Ashley tugged at his whiskers.

He felt their grief, and he recognized it, because it was tangled with the loss of his own sister. What would he have done if Maura and Sophia had chosen Frank and Vivian instead of him, and he'd known they'd never let him near the twins? He would have fought with everything he had.

He didn't want to understand Frank and Vivian. He didn't want to care about them. But at the same time, he didn't have grandparents to give to the girls. And Frank and Vivian were their only connection to Sophia.

He looked at Leila. "What would Maura want me to do?"

She smiled, her eyes full of tears. "You know what she'd want."

He did know. Maura had a huge heart, and she'd always told Sophia not to give up on Frank and Vivian. She'd told Sophia repeatedly that she forgave Frank and Vivian, and that Sophia shouldn't ever feel that if she wanted to resume ties with them that she had to choose between Maura and them.

He looked down at his daughters, his gorgeous, sassy daughters, and he knew that he'd never forgive himself if he took away any chance they had to connect with the family that they'd lost.

He looked up at Frank and Vivian. "I need you to write a letter to Maura and Sophia. I need you to write them the letter they deserve. Tell them you love them. Ask for forgiveness. Accept them fully, their relationship, their love. Give Maura the love you always denied her."

Leila squeezed his hand, and he had to take a moment to compose himself.

"If you do that, if you can welcome them both to your hearts, and love them both, as they were, then..." He paused, knowing he couldn't take back the offer. But he knew it was right. "Then we can work out a way for you to be a real, vital part of Aimee and Ashley's lives."

Vivian let out a cry and went to her knees. Frank caught her arm and knelt beside her, holding her as she cried onto his shoulder.

Leila squeezed his arm, and he looked over at her. "I'm so proud of you," she whispered. "I'm sure that was the hardest thing you've ever done."

"Not yet, but this will be." He handed Ashley to Leila, then stood up. He flexed his hands, then walked across the hotel room to the kneeling couple.

He went down on his knees beside them, and they both turned to look at him.

He cleared his throat. "I loved my sister, and I loved your daughter. They were the best parents I ever knew, and their relationship was pure love, light, and laughter. I miss the hell out of them, and my parents suck, so I'll take you guys instead." His voice was rough, his words tangled with emotion. He wasn't even sure his words made sense, but suddenly, Frank and Vivian were hugging him and he was hugging them back.

In their arms, he cried for his sister, and for Sophia, and for the light that had been lost that day such a short time ago. He cried in a way he'd never let himself cry for them before.

And they did the same.

He didn't want to feel that pain, but he couldn't stop it anymore.

Then he felt Leila's arm slide around his waist. He released Frank and put his arm around Leila, bringing her into their circle. The moment she was pressed up against his side, he knew he was going to be all right.

That they were all going to be all right.

————

A SHORT WHILE and lots of aching emotions later, Leila walked back over to Blue to get the girls. He was bouncing them on his knees, and they were giggling with laughter.

Blue regarded Leila with his thoughtful gaze as she picked up Ashley. "Well done, Leila," he said quietly, low enough that the threesome talking on the other side of the room couldn't hear him.

She shook her head, her emotions heavy in her chest, but also lighter. She knew that Dash had a long way to go with Frank and Vivian, but the path had begun. "It was Dash. He did it."

"It wasn't Dash. Dash wanted to kill them. I saw the way he was holding himself when we were walking over here. I told him I was going to take him down before I'd let him hurt anyone, and he agreed."

Leila tucked Ashley against her hip, smiling as the little girl grabbed her hair. "I heard that exchange."

"But when you guys were sitting on that bed, I saw him look at you multiple times. He was desperate for control, and you gave it to him." Blue held up Aimee. "You talked to him last night, didn't you?"

"I did," she agreed as she took Aimee in her other arm. "Hi sweet girl," she said, grinning when she got a smile back.

"I'll tell you something," Blue said. "Dash is a great man. I love the hell out of him. But he's been through hell and back, and sometimes that breaks a man at a level he can't fix. But with you by his side, he can do it."

Her throat tightened. She was well aware of what Dash had done in the last hour. She knew how hard it had been for him, and she'd fallen so much more in love with him. What he'd done had been so incredibly difficult. She wasn't sure she would have had the strength to forgive Frank and Vivian if she'd been in his situation, but she knew it was the right thing to do. "He has the best heart," she said.

"He does. Don't stay with him out of pity," Blue said. "But

don't run away because you're scared. I had to fight to be brave enough to take on Chloe and all the girls, but it's worth every minute, I promise you."

Leila had witnessed Blue with his family, and she knew he was speaking from his heart's truth. Her heart tightened. "Were you really scared?"

He grinned. "I was completely broken. Completely lost. And letting Chloe in saved my life. You don't need to have it all together to be enough for them, to be deserving of giving yourself the chance to be happy."

She managed a laugh as she juggled the girls. "Well, that's good, because I don't have anything together."

Blue raised his brows. "No one ever feels like they do, but that doesn't mean they don't deserve love and happiness. Be brave enough to take the chance you want, if you want it."

She met his gaze. "I—"

Dash walked up beside her. "I told Frank and Vivian we'd take the girls to the beach this morning. You up for that?"

Leila met Blue's gaze. A morning at the beach with her husband, his kids, and their grandparents? Her heart raced, and a part of her wanted to say yes, to see what it would be like to be part of this little, new family. But another part of her wanted to refuse, to let them meet each other. "It's your time to bond with them. I would be in the way."

Emotion flickered in Dash's eyes. "In the way?"

"Yes." She lifted her chin. "Take your daughters. I'll wait here with Blue."

Dash leaned in and kissed her lightly. "I want you there, Leila. No pressure. Just come. Try it. See."

Her throat thickened. "Dash, I don't—"

"Do you love me?"

"Yes, you know that."

"Then isn't it worth trying? You need to stay around for thirty days anyway. Might as well give it your all."

At that moment, Ashley grabbed Leila's necklace, and she

quickly protected the chain before the little girl could break it. She met Ashley's gaze, and saw the twinkle in her eyes. The joy of life. Suddenly, Leila saw herself in this little girl. A fragile, beautiful soul who needed to be loved.

And in that moment, her fear dissolved, replaced by a deep knowing that the two little girls in her arms were put in her life for a reason.

She couldn't run away from them. She wouldn't run away from them.

Dash touched her arm, and she looked over at him. "You okay?" he asked.

Tears filled her eyes. She nodded, and then said the words that had been growing within her, stronger and stronger. "I want to try," she whispered. "I really, *really* want to try."

A huge smile lit up his face. "Me, too." Then he leaned in, kissed each of his girls, and then slid his arm around her waist and kissed her.

In that moment, in his arms, holding the two little girls, Leila knew that she'd come home.

Deep in her heart, she knew it, and she knew that she would fight for it, fight to be brave enough, strong enough, and healed enough to be able to stay with them. To open her heart to all of them.

To let herself be happy.

Dash smiled. "To the beach, then?"

She nodded. "To the beach."

CHAPTER 28

"One more stop before we go back home and relieve Eppie from babysitting," Dash said a few weeks later.

Leila leaned back in the seat, feeling happy and sated. "Dinner was amazing. It was so nice to be out."

"I told you, I want to date you. It's important that we make time for each other," he said.

Leila turned sideways to look at him. He looked so much younger than he had when she'd first run into him a few weeks ago. "Fatherhood looks good on you."

He smiled. "Who would have guessed I'd like it so much? I should have started accumulating kids years ago."

She grinned, feeling his joy. He was such a great dad. He'd taken a few weeks off from work to focus on acclimating the girls, and he'd been so happy.

She'd been happy too, but torn at the same time. "Dash," she said quietly. "I love the girls. I love you. I love being a part of our family, but I'm having difficulty being in town. My past feels like it weighs on me."

"I know." He drove past their house and put on his blinker. "That's why we're making this stop."

She sat up, fear hammering at her when she realized he

was pulling into the driveway of her old house. "I don't want to be here."

"But you need to." He parked in front and turned off the truck. "We're going inside."

"What? No." She shook her head frantically. "I can't."

"You have to." He took her hand and pressed a kiss to her palm. "Leila, your nightmares wake me up at night. I know you're dreaming of your stepdad. I know he haunts you."

Tears filled her eyes. "I'm sorry, Dash."

He leaned in to kiss her. "Never be sorry," he said. "'I know you have to see this house every day, every time you walk outside our front door, and that's been grueling for you."

She nodded. "I'm so happy with you and the girls. I want to stay. I love that Clare and Emma asked me to help them market their creations, and that I'm starting a business to help women artists develop an online business. It's wonderful, but…"

"He haunts you."

"Yes."

Understanding filled his eyes. "Leila, we both went through hell with our parents. You don't need to pretend that you're okay when you're struggling. Healing takes time."

"I know. I just…I don't know if I can stay here." The words hurt when she said them, but at the same time, it felt like a relief to say them aloud.

He kissed her lightly. "Come on." He opened his door and got out.

She bit her lip as she watched him walk around the headlights. He opened her door and leaned on it, looking adorably sexy. "Come on, darlin'."

She couldn't help but smile. He always somehow made her want to laugh, no matter how upset she was. "Are you a cowboy now? One of those Hart billionaires who are always in the news?"

He grinned. "A billionaire next year. Cowboy, never." He

held out his hand. "Come on, my darling. I have something for you."

"In there?" She pointed to the house.

"Yep."

"How about if I decline?"

He wiggled his brows. "Do you trust me?"

She sighed. "I really hate it when you play that card."

"Right? Because I'm impossible to resist."

"Being irresistible isn't fair."

"Sure is. Because you're irresistible to me, so my charm makes it a level playing field." He fluttered his hand to encourage her. "Come on, sweetheart. One little outing and then I'll make love to you for at least five minutes before we both fall asleep or one of the girls need something."

"Five minutes?" She put her hand in his and let him pull her out of the truck. "That's all you're good for these days?"

"Maybe six. I'm a man being pulled in many directions." He pulled her in his arms and kissed her, long and thoroughly, until her toes began to tingle. He pulled back. "Married for fifteen years and still hot as hell. How do you do it?"

She laughed and hit him in the chest. "You're so sassy. Go away."

"Never." He took her hand. "Come on."

Leila clutched his hand, but allowed him to lead her along the stone walkway to the front door of the little house she'd lived in growing up. She paused, staring up at it. "This is the first time I've really looked at it since I've been back."

"What do you think?"

"It's smaller than I remembered. Less scary," she said honestly. "We moved here when I was a baby. My mom and my dad. Then he died and my mom remarried. I don't really remember my dad, but that's what my mom used to say. That he was a good man. And then she married *him*." She didn't use his name. She never did. He didn't deserve it.

Dash's hand tightened around hers. "I hired someone to find him."

Shock rippled through Leila. "Where is he?"

Dash met her gaze. "He's dead, sweetheart. He can't ever hurt anyone again."

Leila's heart clenched. "He's dead? Really?"

"Yep. Died in a Florida prison, actually. That's why he never came back here and the house was abandoned."

Something inside her that had been held so tightly for so long began to loosen. "He's really gone." Tears spilled over. *"Dash."*

"I know, baby. I know." He pulled her into his arms and held her while she cried. While so many years of tension fell away. Emotions she'd kept tightly gripped for so long. Suddenly, they all tumbled free, safe to be unleashed in Dash's arms.

Eventually, finally, the tears subsided, and she could breathe again.

Dash kissed the top of her head. "I love you, Leila."

She nodded, resting her cheek against his chest. "I know. Thanks for finding that out."

"It's not all I found out."

She looked up at him, her heart clenching. "What else?"

He put his arm around her and turned her toward the house. "This house is yours."

She blinked. "What?"

"Apparently, it was always yours, same as the money. When I married you, the house was yours, too. But we were young and didn't have a good lawyer, and believed his lies, so we didn't know. But it's yours."

"Mine." She stared at the house, stunned. "I don't want it."

"Come inside for a sec." He grasped her hand and headed toward the front door.

Reluctantly, she followed him, pausing for a split second when he turned on the inside lights, when they momentarily blinded her. When she could see again, she realized he'd guided her into the living room, the main room of the house.

The room had been stripped of all the furniture from her childhood. It had been freshly painted a pale blue, with rainbows and unicorns on the walls. There was a thick blue carpet on the floor. Several brightly colored beanbag chairs were arranged in a circle, and a giant teddy bear sat on a huge, sectional couch decorated with pretty, flowered throw pillows.

It was warm, inviting, and full of heart and love. "Did you do this?"

"Yeah." He grinned. "It's not easy to work on the house across the street without you noticing, I'm not going to lie."

Leila walked into the room, looking in stunned wonder at the magical place he'd made. "It's incredible. What's it for?"

"It's for whatever you want it to be." He leaned against the door jam, grinning. "I wanted to give it heart, so you could see its potential. You could sell it to a great family. You could work with Blue and Chloe to make it into a little summer camp for girls in the foster care system. We could redo it and move in, since it has lake front and Bea's house doesn't. You could use it for the office for your marketing firm that we both know will be a success. All great things that fill the space with love and possibility."

She spun around, looking at all the little details he'd put in. Along the wall, light bulbs were glowing in beautiful iron sconces that she recognized immediately. "You made those!"

He grinned. "I did."

"And the fireplace andirons." There were gorgeous, carved loons in her fireplace.

"I needed to put some love in here." He pointed at a blanket on the couch. "Eppie knitted that. There are a few more coming, but they aren't ready yet."

Leila picked up the blanket and unfolded it. It was pink and blue, with hearts and princesses on it. "I love it."

"She made it specifically for this house," Dash said. "She wanted to bring love and empowerment into your house."

Leila kicked off her shoes, and her feet sank into the thick carpet as she walked across the room to look at the white and blue curtains hanging on the windows. "Who made these?"

"Judith was in charge of those. I think it was a team effort." He pointed at the mantle. "Clare didn't want to be left out, so she donated cupcakes."

"Cupcakes?" Leila picked up the box and opened it, then started laughing. "More hearts? I'm sensing a theme."

"Everyone wanted the place to be filled with love," he said. "And me, too. Look at the andirons closely."

She handed him the box of cupcakes, then knelt in front of the fireplace. It took her a moment, and then she realized that there were dozens of hearts woven into the iron. All sizes, angled in different directions. Every single line in the swirls was a heart. Then she saw a D and an L intertwined on the left one, and two As on the right one. She looked up. "Our initials are in there?"

"Yep. You and me, and the girls." He set the cupcakes back on the mantle and knelt beside her. "I thought a lot about what to do when I realized you owned it. I toyed with having the fire department meet us here for a controlled burn to burn it down. Or to knock it down myself."

Leila turned to face him, touched by how much thought he'd put into it.

"But then I thought about how you taught me that working with Frank and Vivian helped hold onto more light than putting them in jail did. So, I knew you loved your mom, and your dad was a good man, so I thought maybe if we could bring love back into the house, it would make them shine brighter than what happened afterwards."

Tears filled her eyes. "Oh, *Dash*."

"But if you want to burn it down, I got that cleared as well." He took her hand and pressed his lips to her knuckle. "I know this doesn't solve everything, but it's my promise to you that you're not alone. You have me, and a whole bunch of other folks behind you. Life is a muddy, complicated mess, and then, when you least expect it, you find sunshine. You're my sunshine, Leila. Let me be yours. We can do it together."

Her heart turned over, and suddenly, she knew, for absolute certain, that he was the man, and this was the life that her heart had always wanted. It wouldn't be easy, but she was willing to stand where she was and let it heal her. "I love you, Dash Stratton."

He grinned. "I love you, my darling."

"Thank you," she whispered. "Thank you for being you, for loving me, and for caring the way you do."

He grinned. "Back at ya, sweetheart."

Her heart melted with that smile. "You know what I think I'd like to do with this house?"

"Tell me."

"I don't want to burn it down. I want to create new memories that are beautiful and wonderful."

His smile lit up his face. "I love that. I'm in. However I can help."

"Let's start right now." Then she pulled him toward her and kissed him.

He figured out the memories she had in mind immediately. Because her husband was a very clever man.

CHAPTER 29

A LITTLE OVER A WEEK LATER, Leila was in the kitchen pulling a lasagna out of the oven when she heard Gordon's familiar voice ring through the house. "Yoo hoo! Babycakes! Are you home?"

"Yes, come on back!" She set it on the hot plate, then smiled when Gordon and Otto walked into the kitchen, all smiles and joy, as they had been since the day they'd run into each other in the driveway in front of the house a month ago.

On that day, Gordon had just arrived with Leila's car, which he'd driven home from New York City after Leila had chosen to drive back to Birch Crossing with Dash and the girls. Otto had just flown in from New York to get a better look at Dash's art. He'd shown the photos to a few clients, who had been so impressed with it, especially the installations, that he'd immediately booked himself a flight to Birch Crossing to see for himself what was so special about it.

Gordon had hopped out of Leila's car in jeans and flip flops.

Otto had untangled his long legs from his black rental, and the moment he'd set his polished black loafer on the ground, the connection between the two of them had been instant.

And now the girls had two uncles, one of whom was making everyone very rich with his ability to match uppity New Yorkers with Dash's incredible artwork. He'd also taken on Emma as a client, and he'd sold two of her paintings for a tremendous amount of money as well. He'd hired Leila as a marketing consultant, and she'd already made a big difference, which felt amazing. She was opening her own business, and no one would ever be able to take it from her.

Gordon sashayed into the kitchen and wrapped Leila up in a hug. "My darling! You look radiant."

She grinned as he released her. "You're the one who looks radiant. Love agrees with you."

"Oh, it does," Gordon said. "Who knew?"

"I knew the first moment I saw you." Otto, with his pressed white shirt and black trousers was more subdued, but the happiness in his eyes was equally as touching. He raised a bottle of champagne and held up a set of gold balloons. "We came to celebrate!"

"Me, too!" Eppie marched into the kitchen, carrying a big salad. Her hat had little stuffed panda bears sewn to it, and she was wearing a panda-bear blouse that made Leila smile.

"And us!" Behind her, came Clare, with her husband and kids. She was carrying several boxes of cupcakes.

"We brought more balloons!" Chloe and Blue came in behind Clare and her family. All their little girls were with them, foster and adopted, balloons clenched in their little fists.

Next were Astrid and her family, Emma and hers, and Jackson Reed and his, and even Ophelia, who ran the café at Wright's. All the people Leila had gotten to know over the last month, helping her with baby advice, knitting lessons, and teaching her about friendship, belonging, and kindness.

Everyone had brought main dishes, dessert, drinks, and

plates, and had immediately started setting up on the kitchen island.

After a month in Birch Crossing, the spontaneous influx of people into her house didn't surprise Leila at all. She loved it. "I do love a party. What are we celebrating?"

"Thirty days," Clare said. "You guys made it thirty days!"

"We did?" She hadn't even been keeping track.

"You can sell the house," Eppie said.

"Sell it?" Leila looked around at the full kitchen. "I don't think—"

"Where's Dash?" Gordon interrupted. "We need to celebrate with him!"

"He's outside with the girls," she said. "He was giving me a break so I could make dinner."

Eppie walked over to the back of the house and looked out the window. "He's in the yard. Let's go get him."

"Yes, let's!" Gordon and Otto raced out the back door, and everyone else followed, leaving Leila standing in the kitchen alone, wondering what had just happened.

She tossed her potholders on the table and followed everyone outside. She stepped out the back door, then stopped when she saw everyone lined up on the grass, creating a pathway toward Dash's workshop. The balloons had been spread out so that there were balloons every few feet. Dash and the twins were nowhere to be seen.

She narrowed her eyes suspiciously. "What's going on?"

"Dash must have gone into his workshop," Eppie said brightly. "You should go get him."

"Should I?" Leila looked around at everyone, a smile quirking her lips. She loved all these people so much. "What are you guys up to?"

"Just go find Dash!" Eppie said. "Go, go, go!"

Leila grinned as she headed down the pathway they'd made, but she couldn't help but roll her eyes. They might be up to something, but there was so much laughter and giggling that she found herself laughing as well. "You guys are crazy."

"Of course," Eppie said. "That's life in Birch Crossing!"

"That it is." Still smiling, Leila grabbed the door of Dash's workshop, pulled it open, and stepped inside, then her heart turned over.

There was a white runner carpet down the middle of his studio, covered in white and red rose petals. And the end of the runner, Dash standing in his shorts and flipflops, looking ridiculously handsome. On either side of him stood Frank and Vivian, each holding one of the girls.

Leila's heart started racing. "What are you doing, Dash?"

He grinned. "Why don't you walk down here and find out?"

Behind her, the rest of their visitors snuck inside, giggling and laughing, and whispering.

Leila grinned and walked down the soft carpet to Dash, her bare feet sinking onto the whisper-soft rose petals. Dash's art was pushed to the side, but a few of the pieces had been set along the sides of the carpet, guiding her way.

She walked up to him, laughing at the smile on his face as she kissed each of the twins. "What's the big grin for?" she asked Dash.

"It's been thirty days."

"Yes, I've been informed of that." She cocked her head. "Were you keeping track?"

"I was." He took her hand. "Leila, thirty days ago, we told each other we loved each other for the first time, even though we were married so long ago. I told you I wanted forever, and I asked you to think about it."

Her heart warmed. There was so much love in his eyes, it would have made any woman melt. But his love was for her, only for her, and it was incredible. "I remember that." She smiled. "You know how I feel, Dash. I'm not going anywhere."

"I know that." He winked at her, then, to her surprise, he went down on one knee.

She put her hand over her mouth in surprise. "Oh, Dash."

He winked at her, that silly little wink he did that always made her want to laugh. "Leila, when I married you a zillion years ago, I had no idea how completely I would fall in love with you. I didn't know that I was going to want nothing more in my life than to build a family with you, starting with the two little gremlins who are keeping us up at night."

Her throat tightened, and tears started to fill her eyes.

"As it turns out, you're the woman I was always meant to marry, love, and build a glorious life with. I'm sorry that we missed out on fifteen years, but I'm excited to start now."

She smiled. "Me, too."

"Last time, deciding to get married at the kitchen table with you, Bea, and Maura plotting like thieves was perfect, but that's not perfect for now." He reached into his pocket, and pulled out a beautiful diamond ring. "Leila Kerrigan, will you be my wife, for real, in every sense of the word? Raise these little darlings together, worry about them, make them into badass powerful women who will take care of us and the world when we get old?"

She started laughing, joy bubbling up inside her. "Yes, of course I will. I can't wait."

"Wahoo!" The place erupted into cheers.

Dash's face lit up, and he slipped the ring on her finger. Then he bounded to his feet, swept her up in his arms, and spun her around in a circle. "I love you, Leila. We're going to rock this life together."

She locked her arms around his neck. "We definitely are. Even when we stumble."

"Even when we stumble," he agreed.

He leaned in and kissed her while their little group of friends cheered. She knew why he'd invited everyone. He'd wanted her to remember that she wasn't just marrying him.

She had a whole posse of family and friends who would fill her life with love, laughter, and chaos.

Exactly what she'd always wanted...even if it had taken her fifteen years to realize it.

Home was home, no matter what the path was to get there.

————

IF YOU'RE **new to Birch Crossing** and want to start at the beginning, grab *Unexpectedly Mine* today!

If you want more small-town, emotional feel-good romances like the *Birch Crossing,* you'd love my small-town cowboy series, too! ***Wyoming Rebels* series about nine cowboy brothers** who find love in the most romantic, most heartwarming, most sigh-worthy ways you can imagine. Get started with *A Real Cowboy Never Says No* right now. You will be sooo glad you did, I promise!

***Hart Ranch Billionaires* is a series about found family, loyalty, and cowboys,** with a dash of suspense thrown in. The newest book,*A Rogue Cowboy Finds Love,* just came out (skip ahead for a sneak peek), but you can get started with the first book, *A Rogue Cowboy's Second Chance.*

Are you in the mood for some feel-good, cozy mystery fun that's chock full of murder, mayhem, and women you'll wish were your best friends? If so, you'll fall in love with *Double Twist,* or read a sneak peek of the newest mystery, *Gone Rogue* by skipping ahead to a sneak peek.

Are you a fan of magic, love, and laughter? If so, dive into my paranormal romantic comedy *Immortally Sexy* series, starting with the first book, *To Date an Immortal.*

Is dark, steamy paranormal romance your jam? If so, definitely try my award-winning *Order of the Blade* series, starting with book one, *Darkness Awakened.*

• • •

FOR INFO on Stephanie's newest releases, join her newsletter today!

Sign me up for Stephanie's Newsletter

KEEP SCROLLING for sneak peeks of three Stephanie Rowe books! You might find your next binge-read right here!

SNEAK PEEK: A ROGUE COWBOY FINDS LOVE

★★★★★ "The story just had it all. Sooo much suspense, such great characters, and so many touching moments."
Goodreads Review (Riding Reviewer)

To protect her daughter, a single mom must hide out at the ranch of Jacob Hart, a reclusive loner who doesn't like people, chaos, or anyone in his space. What better place for a single mom, her sassy six-year-old, and their rambunctious puppy to spend a few days? Healing, hearts, horses, and smexy times abound!

———

Jacob Hart needed to get away.

From people.

From his memories.

From noise.

Anger coiling through him, Jacob urged his horse faster, allowing the rescued gelding to unleash the monster that haunted him. Together, they raced across the barren terrain, both of them breathing hard as they sought the elusive peace that they could never find.

Farther and faster they went, carving their way across the massive Hart Ranch, heading toward the most distant corner where no one else ever went, where everyone knew to stay away.

Toward the remote hideaway where Jacob had chosen to build his home.

The massive pitch-black gelding galloped hard and free, a magnificent beast who hadn't been able to walk when Jacob had broken into that shack and pried him free of the life that had tried to claim him.

And now. Galloping fast. Free. The ultimate rescue success.

And yet all the shadows still clung to the horse's cells, his skin, his soul.

Just like Jacob.

He clenched his jaw, focusing on the wind whipping at his cheeks, knifing the front of his neck where his jacket had flapped open, but it was never enough to change his moment, his existence in this world that he couldn't embrace.

Ahead of them, Jacob's cabin loomed, with the luxurious attached barn that he'd designed and built for the horses he claimed, his own private rescue for the most damaged, the ones no one else could help.

His mount, who he'd named Freedom, eased off the

frantic gallop as their home came into sight. Freedom, who would never be sent away from this new home Jacob had given him. Freedom, who didn't yet trust that he could put down roots and breathe deeply of the oasis he lived in.

Just like Jacob.

Freedom slowed to a jog, his breath like white bursts of angel breath in the cold, high desert early morning air of eastern Oregon. Jacob settled back in the saddle as he ran his hand along Freedom's shoulder. His hands were like ice, in need of the gloves he hadn't bothered to put on when he'd bolted from the house, desperate to get out and away from the noise that sometimes closed in on him when he was alone.

The only time it quieted was when he was with his family, his brothers and sisters, Harts by choice and not by blood, but even that relief only lasted for so long.

Especially after the news he'd just gotten.

Jacob needed to be in a place where conversation didn't need to happen, where meals could be taken with nothing but the sunset and the fresh air around him, where he didn't have to pretend he understood how to be social.

Not that the Harts asked him to be what he wasn't. They understood. They accepted. They loved him.

But still, he'd had to build his house at the far end of their massive ranch. Small. A fraction of the size of the others. Two bedrooms. One bathroom. An open living space. Sparse. No clutter. Just an oasis to breathe, to stabilize, to be alone.

His sanctuary was needed even more, now that two of his brothers had found partners, one of whom had a sixteen-year-old daughter. He loved both women, and the kid, but their presence at family events shifted the dynamic in a way he struggled with.

He pulled a remote out of his pocket. With the push of a button, the huge barn door began to slide open, and he rode Freedom straight into the entry of the barn. He paused the gelding in the foyer, waiting as the door closed behind him.

The moment it shut out the cold air, the interior door opened, welcoming them. The motor was silent as the doors moved, cutting-edge technology that he improved and modified regularly.

Three of the four horses he currently had looked over their stall doors in greeting as he reined Freedom to a stop, the gelding's hooves silent on the state-of-the-art shock-absorbing mats that covered every inch of flooring for his horses. The fourth was a pony, too small to see over the door, but Jacob was going to fix that in the morning.

Every animal needed the freedom of being able to connect with the others, and the pony was no exception.

The air was fresh and clean, the barn sparkling with the best of everything for his animals. Literally everything. Organic food that he contracted out to be hand-mixed and delivered twice a week. Hay that he had privately grown in nearby fields, devoid of any toxic chemicals, stored in the most pristine conditions.

He breathed deeply into the silence, into the soft snorts of welcome, into the peaceful presence of living creatures that gave him companionship, but demanded nothing of him.

"Only the best for you guys," he told Freedom as he uncinched the girth to remove the saddle.

Did having only the best chase away their demons? He did all he could for them, for the fragile creatures who needed him.

Talking quietly to the horses, he stripped down Freedom and went to work brushing him, cleansing the dirt and cold and sweat they'd churned up. Freedom relaxed under the grooming, his back foot cocked and his head down, embracing the attention.

Jacob smiled, remembering how Freedom had been terrified of any physical contact when he'd first arrived. "I remember what that was like," he said. "It's a tough lesson to unlearn, isn't it?"

Freedom swung his head around and snuffled at Jacob's back pocket. He laughed softly. "I already gave you all the treats I have." He moved his hand slowly so as not to startle Freedom, and the horse didn't flinch as Jacob rubbed his ears. "They say time heals all wounds. You think that's true? That wholeness is possible?"

Freedom pressed his head against Jacob's side and sighed, his ribs expanding with the deep breath of contentment.

"I'll take that as a yes." The horses gave him hope.

Without hope, he had nothing.

With hope, he had a reason to get up every day, take care of his horses, and play with technology. Because maybe this time, something new would happen. Something would change. Inside him. Outside him. Whatever it took.

His phone rang, and he looked over at the feed room where he'd left it.

He didn't take it with him most of the time, because he didn't want to be found. Didn't want to have to talk when he didn't want to talk. He never let a call from his family go unanswered, but if he didn't have his phone, he didn't have to answer.

The ringtone echoing through the barn was the one he used for his family, which meant he had to answer.

He gave Freedom a little pat. "I'll be right back."

He kept his eye on the horse as he walked across the barn. He never cross-tied his horses, because he didn't want them to feel trapped. He asked them to stay for him, and they did.

The phone went into voicemail before he reached it, but he saw from the screen that it was his brother Dylan. He immediately called him back, because his connection with his family was something so ingrained in him that he never blocked them.

Dylan answered on the first ring. "You have to start taking your phone with you on rides."

Jacob smiled and sauntered back across the floor. "Nothing is ever that urgent."

"Except now."

Jacob's smile dropped off his face at the tension in his brother's voice. *Son of a bitch.* He gripped the phone with sudden alarm. "What's wrong? Who's hurt? Who's in trouble? I'm on my way. Tell me where." He started running toward the door, panic hammering in his chest, terror that his little family, his precious world, had been shattered.

"Stop." Dylan's voice was calmer now, but Jacob could feel he was concealing his urgency. "No one in the family. Everyone is fine. I need your help with something else."

"Fuck." Jacob stopped and leaned over, bracing his hands on his knees, fighting to keep his composure as the relief swarmed him. "Don't do that to me."

"Shit. Sorry. I wasn't thinking. Look, I've got a situation."

Freedom walked over and blew in Jacob's ear. Jacob wrapped his arm around the horse's head and closed his eyes. "What kind of situation?"

"You know Eliana, right?"

Jacob nodded. "The woman you're in love with but will never make a move on because you're afraid you'll lose her friendship forever, and your platonic friendship is better than losing her? That Eliana?"

"Funny guy," Dylan said. "We're just friends."

"You know you'll never get her unless you tell her that you love her."

"Dating advice coming from the guy who hasn't gone on a date in years?"

"Yep." Jacob rose to his feet, then set his hand on Freedom's neck to guide him toward his stall. "What's going on?"

"You know how she helps women escape from abusive situations and then disappear?"

"I do." Eliana was an absolute badass. Jacob had the highest respect for her. She understood the edge that ate away at Jacob, and most of his siblings, because she spent much of her time in the same marshy world. That connection helped Jacob be comfortable around her. She'd be perfect for Dylan, if the two of them ever got out of their own way. "What's up?"

"She didn't give me the details—"

"She never does."

Dylan ignored his comment. "She has a woman and a young girl living not too far from our ranch, but some guy just got out of prison. She's worried that he's going to go after them. She needs them off the radar until she can be sure they're safe."

"You need to borrow my truck?" Dylan owned a private detective firm, and he often helped out Eliana with her clients.

"No, I'm out of the country right now. I need you to go get them and bring them to your house."

Silence reigned.

"Jacob?"

"Did you just say you want me to go get a woman and a child and bring them to my house and have them stay here? With me?"

"Yes."

"Here? Bring them *here*? For how long?"

"A few days? A week? I don't know. Eliana didn't tell me."

"I can't have them in my house."

"You can."

Jacob shut Freedom's door. "You need to know that I got a call that my dad got out of prison yesterday."

Dylan let out his breath. "You okay?"

"Yeah."

"Heard from him?"

"No." Not that he would answer if his dad did reach out. "I'm sure he has no idea that his son is the billionaire rancher Jacob Hart. He'd never expect I could have been that guy."

"And if he did, he has no power over you anymore."

"I know." But the release of his dad from prison brought back memories that Jacob had thought no longer controlled him. "So, yeah, not the best time for me to take on a woman and a kid."

"Crises never ask ahead to make sure the timing is good. I need you to do this."

Jacob swore. "Did you call the wrong brother? I'm not the guy who takes in women and kids."

"You're the guy who takes in horses."

"Hell, Dylan—"

"I've known you for almost twenty years. I know exactly who you are and how difficult this will be for you. So you know that if I'm asking, I don't have a better option right now."

Jacob leaned against the stall door and closed his eyes. "Fuck."

"Bring a gun."

His eyes opened. "A gun?"

"If this guy finds them, he's likely to try to kill them. So, yeah, a gun. He got out of prison an hour ago, and Eliana has already lost track of him. None of her contacts can find him, so he could be on his way right now. Apparently, he has money and connections."

Memories flashed though Jacob's mind, galvanizing him. He strode over to the cabinet, let it scan his face, then the door swung open for him. He reached inside and pulled out his gun. Then a second one. "Where are they?"

"The town of Blackthorn. It's about an hour away."

"I'll be on my way in two minutes. Text me the address and any info I need."

"Will do. And one more thing..."

Jacob was already running for the door, setting the alarm for the barn on his phone as he ran. "What?"

"This woman uses her phone about as much as you do. Eliana hasn't been able to reach her yet to tell her what's going on. So, when you show up, she might not know why you're there, or that you're a good guy."

Jacob burst outside into the cold night, his boots thudding on the frozen gravel as he ran for the garage where he kept his truck. "So, I'm supposed to sweet talk a woman and kid?"

"Pretend they're horses. You'll do great. And, Jacob?"

Jacob ducked under the garage door as it opened and leapt into his truck, which he'd remote-started already. "What?"

"Thanks."

Jacob put his truck in reverse. "No little girl dies on my watch. Not ever again."

Then he hung up and hit the gas.

One-click now to get started!

SNEAK PEEK: GONE ROGUE

A MIA MURPHY MYSTERY

"**So much darn fun!**" Five-star Goodreads Review (Penny)

CHAPTER ONE

My phone rang just as I hopped out of Turbojet, my well-used, antique pickup truck I'd acquired along with my new business, the Eagle's Nest Marina. I saw the call was one of my new besties, Hattie Lawless, so I answered. "What's up?"

"Mia. It's been ten days since we've had to deal with a corpse. Are you getting as bored as I am?"

Alarm shot through me, and I hung up on her.

Hattie was a seventy-something race car driver who owned and operated a café in my marina. She was sassy, irreverent, and an unstoppable force, which I greatly admired. Except when it got me almost killed. Which seemed to happen a little bit too often.

She called again, and I almost didn't answer. But what if Hattie was in trouble? I couldn't take the chance. "What?"

"No one has tried to kill you in ten days either. You have to ditch your new bodyguard. I think he's repelling fun."

I hung up on her again. Hattie was like a siren. The entire world seemed to want to bend to her will, not because she tried to control it, but because it *wanted* to be her friend. If Hattie invited murderers into our lives, they would probably come.

Not that I was superstitious, but Hattie was…Hattie.

My phone rang before I managed to get it back in my pocket. I answered it as I wandered away from Turbojet and headed toward the Bass Derby town green, which was teeming with people, music, tents, and small-town festivities. "Hattie. I love you. I don't love murderers."

"Yes you do. If you didn't, you wouldn't have gone undercover for the FBI against your drug lord ex for two years."

That had not been an entirely voluntary situation for me. "They made me."

"Hey! Don't give away your power by lying to yourself like that! No one makes you do anything. You wanted to because you crave excitement, my thieving friend."

I smiled at the affection in her voice. I'd been so scared that she and Lucy Grande, my two favorite people in the world, would reject me when they found out about my criminal childhood, but my pickpocketing past had been a great hit with both of them. "I just arrived. Where's your tent?"

"Pink and white striped tent at the near end of the first aisle. Best spot of the festival. You can't miss it."

"Of course you got the best spot."

"Always," she agreed cheerfully. "The world is my playground."

Up ahead, I saw the awning in question. "I see you. Coming over."

"Awesome. Ditch Ivan in the crowds, though. Seriously."

I glanced behind me at the six-foot-four jacked-up, federal agent-type suit-wearer who had been shadowing me for the last ten days, shooting looks of "I will take you down if you mess with Mia" to anyone who came close to me. I smiled at him, but he ignored me. Ivan didn't mess around, which was a great trait in a bodyguard. "I'm not ditching Ivan. You'd be so sad if I was assassinated."

"Would I, though? That's such a complex, loaded issue."

I laughed. "Bye. I'll see you in a sec." I hung up as I merged with the crowds streaming onto the grass. Tonight was the opening night of the three-day Bass Derby Strawberry Festival, an annual event that drew people from all over the state to celebrate, culminating in the crowning of the Strawberry Shortcake Bake-Off Champion on Sunday afternoon.

How adorably small-town was that?

I was so excited. The crowds were boisterous. The tents were so cute, local vendors selling crafts, artwork, pottery, candles, pizza, sandwiches and everything else that one could create. There was a big contest tent for the competitors. Tonight was round one, the strawberry contest, where contestants would present home-grown strawberries for judging. Saturday was the biscuit contest. And Sunday was the Strawberry Shortcake Bake-Off, which was the biggie. Plus, there was a palooza of other events planned for the weekend as well.

A band was playing on the gazebo, and the local baton-twirling team was performing routines. Pickup trucks lined the parking lot, and people were tailgating with barbeques and beer. The mid-June night was warm, the evening sun casting glorious light across the water, and the adjacent town beach was full of kids and families playing in the water.

It filled my soul with all the warmth and belonging that I'd wanted my whole life.

This was why I'd turned down witness protection and moved to Bass Derby.

This was why I'd bought the run-down Eagle's Nest Marina, so that I could be here, becoming a part of a community for the first time in my life, rehabbing the marina to make it my dream.

I'd even managed to grab a last-minute volunteer spot. I was part of the team patrolling the contest tent to make sure that all the competitors had what they needed. My shift started in ten minutes, and I was so pumped. I was proudly wearing my volunteer badge, and I was pretty much giddy with excitement.

I jogged over to Hattie's tent, breathing in the scent of the fresh bread Hattie was so magical at creating. She was behind a well-stocked table, and there was a line twenty-people long already. "Hey, girl. How's it going?"

"Swamped," Hattie said cheerfully. "Niko and Cris are away at some football camp this weekend, so I'm on my own."

Nico and Cris Stefanopoulos were Greek brothers who worked in her café. They were both headed to college on scholarships, and their grandma, Angelina Stefanopoulos was raising them. As a staff member at the police station, she'd been helpful to us on more than one occasion.

Today, Hattie was sporting fuchsia hair, to match her Hattie's Café T-shirt. I didn't know many seventy-somethings who could carry off fuchsia hair, but Hattie definitely could. "Jump in and help. I'll give you free food."

Hattie never gave away anything for free, so the offer was tempting. But… "My shift starts in ten minutes."

"How long is your shift?"

"Two hours."

She shook her head. "No, that won't work. I need help now. Ditch your shift."

I blinked. "I can't. I promised I'd do it—"

Hattie leaned on the table. "I need you. I thought we were friends."

"We are friends." I would never turn down a request from Hattie, but I'd been excited at the chance to volunteer, as if I actually belonged to the community. "Hattie, I—"

"Hey!" A low voice barked out the single word.

We both turned to see three twenty-something gang member-ish dudes striding across the grass toward us, wearing heavy motorcycle boots, leather jackets, gold chains, with possible gun bulges in their jackets, and enough swagger to trigger a tidal wave in Diamond Lake.

A path had cleared, and people's jaws were open in stunned shock, clutching their babies and dogs as if the trio was there to mass murder everyone. The approaching trio was so out of place that I could practically feel the earth shifting to expel them.

The woman at the front of the line hugged her loaf of Hattie's rosemary focaccia bread to her chest. "Are they coming here? They look like they're heading here. They're not getting my bread."

As she spoke, the trio strode right up to the table and stopped, arms folded, jaws jutted out, shoulders back. Every line of their bodies said that they expected to be thrown out.

I'd spent most of my first seventeen years with that stance.

They did not tackle anyone for their bread, babies, or dogs. Instead, they focused entirely on Hattie. The tallest one spoke first. "You owe us. We're here to collect."

A woman behind me made a noise like she was slowly dying, and I heard someone whisper to find Chief Stone. I heard someone else say something about me being a drug dealer, which hurt my innocent little heart just a bit.

Hattie set her hands on her hips. "Mia? Do I owe these guys?"

I'd been with her when we'd met them a couple weeks ago. I knew what she was doing, but at the same time, I felt for these guys, because that had been me. They wouldn't interpret her response the way she meant it. I knew that, because I'd been them. "Um, guys? Vinnie?"

The tallest one looked over at me, then his brows went up. "I remember you."

More people started whispering, which bothered me a little bit. Honestly, life was so much more complicated when you cared what people thought, when you were trying to put down roots. "Hattie, for heaven's sake, stop being difficult. Vinnie, you, too. You're like two alpha dogs who want to pee on each other."

Both Hattie and the guys looked at me. "You're calling me a dog?" Hattie said.

"I am. An alpha dog, though. Top of the heap."

"A Cane Corso? I'd like to be a Cane Corso."

Of course she would choose to be a one-hundred-and-fifty-pound guard dog. "Sure."

"You're calling *me* a dog?" Vinnie didn't look as thrilled with the news as Hattie had been.

"Yes. I am." I put my hands on my hips. "Vinnie, Hattie promised you a free sandwich at her café in exchange for the favor you did. Instead, you chose to show up at the strawberry festival and try to scare everyone. But Hattie's the alpha dog, and she has to prove it by not feeding you here, since she's not at her café. So, she's going to say no to the sandwich, and then you're going to get all mad and think that no one is trustworthy. But that's a bunch of crap, because Hattie's completely loyal and amazing. We all know you're not a jerk, because you saved our lives and hers. So give it up. You two are both cute little puppies who need to go romp on the beach together instead of peeing on each other."

Everyone stared at me.

I smiled. "But Hattie needs help at the booth right now and she offered me free food to help her, so maybe you guys can make a trade."

Vinnie's eyes widened. "Work here?" He looked around, and we all did. I could see that he didn't believe Hattie would let him get behind her table, handle her food, work with customers, and take their money.

But he didn't know Hattie like I did.

Sure enough, Hattie's face lit up. She liked to nurture people with potential, and these guys were no exception. She knew goodness when she saw it, and she didn't give a hoot what anyone else thought. So what if Vinnie probably liked to steal cars in his spare time? He had a good heart buried under that gang activity, so that was all that mattered to Hattie. "Yes!" she exclaimed. "Great idea! Vinnie, get your team back here. Let's do this! One free sandwich for every hour you work the booth."

Vinnie stared at her. "You're serious?"

"I never joke about food."

Vinnie went silent, then looked at his friends. They both shook their heads and headed back down the aisle toward the parking lot. But Vinnie shrugged off his leather jacket, revealing massive, tattooed biceps that set the whispers going again. "I'm in."

Two minutes later, Vinnie and his muscles were wearing a fuchsia Hattie's Café T-shirt that was a little too tight, a matching visor, and he was holding a credit card reader and taking money.

Hattie grabbed a muffin and handed it to me without a word.

Her way of thanks. Lucy and I owed Vinnie our lives, and Hattie was as happy as I was to offer more than a sandwich to him.

I winked at her and swiped a cookie, feeling all sorts of warm fuzzies in my heart. I was so happy to be in a position to offer belonging to someone who was an outsider, after a lifetime of being the one on the outside.

If I had tried to hire Vinnie, my marina would have paid the price in lost business. But Hattie had the power to do whatever she wanted in Bass Derby, and she'd just given Vinnie her stamp of approval.

It felt good to be a part of that.

"Mia! Hattie!"

We both turned as the third part of our trio of awesomeness, Lucy Grande, ran toward us, ducking around people. It took me only a split second to register her tension and to realize she was running hard. Alarm shot through me as she reached us. "What's up?"

"It's Rogue!"

I glanced at Hattie. "Rogue? What's wrong with Rogue?" Rogue, whose real name was Esther Neeley, was about Hattie's age. She was obscenely rich and not afraid of owning it. She was sassy, irreverent, and a member of the Seam Rippers, a local quilting group who loved margaritas, loyalty, and adventure. I adored Rogue, and she'd helped save my life ten days ago. Different situation than when Vinnie had stepped in, but equally as helpful.

"The strawberry judging starts in a half hour, and Rogue's not there. Her table's not set up. I've looked everywhere for her, and no one has seen her." Lucy looked worried. "I tried to call her, and her phone went right into voicemail."

"She should have been set up hours ago." Hattie swore. "We need to check her house. Something's clearly wrong."

Their worry was contagious. "What are you guys talking about? What table?"

"I'll drive," Hattie said. "Vinnie. You're in charge. The reputation of Hattie's Café is on your shoulders. If you blow it, I will hunt you down, and you won't like it one bit."

The gun-wielding gang leader's eyes widened, and he looked slightly alarmed. "Run your tent?"

"Yes, I'll be back soon." Hattie grabbed her keys from a corner of the tent. "Let's go!" She broke into a run, and Lucy ran after her.

They took off so fast that I had to sprint not to lose them in the crowd. They were both fitter than I was, but ten days of working out with Rogue had helped me enough that I still had them in sight when Hattie leapt into her massive, jacked-up pickup truck.

Lucy jumped into the back seat, and I grabbed hold of the passenger door and hauled myself in as Hattie hit the gas. "What is going on?" I panted as I dragged the door shut just in time to avoid taking out a telephone pole.

"Rogue has won the Strawberry Shortcake Bake-Off four times," Hattie said as she peeled out onto the main road. "The festival charter states that the championship trophy will be named after the first person to win it five-times."

"She's been entering for years, and she finally won her fourth time last year. There are four others who have also won four times," Lucy said. "Rogue wants that trophy named after her, and she's been planning for this year's festival for the last twelve-months."

"One of the four-time champions is probably going to win this year," Hattie said, the tires squealing as she peeled around the corner. "Rogue needs it to be her."

"Why?"

Hattie glanced at me. "She used to enter with her daughter long ago. It has personal meaning for her. There's no way she'd miss out on the Strawberry Contest."

"Doing well in the first two rounds can help break a tie in the finals," Lucy explained. "Today matters."

"Rogue was planning to get there at six this morning to set up her table," Hattie added. "Presentation makes a difference."

"But her table is empty. Nothing on it at all," Lucy said. "Judging starts at seven."

I glanced at Hattie's dashboard and saw it was six thirty-three. Much like Hattie, Rogue was an unapologetic, unstoppable force, but she had the added benefit of endless financial resources. If she wanted to win that contest, nothing would have kept her from being at that table. "You don't think she changed her mind?"

"No." Hattie swung the truck into the long, white-stone driveway that snaked almost a half mile through Rogue's lake-front property. "No chance."

I pulled out my cell and texted Bootsy Jones, the only other Seam Ripper I had in my phone. *Rogue's missing. Have you heard from her?*

What? No. I'll ask around. I'm at the Festival. I'll look around here.

Great. We're at her house. I set my phone down as Hattie screeched to a stop by the front door.

Rogue's cherry red Lamborghini SUV was parked out front, with the tailgate wide open.

I was the first one out of the truck. "Rogue!"

There was no answer, but the back of Rogue's SUV was loaded with gorgeous strawberries, along with other crates containing what appeared to be table decor. I could see champagne, a velvet table covering, but no Rogue.

Hattie came up behind me. "She told me she was packing her car at five-thirty this morning."

Fear trickled down my spine. "That was thirteen hours ago."

The strawberry crates were neatly arranged, ready for transport that had never happened. The berries were a gorgeous vibrant red, plump, flawless perfection. "The strawberries look really good. Does she grow them herself?"

"Actually yes. She doesn't even let her gardener touch them. They're the best around."

Lucy was at the front door. "No one's answering." She peered through the window beside the door, then swore. "You guys! The furniture inside is knocked over. It looks like someone tore the place apart."

We all looked at each other, and then suddenly, I realized that Ivan, my bodyguard wasn't with us. "We lost Ivan."

"Well, I think that tells you a lot about how useful he'd be in an emergency, right? Because right now, I feel like there's something going on that he might be needed for."

"I agree," Lucy said. "This scene is giving me the creeps. It's like Rogue was plucked right out of her life mid-stride."

A shiver went down my spine, so I immediately cleared my throat and stood taller. Fear was never allowed to win. "It's fine. Whatever it is, we can handle it."

"Damn straight we can." Hattie pushed me toward the house. "Go unlock the door, Mia. See what's going on."

"Unlock it? I mean, yeah, I love a chance to pick locks, but shouldn't we call the police?"

Hattie put her hands on her hips. "How well did that work for us recently? Involving the police in a dicey situation?"

"That was murder!" I stared at them, horror congealing in my stomach. "You don't think—"

"Well, open the door and find out."

With the exception of Griselda, my FBI handler, I didn't trust cops to believe in my innocence. Well, if Devlin Hunt was in town, I might have texted him. But he'd been called away right after he asked me out on a date, and I hadn't heard from him since. The only one we could call was Chief Stone. The fact he was Lucy's cousin didn't mean we could trust him to do what was right and handle the situation correctly.

Quite the opposite.

Which meant if we cared about Rogue, it had to be us.

I grimaced, but pulled out my lock picks, which I now carried with me more often, because life in Bass Derby was turning out to be like that. "Make sure no one shoots us."

"They'd shoot only you. *We* don't have assassins after us," Hattie said, but she took up position next to me, facing out.

Lucy did the same as I went down on my knee and got to work.

I was sure that Rogue had an alarm, but there was no sound as the lock clicked a minute later. I pushed the door open. "Hello? Is anyone there?"

Silence.

I stood up and took a step inside. "Rogue?" My voice faded as I took in the carnage. Her house usually was in pristine condition, gorgeous, designed to emulate cozy, Maine warmth with expensive perfection. But right now, chairs were upturned. Pictures and books strewn on the floor. The rugs askew.

"Go in and check it out," Hattie said. "I'll stand guard out here."

I looked back at her. "Why me?"

She smiled and waved me inside. "You're the FBI special agent. Do your thing."

"I'm not an FBI special agent—"

"Closer than I am. Go, go."

I looked at Lucy, and she picked up a small pot of geraniums and hefted it. "I'll come with you. I'm good at throwing things."

"All right, then. Let's do this." Wishing I had my hairdryer, which I'd recently discovered was very useful as a weapon, I led the way into the front hall. I looked around and saw that the family room was open to the kitchen. "That way." I pointed, my instincts drawing me toward the kitchen.

"Okay." Lucy stayed close to me, her pot ready.

As I walked past an upturned table, I grabbed the lamp off the floor and wrapped the cord around my hand, swinging the lamp gently. It wasn't as maneuverable as a hairdryer, but all corded projectiles were pretty much in my wheelhouse these days.

We stepped into the kitchen and looked around.

"Nothing in here looks like it was touched," Lucy said. "Let's go—"

"No." I knew from my own childhood training sessions with my mom that sometimes the best distraction was in plain sight. "The front hall is a mess, so maybe someone doesn't want us to notice something in here."

"Oh...right...I forgot about that. I gotta work on my criminal mind."

We both looked around, and this time, I saw a note on the center island, with messy handwriting scrawled across the paper. I walked over and peered at it. The message was short and to the point. "I didn't do it," I read aloud.

Lucy looked over. "Who didn't do what?"

"Rogue, I'm guessing. But what didn't she do? Trash her house?" I looked around, and I saw that the pantry door was open at the back of the kitchen. Instinct made my heart start to pound. "In there."

Gripping my lamp more tightly, I forced myself to walk across the kitchen. "If Rogue jumps out of there to scare us, I'm pretty sure I'm going to have a heart attack."

"You and me, both." Lucy edged up close behind me, which I greatly appreciated—

My gaze dropped to the threshold, and fear crept down my belly when I saw something peeking out from the pantry. Limp. Lifeless. Adorned with very high heels. "Are those *feet*?"

"What? Where?" Lucy looked down. "Oh, God. *Yes.*"

We lunged for the door and yanked it open. Sprawled on the ground facedown was a fifty-something woman with raven black hair, gorgeous shoes, and a bunch of strawberries scattered around her.

"Oh, God." I dropped to my knees beside her, but the moment I touched her, I knew.

She was dead.

———

Want more *Gone Rogue*? Go *here* to get it now!

SNEAK PEEK: BURN

"A fast-paced, heart-racing, mind-boggling, sexy read...and I loved it!!!"
~NanaX8 (Five-star Amazon review)

Don't miss this sizzling romantic suspense in which a serial arsonist targets the biological family he found through an online DNA test. In this high-stakes cat-and-mouse game set in the unforgiving Alaskan terrain, a reclusive ex-military tech expert must protect a spunky, sexy tavern hostess from the killer who has already wiped out the rest of her family.

"A M A Z I N G...A fast-paced adventure all wrapped up in scorching hot romance. This entire series is a must-read!"
~Christa S. (Five-star Amazon Review)

———

MACK CONNOR HAD BEEN IN ALASKA for less than an hour, and he was already restless. He wanted to be back in Boston, but when Ben Forsett asked for his help, he got it.

Always.

Every single time.

No matter what.

It had been that way since they were kids, both of them trying to survive the streets, the drugs, and the gangs long enough to get the fuck out of the hell they'd grown up in. Ben had gone to college and law school. Mack had gone into the military and become one of the world's renowned experts on security tech, and all the shit that went with that.

Their connection had never faltered, even when life had blown up around them. Ben was the only friend Mack counted, and the only one he needed.

They always leaned on each other when the shit got real. Always. Until last month when Mack had uncovered a living hell...

"You okay?" Ben looked over at him, his brow furrowed.

Mack cleared his throat and looked out the window at the trees rushing past. So many damn trees. "Yeah. Fine."

"What happened last month?"

Mack shot a sharp glance at Ben. "Nothing."

"Bullshit. Something fucked you up. What was it?"

For a split second, Mack was tempted to tell Ben the truth, to rip the darkness out of him and throw it onto his friend.

But just as quickly, he shoved it back down inside him, deep and hard, where it couldn't see the light of day.

"Nothing." He wasn't going there. He just fucking wasn't.

He hadn't told Ben about it then, and he wasn't going to tell him now.

Darkness settled in him, and he growled as he dragged his thoughts away from the nightmare that had jerked him awake every single night for the last month. "How about you?" Ben had been through hellacious year.

Ben hesitated, and Mack saw the moment that he decided not to push Mack for more answers. "Better. Mari helps. A lot."

Mack nodded. "Good." He was glad Ben had found someone who fit him. "I can't believe you proposed to her."

Ben smiled, a legit grin that lit up his face. "She changed my world, bro. She's a gift."

A sliver of envy flickered through Mack at the happiness on his friend's face. He'd never seen him like that before. It hadn't even occurred to him that either of them would ever feel that, that it could be a part of their lives. "Damn, man," he said softly. "I'm almost jealous of that stupid grin."

Ben's smile faded into seriousness. "I'm staying in Alaska. I've found peace here."

"Not coming back to Boston?" Mack felt darkness settle in him again. He and Ben had both been in Boston for the last few years, and it had settled him to have Ben around again. Having him move to Alaska? *Shit.* But he grinned at his friend anyway. "Good for you." He meant it, too.

Ben cocked an eyebrow at him. "You might like it here, too. It's an amazing place."

Mack snorted and jerked his thumb at mountains in the distance. "Where are my skyscrapers? No fucking way."

"That's what I thought, too. Things change."

"Not for me." Mack shifted, suddenly restless to get back to topics he felt comfortable with.

They'd spent the first part of the drive from the airport going over the serial killer he'd helped Ben track a few weeks ago, and now it was time to focus on the present.

"Talk to me," he said. "What do you need me for?" He knew it must be bad for Ben to ask him to fly to Alaska for it. The fact Ben had refused to give any details over the phone about why he needed him had jacked up his adrenaline even more.

Ben glanced over at him as his truck bounced over the rutted dirt road. "Mari's friend. Charlotte."

Charlotte. Mack liked the name. He wasn't sure why. It was soft and strong at the same time. He knew nothing about soft, and he didn't particularly want to, but her name seemed to settle in him whenever he heard it.

"The one who got kidnapped." He'd tracked her phone for Ben to help find her. "She doing okay?"

Ben inclined his head. "Sort of."

Mack narrowed his eyes, studying Ben. "You brought me here for her?"

At Ben's nod, Mack settled into the familiarity of business mode. "What's she into?" He unzipped his backpack and pulled out his computer. It booted up instantly, and he created a file with her name. "Her last name is Murphy, right?"

"Yep." Ben rattled off her address, and Mack entered it into the computer.

"What else?"

"That's it."

Mack looked up. "What do you mean, that's it? What's going on with her?"

"I don't know." Ben took a right, the truck lurching over a big rut in the dirt. "It's something though. Something from her past."

Mack frowned. "A person? A man? Something someone else did? Something she did?" The last question stopped him hard. He knew all about someone who had done something bad, something that came back to haunt him. He was not getting involved with someone who had done bad shit. Not again. He cast a suspicious look at Ben. "How well do you know her?"

"Not well, but she's good. She's been Mari's friend since the day she arrived in town."

Not well. Mack closed the lid to his computer. "Look. I owe you a thousand times over, but I'm not feeling this one."

"You will." Ben slowed the truck. "I arranged for you to stay at her place with her."

"No." Mack put his computer away and zipped up his backpack. "Absolutely not. I live alone. I hate people, except for you. And even you I don't want in my space."

At that moment, Ben's phone rang. He hit the speaker button. "Hey, sweetheart."

Sweetheart? Mack frowned at his friend as a woman's voice filled the car.

"Hey, babe. We have a problem," she said. "Charlotte says Mack can't stay with her, and she's leaving town. She's inside packing right now."

Mack couldn't help but grin. He liked the fact that Charlotte was refusing to be railroaded by Ben. The woman had backbone. "See? It's been decided."

"Mack? Is that Mack?" The warmth in Mari's voice surprised him. "I'm so glad you're here. Ben's told me so much about you. Charlotte needs you."

Her words ripped the smile off his face. "Charlotte appears to disagree with you both." He tried to sound civil, but he knew he wasn't particularly good at it.

"She freaked out when we got here, Ben," Mari said, ignoring Mack so completely that he got a little more respect for her. "I thought she was going to leap out of her skin when I knocked on her window. She was scanning the woods like she knew someone was watching her. It freaked me out, too."

Her words piqued Mack's interest, despite his reluctance. A woman in danger was a dangerous trigger for him right now, even more than usual. "You think it was nerves from the attack?"

"No." Her convocation was absolute. "It definitely had to do with someone else. Whoever it was that she said would be coming back for her."

"Coming back?" Mack leaned forward, listening more intently. "When did she say that?"

"At the hospital, when she found out that the story had been in the papers and on the Internet. She said he'd see it, and he'd come back. She was so freaked when she got home."

Ben swore under his breath and shot a scowl at Mack, as if it were his fault.

"Joseph found me," Mari said, her voice cracking slightly. "There's nowhere to hide if someone wants to find her. We all know that."

Mack did know that. He was one of the ones who could find anyone. And he'd completely fucked it up a month ago.

"We'll talk to her when we get there." Ben's voice was gentle, gentler than Mack had ever heard him use. "You doing okay, Mari?"

"Yeah. She kind of wigged me out, but Haas is here, so I'm okay."

"Haas Carter?" Mack repeated the name, fighting the temptation to open his computer back up and add it to Charlotte's file. Ben had such praise for the old-timer Alaskan that Mack was actually interested in meeting him.

"Yes, he's here—" Mari paused. "Charlotte's coming out the door now with a bag. Haas says he won't shoot her to make her stay. How far away are you?"

"We're here."

As Ben spoke, the truck rounded a bend, and a well-worn log cabin came into view. A second building had part of the frame up, a couple trucks were in the driveway, and an old man and a woman were next to the bigger one.

But what caught Mack's attention was the woman

jogging down her front steps with a duffel bag that was twice as big as she was. On her heels was a gorgeous German shepherd, glued to her side as if it were trained to perfection.

But it wasn't the dog that riveted his attention.

It was the woman. Charlotte.

It wasn't the gorgeous dark waves of her hair. Or the rigid set of her shoulders that told him of a raw, inner strength. Or the way her jeans hugged her hips like they were made for her.

It was the way she stared at the woods, terror etched over every line of her body as she came to a sudden stop.

She spoke to the dog, who took off at a sprint, nose to the ground as he bolted into the trees.

Mack was peripherally aware that Ben and the two folks in the driveway had paused to watch the dog.

He didn't.

He watched Charlotte.

She remained still, but she wasn't watching the dog either. She was carefully scanning her property, her gaze focused and methodical, as if she knew exactly what she was looking for while she waited for the dog to finish.

After her survey, he saw her shoulders loosen infinitesimally. She then raised her gaze to the dog, who was trotting back, his body at ease, and his tail waving peacefully.

She relaxed more, and held out her hand to the dog, who ground his head affectionately into her palm as she spoke softly to him.

The brief moment had told Mack much.

She was strong.

She was smart.

She was good to her dog.

And whoever was hunting her had been doing it for long enough that she'd developed a defense system, one that she no longer believed could keep her safe.

He swore under his breath as Ben pulled up beside an old, battered pickup truck that he assumed belonged to Haas.

Charlotte looked up and saw Ben's truck. As soon as she realized he was there, for a split second, she relaxed, a full and complete release that made her face soften.

Mack knew it was because Ben's appearance made her feel safe, and for that split second, she leaned into it, grasping for a respite from being constantly on edge. He liked that she trusted Ben. It showed she had good sense. Ben was the only person he trusted, so he appreciated that Charlotte could see that about him as well.

Then her gaze went to the passenger seat, and she realized Mack was with him.

Her jaw immediately jutted out. She pulled her shoulders back. And she set her hands on her hips. A fighting stance that made him grin.

"She's ready to kick you out before you even move in," Ben said, resting his forearms on the steering wheel.

"I see that."

Ben cocked an eyebrow at him. "What are you going to do about it?"

Mack leaned forward, watching Charlotte. She was too far away to see clearly, and he knew she couldn't see him well behind the windshield. "She believes she'll be attacked in her own home," he observed.

"I agree." Ben drummed his fingers on the dash. "What if you walk away, and that happens to her?"

Mack was unable to take his gaze off her as she stared him down. She was attitude and sass, even when she was scared shitless. He respected that. Which made Ben's question jab right into his gut and twist its blade. *What if he walked away, and she was killed?* "Really? That's the line you're throwing my way to get me to stay?"

"Yep." Ben cocked an eyebrow. "Did it work?"

Mack sighed and picked up his backpack. "Fuck you,

Forsett." He grabbed the door handle and stepped out of the truck.

Ben leaned across the seat, grinning at him. "So, that's a yes? It worked?"

Mack's only answer was to slam the door in his friend's face, but he was grinning as he heard Ben's laughter.

Yeah, it had worked.

Charlotte Murphy was officially his next case.

Like it? Get it now!

A QUICK FAVOR

Did you enjoy Dash and Leila's story?

People are often hesitant to try new books or new authors. A few reviews can encourage them to make that leap and give it a try. If you enjoyed *A Rogue Cowboy Finds Love* and think others will as well, please consider taking a moment and writing one or two sentences on *your favorite etailer and/or Goodreads* to help this story find the readers who would enjoy it. Even the short reviews really make an impact!

Thank you a million times for reading my books! I love writing for you and sharing the journeys of these beautiful characters with you. I hope you find inspiration from their stories in your own life!

Love,
Stephanie

BOOKS BY STEPHANIE ROWE

<u>MYSTERY</u>

MIA MURPHY SERIES
(COZY MYSTERY)
Double Twist
Top Notch
Gone Rogue
Margarita Mayhem

<u>CONTEMPORARY ROMANCE</u>

WYOMING REBELS SERIES
(CONTEMPORARY WESTERN ROMANCE)
A Real Cowboy Never Says No
A Real Cowboy Knows How to Kiss
A Real Cowboy Rides a Motorcycle
A Real Cowboy Never Walks Away
A Real Cowboy Loves Forever
A Real Cowboy for Christmas
A Real Cowboy Always Trusts His Heart
A Real Cowboy Always Protects

BOOKS BY STEPHANIE ROWE

A Real Cowboy for the Holidays
A Real Cowboy Always Comes Home
SERIES COMPLETE

THE HART RANCH BILLIONAIRES SERIES
(CONTEMPORARY WESTERN ROMANCE)
A Rogue Cowboy's Second Chance
A Rogue Cowboy's Christmas Surprise
A Rogue Cowboy Finds Love
A Rogue Cowboy's Heart

LINKED TO THE HART RANCH BILLIONAIRES SERIES
(CONTEMPORARY WESTERN ROMANCE)
Her Rebel Cowboy

BIRCH CROSSING SERIES
(SMALL-TOWN CONTEMPORARY ROMANCE)
Unexpectedly Mine
Accidentally Mine
Unintentionally Mine
Irresistibly Mine
Secretly Mine

MYSTIC ISLAND SERIES
(SMALL-TOWN CONTEMPORARY ROMANCE)
Wrapped Up in You (A Christmas novella)

CANINE CUPIDS SERIES
(ROMANTIC COMEDY)
Paws for a Kiss
Pawfectly in Love
Paws Up for Love

SINGLE TITLE
(CHICKLIT / ROMANTIC COMEDY)

BOOKS BY STEPHANIE ROWE

One More Kiss

PARANORMAL

ORDER OF THE BLADE SERIES
(PARANORMAL ROMANCE)
Darkness Awakened
Darkness Seduced
Darkness Surrendered
Forever in Darkness
Darkness Reborn
Darkness Arisen
Darkness Unleashed
Inferno of Darkness
Darkness Possessed
Shadows of Darkness
Hunt the Darkness
Darkness Awakened: Reimagined

IMMORTALLY DATING SERIES
(FUNNY PARANORMAL ROMANCE)
To Date an Immortal
To Date a Dragon
Devilishly Dating
To Kiss a Demon

HEART OF THE SHIFTER SERIES
(PARANORMAL ROMANCE)
Dark Wolf Rising
Dark Wolf Unbound

STANDALONE PARANORMAL ROMANCE
Leopard's Kiss
Not Quite Dead

BOOKS BY STEPHANIE ROWE

FUNNY URBAN FANTASY
Guardian of Magic
The Demon You Trust

DEVILISHLY SEXY SERIES
(FUNNY PARANORMAL ROMANCE)
Not Quite a Devil

ROMANTIC SUSPENSE

ALASKA HEAT SERIES
(ROMANTIC SUSPENSE)
Ice
Chill
Ghost
Burn
Hunt (novella)

BOXED SETS

Order of the Blade (Books 1-4)
Protectors of the Heart (A Six-Book First-in-Series Collection)
Wyoming Rebels Boxed Set (Books 1-3)

For a complete list of Stephanie's books, click here.

ABOUT THE AUTHOR

NEW YORK TIMES AND *USA TODAY* bestselling author Stephanie Rowe is the author of more than sixty published novels. Notably, she is a Vivian® Award nominee, a RITA® Award winner and a five-time nominee, and a Golden Heart® Award winner and two-time nominee. She loves her dogs, tennis, and trying to live her best, truest life. For info on Stephanie's newest releases, join her newsletter today at www.stephanierowe.com.

www.stephanierowe.com

ACKNOWLEDGMENTS

Special thanks to my beta readers. You guys are the best!

There are so many to thank by name, more than I could count, but here are those who I want to called out specially for all they did to help this book come to life: Alyssa Bird, Ashlee Murphy, Bridget Koan, Britannia Hill, Deb Julienne, Denise Fluhr, Dottie Jones, Heidi Hoffman, Helen Loyal, Jackie Moore Kranz, Jean Bowden, Jeanne Stone, Jeanie Jackson, Jodi Moore, Jodi Bobbett Judi Pflughoeft, Kasey Richardson, Linda Watson, Regina Thomas, Summer Steelman, Suzanne Mayer, Shell Bryce, and Trish Douglas. Special thanks to my family, who I love with every fiber of my heart and soul. And to AER, who is my world. Love you so much, baby girl! And to Joe, who keeps me believing myself. I love you all!

For all the women out there who need a little reminder that you're awesome, you matter, and you never, EVER need to apologize for who you are, what you want, or how you feel. Because you're amazing, exactly as you re.